The Thing About Thugs

Born in 1966 and educated mostly in a small town of Bihar, India, Tabish Khair is the author of various critically acclaimed poetry collections, studies and novels. Winner of the All India Poetry Prize and fellowships at Delhi, Cambridge and Hong Kong, his novels—*The Bus Stopped* (2004), *Filming: A Love Story* (2007), and *The Thing About Thugs* (2010)—have been translated into several languages and shortlisted for major prizes in five countries, including the Encore Award (UK), the Crossword Prize, the Hindu Best Fiction Prize, the DSC Prize for South Asia (India) and the Man Asian Literary Prize (Hong Kong). His latest novel, *How to Fight Islamist Terror from the Missionary Position*, has been recently published by HarperCollins India. Khair lives in Århus, Denmark.

Praise for *The Thing About Thugs*

'[The] world Khair creates seems so real [partly] because foggy Victorian London is so well entrenched in the imagination. However, much more is due to Khair's own peculiar genius. He ... has a rare gift for prose. He can, in a few words, a brief alliterative phrase, conjure up a picture, inspire horror, pity, fear or love. He has crafted a novel full of suspense where the various strands of mystery, human relationships and crime are expertly woven into one absorbing and fast-moving tale. This book deserves to stand the test of time and join the other masterpieces of Victorian London' – *India Today*

'Contains a mind-boggling number of literary styles, literary references and narrative voices ... The great "thing" about Khair's novel is his ability to construct a narrative that works on multiple levels ... [It] offers a profound, even esoteric, meditation on the complex, reflexive relationship between the colonizer and the colonized' – *DNA*

'A multilayered dissection of the Victorian empire that is only tangentially about thuggee ... [it] makes for intellectually satisfying reading, by virtue of its redoubtable research and excellent atmospherics. By reintroducing imagination to the Indian novel in English without sacrificing relevance, Khair has done us all a favour' – *Mint*

'Khair is adept in showing us how the narrator dreams of this work through a clever juxtaposing of the books he has read and the people he has met. The atmosphere of foggy London is ably evoked' – *Hindustan Times*

'Stylistically and intellectually fearless, *The Thing About Thugs* hurls itself forward to challenge history and fiction. Absorbing and exciting, the book is an ambitious attempt to excavate a long-forgotten past' – *First City*

'*Thugs* is a period thriller with an engaging (if somewhat grisly) plot ... Hitchcock would have been proud of the way Khair leads ordinary people to crime ... Definitely a book worthy of more attention' – *Deccan Herald*

The Thing About Thugs

Tabish Khair

HarperCollins *Publishers* India

First published in India in 2010 by Fourth Estate
An imprint of HarperCollins *Publishers* India

First published in paperback in 2012

Building 10, Tower A, 4th Floor, DLF Cyber City, Phase II,
Gurugram Haryana – 122002, India
www.harpercollins.co.in

2 4 6 8 10 9 7 5 3

ISBN: 978-93-5029-326-3

Typeset in 11/15 Adobe Jenson Pro, Wamock Pro,
Apple Chancery and Times New Roman
Jojy Philip New Delhi 110 015

Printed and bound at
MicroPrints India, New Delhi

In memory of
Anny Ø. Jensen
and
Meenakshi Mukherjee,
and for
Poul Einar Jensen:
Because stories outlive us.

With thanks to
Isabelle Petiot, Sébastien Doubinsky, Mita Kapur,
Simon Frost, Dominic Rainsford, Pankaj Mishra,
V.K. Karthika, Anne Sophie Haahr Refskou,
Aamer Hussein, Neelini Sarkar and
Shantanu Ray Chaudhuri.

'...since history has devoted
Just a few lines to you, I had more freedom
To fashion you in my mind's eye...'

C. P. Cavafy, *Caesarion*, 1916–18

'The man who stood in front of me in that hospital room was a fine specimen of the Asiatic type: compactly-built, of average height, with dark brown hair and limpid mascara-touched eyes. He had a sharp moustache and wore a loose turban; he was dressed in an embroidered kurtah and pyjama, both rather dirty, and he was barefoot, either because he did not wear slippers or because he had taken them off, as is the custom in these parts, before entering the building. He obviously belonged to one of the higher castes, for his complexion was almost fair; he might even have passed for an Italian back home. But this man was no child of the Enlightenment. No, the deities he worshipped were different. His religion was terror; his goddess was terrible. From his cradle, he had been brought up to rob and murder and terrorise. In front of me there finally stood, gentle reader, that most dreaded of men in India, that relentless practitioner of terror and murder and deceit, a Thug.'

—William T. Meadows, *Notes on a Thug: Character and Circumstances*, 1840

'But, Mousie, thou art no thy lane
In proving foresight may be vain:
The best laid schemes o' mice an' men
Gang aft a-gley...'

Robert Burns, 'To a Field Mouse', 1785

Acknowledgement

Ghosts are said to be white. Like the house in which this story began: like all stories, this too began elsewhere. It began in a house with a driveway of reddish pebbles, beds of stricken roses, groves of sour oranges and lush mangoes; a ghostly white house in Phansa.

Phansa is a wretched little town in Bihar, an ancient town. It is mentioned in the Puranas, which makes it older than Jesus but by no means as famous. Like all ancient towns, it is filled – no, not with temples, or mosques, or forts: it is filled with stories.

The whitewashed house is also old and it, too, is full of stories. What else but shadows and stories? For shadows accrete to stories as surely as stories emerge from shadows.

There are stories outside that house too. You can feel them in the narrow paths, winding between the neglected rose bushes and seasonal dahlias, lilies, chrysanthemums, which stretch along one side of the house; in the driveway covered with red stones; in the grove of fruit trees behind: mango, guava, orange, pomegranate; in the towering jackfruit tree, the neem, and among the nameless bushes that have been poaching, growing, growing back over the years. But it is the stories inside the house that concern me here. It is these stories, trapped in a house whose live shadows are gradually slipping away unnarrated, that reach out their bony fingers and touch a face or two across a century, whisper with the ghostly voices (real or fraudulent?) of another place.

The whitewashed house belonged to my grandfather, who has been dead for many years. My grandmother lived in it, refusing to move into the more modern homes of her two sons and three daughters. She lived on the second floor, almost the last of the live shadows still inhabiting the house. The ground floor was kept locked. In particular, one damp, shady room in a corner, with a peeling veranda of its own. Not only did the doors to this room bear heavy rusted padlocks, but the two dozen wooden cabinets inside were locked as well.

When my grandmother was in a good mood, and if she felt that a visiting grandchild deserved it, she would walk down the stairs with a bunch of metal keys jangling like bangles, and with painstaking care unlock the cabinets. They had glass panels. Inside, there were books, protected by white mothballs in small perforated plastic bags. Books in Urdu, Arabic, Persian, Hindi and English. My grandfather, it was often recounted, had not just been a doctor; he loved to read and tell stories.

I was the grandchild rumoured to have inherited his love of stories. This was strange, for I lacked most of his languages, which had been reduced to shadows in the glare that the English language cast on my generation. I had the cabinets unlocked for me time and again, over the years. It was there that I first read rumours of the story I will tell you in these pages, while a gecko clicked on a wall, a moth butted its head against the false sky of the windowpane, and the antique ceiling fan chattered and sighed in turns.

Yes, in those cabinets, in their dark corners, in the fingerprints of dust on the shelves, in the scuttle of sly silverfish, in the brittle paper of those books singed by time.

Not all the books, for I knew no Arabic and I was lazy with the Persian and Urdu that I was taught outside school hours. My school taught us only English, and some grudging Hindi.

As the Hindi books in my grandfather's library were few and pedantic, it was mostly the English books that I read. Russian and French classics in translation, and the Bröntes, Austen, Collins, Dickens, Kipling, Conrad. And then stranger books, like Taylor's *Confessions of a Thug,* William T. Meadows' *Notes on a Thug: Character and Circumstances,* Wells' *How to Read Character,* and Mayhew's voluminous accounts of the London poor, which neither I nor anyone else in Phansa had ever heard of.

I think it was in the pages of one of these books that I found the handwritten Persian notes which, once I had deciphered them with some difficulty and assistance, gave me the first piece of the jigsaw that I have tried to assemble in this book. And it was in another of these books that I found the yellowed cutting from a London newspaper announcing the disappearance and presumed death of Lord Batterstone, during a voyage to Africa. It was wrapped in a pamphlet announcing the seemingly unrelated murder by decapitation of a 'Creole or Gypsy' woman in a place called Spitalfields that no one in Phansa could place on any map.

This is what the clipping said:

> We have also this week to publish, with feelings of regret and sympathy, the news of Lord Batterstone's untimely demise. Lord Batterstone, a renowned scholar of the phrenological science, was last seen on the deck of SS *Good Hope*, when it

> was caught in a sudden squall only a few hours from sighting land off the vernal coasts of the Congo. In the 57th year of his age, and leading a private expedition of exploration into darkest Africa, His Lordship is most deservedly regretted by his peers, and deeply lamented by his relations and friends.

The rest of this novelized history comes from other volumes in the library, from Dickens and Mayhew and (much later, in other libraries) from more recent books by Rozina Visram, Judith Flanders, Peter Akroyd, Jerry White, Michael Moorcock, S.I. Martin and others. Sometimes, though not often, the locks on the past can be opened with keys that lie buried in the present.

As for the notes, written by hand on stiff, parchment-like paper, in Farsi, over a hundred years ago by someone called Amir Ali, how can I explain their presence in my grandfather's library? Were they inherited, or were they collected? For, my grandfather collected manuscripts and artefacts like so many other men of his generation and class. And how did the notes, written by someone so far away – in London in the first half of the nineteenth century – find their way back to a private library in the region of origin of their writer?

The notes, of course, were not sufficient. Notes never are. I had to fill many gaps in them. I also had to fill the gaps between the notes – with voices that, surprisingly, I found to hand.

You might ask, as you may also ask about the provenance of the notes, are these voices authentic?

How can I answer that question? Neither I nor anyone else has heard the voices of England or India in the 1830s. To me, these voices are as authentic as the voices of other characters in books about other places, say, about midnight India in the light of

English. Like the authors of those other characters, I write from between texts and spaces, even though I am located in the space of their narration and they in mine. Our mutual commerce runs in opposite directions – and hence, perhaps, your doubts about my authenticity. I accept your doubts with a doubtful smile. And I answer: whether authentic or not, these voices are true. For, in a very basic sense, any story worth retelling is a true story.

It is the ghost of a true story that I tell in these once white pages.

Time Past: Text

'You ask me, sahib, for an account of my life; my relation of it will be understood by you, as you are acquainted with the peculiar habits of my countrymen; and if, as you say, you intend it for the information of your own, I have no hesitation in relating the whole...'

Time Present: Context

1

This is what I see across time and space. This is what I see from the gloaming of my grandfather's library, surrounded by Dickens and Collins; this is what I see from a whitewashed house in Phansa. I see a place in London more than a hundred years ago. In... what year is it... in 1837, the year of the coronation of Queen Victoria. I see a room. I see – what is that?

Perhaps it is a tattered shirt hanging from a nail hammered into the cracked windowpane. Or a window curtain, ragged, netting the dregs of the light which, dying a lingering death all day, still manages to creep into the room from the grimy court in a corner of the rookery, at this late hour.

The man reclines across a sagging bedstead. He is dressed in expensive clothes, or clothes that seem expensive in this tawdry room. Also lying (dressed in shabbier clothes of varying cut) are a Chinaman, a lascar with a long, white beard and a haggard woman. The first two are asleep, or only half awake, as if in a stupor, while the woman is blowing at a kind of pipe, trying to kindle it. She shades it with her bony hand, concentrating her breath on its red spark of light that serves as a lamp in the falling night, to show us what we see of her face. It is wizened and wrinkled, an old woman's face, though her body has the agility of someone younger. Her hair is matted and clumpy, as if under it the bone was uneven and indented. A sweet, sickly smell pervades the room.

'Another?' says the woman in a rattling whisper, extending her pipe towards the men. 'Have 'nother?'

The well-dressed man stirs slightly, and makes a gesture of repugnance.

The woman laughs and lazily retracts the pipe. She pulls at it herself.

'He'll come to it,' she says to the Chinaman and the lascar, who show no sign of hearing her. 'Always does. I sees his kind coming here, angry-like, and I ses to my poor self, I'll get 'nother ready for him, for there's a gentleman. Not like you lot, no better'n me you are, though I'as nothing 'ginst you. A few years in dust and smoke and toil and who can tell yer skin from mine? Ha. But he's a gentleman. He'll remember like a good soul, won't ye, sir, that the market price is dreffle high just now. And I makes my pipes from old penny ink-bottles, ye see, dearies – with me own two hands – and I fits in a mouthpiece, all clean, sir – see, like this – and I takes my mixter out of this thimble with a little silver horn... Not every place is like this, sir. I sets the pipe going myself, with me own breath, like this, see... Here y'are...'

Having prepared a new opium pipe, she tries to pass it to the gentleman, but he pushes it back, so abruptly that the pipe falls to the dirty ground, and embers fan out like fireflies released from a bottle, waking the Chinaman, who starts stomping on them alongside the woman, both of them muttering and cursing.

Our gentleman sits up and watches the spasmodic shoots and darts of the embers on the floor, the unsteady stomping that extinguishes an ember in one place and sends another whirling into the murky air. He does not know who he hates more, himself for being here, or these people. When the Chinaman stumbles into him in his drugged stomping out of the embers, the gentleman pushes him so hard that the wizened old opium-smoker bounces off the opposite wall, knocking down a pan in the dark, and crumbles into a heap, quivering but not getting up again.

This makes the old woman indignant. She protests that she runs a respectable house and not even the 'lascars, moors and Chinamen who come here with nary a word of English, sir', take such liberties with each other in her presence.

The gentleman puts one finger to his lips and holds out a coin in the other hand. He beckons to the woman. A crafty light steals into the woman's eyes and she sidles up to the man, simpering. He holds her at arm's length and with the other hand, still holding the coin, probes her hair. Perhaps she takes it for a caress. She certainly tries to make the appropriate noises, smiling seductively. But the man is not caressing her. He probes her skull with knowing fingers and if she had been able to look up, she would have been struck by the expression on his face. Then suddenly, the gentleman pushes her away. As she begins to remonstrate again, more loudly this time, he tosses the coin at her and walks out of the room.

The long-bearded lascar continues to sleep on the sagging bedstead.

(I see him. I distinctly hear his hoarse breathing in my grandfather's half-gagged library in Phansa.)

2

The man, unusually well-dressed for the neighbourhood but perhaps not really a gentleman in the esteem of politer circles, crosses the grimy court at a brisk, angry pace, and walks into a dirty little street, pushing away an urchin who gets in his way. The urchin shouts at him, but runs away when the man makes as if to stop. The man continues down the street, walking with some care to avoid the horse droppings and muddy tracks left by carriages and carts of all sorts.

Look. Night is descending on the streets of London in the likeness of a steaming darkness, capped by a laggard mist a little way up in the air, which drops fine particles of soot that settle on the dirty yellow hair of our bareheaded gentleman and on his clothes. He walks on; the streets here are dark. After some time, he turns into a broader street where the gas has been started up in the shops, and the lamplighter – lighting rod slung across one shoulder like a gun – scampers along the pavement. Another turn and he is on Old Baileys, for long the preferred thoroughfare of sheep, cattle and drovers walking down from the market at Smithfield, and even now occasionally containing more animals than human beings, despite the appropriation of public spaces solely for the use of bipeds and their carriages over the years.

About a hundred metres from the stony grimness of Newgate Prison, near Cock Lane, our man enters a pub under the sign of a gilded wooden cherub: a corpulent, naked boy hanging from the walls, darkened with rain and soot. The sign says Prize of War. Our gentleman is known in the pub – people at two different tables raise their drinks to him, their voiced greetings, if any, drowned in the clatter of crockery and the constant coming in and going out and running about – and the barman-publican, who lacks an arm, nods at him familiarly. The usual, says our man, and he is poured a pint of half-and-half.

Our man does not seem as gentlemanly here as he did in the

opium den. Most of the other men are wearing similar clothes, though our man appears to have taken greater care over his appearance: his whiskers are brushed and clipped, his collars tidy, his cuffs clean, his chin closely shaved.

The barman, polishing a glass on a dirty rag, does not look up, but he utters the name our man is known by: 'John May'. He adds, without once glancing up at John May: 'He is here. Your mystery Lordship.'

'Already?'

'Been here a quarter.'

'The usual parlour?'

The barman smirks instead of nodding. John May takes a hasty pull at his pint, draining half of it in one go, and walks off into a darkened doorway, carrying his drink in one hand and wiping froth from his lips with the back of the other.

John May – that is what almost everyone calls him, not John, and not May, but always the two together – John May walks along a sanded passage to a private parlour: a carpeted room whose inability to stay impeccably neat has been camouflaged with an excess of potted plants, cheap coloured prints of various regents and royal consorts, and an array of stuffed animals – two foxes, a deer, an otter or something like it, and even a dried fish in a glass case.

In one corner of the room, smoking in an armchair, half hidden by the shadows cast by the candles, sits a stoutish man. His lips are parted in a fixed smile, the leer of a satyr.

When he hears John May enter, he gets up, and I can see that he is at least middle-aged, though quite well-preserved, and dressed in such a careful manner, with a fur collar and a hat of substantial size and weight under one arm, and in such expensive fabrics, that John May shrinks visibly and brushes invisible indignities off his own clothes with his free hand. The lack of a hat makes him feel naked in front of this elegant satyr.

But no, this is no mythological beast: I can see that his face is a mask. One of those masks that the young have started favouring for certain fancy parties. It is a mask twisted into a permanent smile.

'You are late,' says the stout gentleman, for there is no doubt that here we have the real item, a gentleman from birth and by deportment; even the mask cannot hide that. John May, who had spoken rather clear English to the barman, apologizes in an accent burdened by the inferiority of some impossible-to-identify dialect.

'It is difficult to find Things, especially after the affair of the Italian boy, and you, M'lord, want only part of them and on certain conditions...' There is a timid effort to bluster on the part of John May.

'I, sir, pay you five times what you would get for all the – what do you call them – Things, and I neither ask how you procure them, nor what you do with the remains.'

John May's incipient bluster vanishes; his voice turns servile.

'M'lord, I am grateful; I am your devoted servant, I am, sire, I assure you. It is just that not only is this business difficult – there was a time when a lifter carted a Thing in a bag to this place, this pub, and left it lying under the table while they bargained over the price...'

'I would rather not have the details of your noble profession,' the gentleman interrupts, his mask not concealing the distaste in his voice. All I want to know is whether you have got the, the Thing, you promised me.'

'I ran into problems, sire. He is not... I can explain...'

'Would another ten crowns enable you to overcome the problems, my good man?'

The cold steel of this interruption is not lost on John May. A crafty look passes across his regular – not unhandsome, but perhaps callow – features. He takes out a large handkerchief and wipes his face. He replies with much eagerness, the words falling too glibly from his lips, which he constantly moistens with his tongue, licking them between sentences: 'M'lord, sometimes graveyards are watched as closely as banks, strange though it...'

'I told you, sir,' the gentleman interrupts again, this time with greater asperity, 'I told you I am not interested in the details of your noble profession. Quote the price and fetch me the Thing.'

'Fifteen crowns would cover it quite neatly, M'lord.'

The gentleman drops fifteen crowns on the table, one at a time, each coin spinning and glinting in the candle flame, the clink of metal on wood suddenly loud between them.

'But I need the, ahem, the top of the Thing before the next meeting of my Society, ready to be exhibited. Do you understand? Ready to be exhibited and demonstrated, and as exceptional as you have made me believe.'

'I assure you, M'lord,' gushes John May, gathering up the coins from the table, the tip of his tongue darting over his lips like a lizard behind a stone, 'I assure you, it will be done. Have I ever given you reason to doubt my character or judgement?'

He looks up for the gentleman's answer but the room is empty. The candle throws mute shadows that probe the corners, the grimacing animals, the heavy wooden furniture, and flee like wisps of cloud across the carpet. But for the cold coins in his hand, M'lord might have been a figment of his imagination, a ghost.

3

Night envelops the streets of London, shrouding even the immensity of Newgate Prison and the courthouse, and the two men – John May and the gentleman who has employed him to procure the 'Thing' – depart in different directions. The gentleman walks a short distance and takes out a whistle when he turns the corner. He blows three sharp notes on it and a fly, evidently waiting for him further down the street, appears out of the darkness and the fog. The gentleman boards it without looking around or taking off his mask.

John May, after another pint of half-and-half, and a round of rum hot with the one-armed barman and two other acquaintances, hails a common cab 'towards Virginia Row' in a moment of extravagance. But he has second thoughts and gets off a little earlier, just before the point where going further into the squalid areas of East London would double the cab fare. Then he proceeds on foot, occasionally jangling the new coins in his pocket. It is cooler now.

If night and the industrial fog of London did not prevent us from seeing either John May or the surrounding buildings and occasional passers-by, not to mention the bundled figures here and there, under arches and on doorsteps, evading the policeman on his nightly patrol, the policeman whose job it is to ensure that those who have houses sleep secure in their possessions – which may only be done by evicting from the city limits those who do not have houses – we would have noticed that John May gets taller and better dressed with every step he takes into the grosser quarters of London. Perhaps, from where I watch him, a hat appears on his head by the time he reaches his meagre house. And why not? Stranger things have happened in this city.

Jolting along in his smart fly, driven by a man of huge proportions and gypsy looks, so fiercely moustachioed and beetle-browed that the flaxen wig on his head seems unreal, and pulled by a horse that is conscious of its superiority on these streets, our stoutish gentleman undergoes no such metamorphosis. He is made of metal that cannot be altered by time and place. He remains what he is everywhere: superior in the cut of his clothes, the tone of his voice, the fashion of his views, in the very colour of the blood that pulses through his veins and that has pulsed through the veins of his ancestors for twelve generations, all bearing with absolute conviction the self-knowledge of one family name and many honorary titles.

What do we call this gentleman? John May calls him M'lord. The heavy portals of his city house swing open almost at the very moment he alights from the fly, as if his servants keep vigil all through the deepening night, and the servant who holds the door open also has no other name for him but 'M'lord'. No name could be more appropriate for him, and dare we decipher from the family arms on the door of the house he alights at, the name that his equals employ to address him?

For, standing across the road of time, we are not his equal, we who live in denuded times; we are the passers-by who raise our hats at him and receive, if anything at all, a gracious nod in reply; we are, at worst, the sweeper-boy who cannot tell the family arms from an alphabet, let alone dare to take the family name in vain; we are, at best, those faceless, vote-less citizens on whom he and his equals seek to bestow the benefits of science and religion. For the time being, what can we, what dare we call him but M'lord?

There are more gaslights on this street than in any other part of London, but not all the spheres of gas can unite to penetrate the stolidity of its buildings. For the light from these sputtering spheres contends not just against the darkness of the night and the fog of London, it also beats against the severity of the mansions lining the street. These are houses that are determined not to condescend to liveliness: the black doors and windows, the ironwork and winding stone stairs, the polished knobs and the empty parks behind them, all conspire to impose a solemnity of purpose, a high-mindedness on all who are capable of such sentiments. As for those who are not, say, the passing sweeps, the occasional raw maidservant from the counties, an ayah or two brought over from the colonies, all such are struck dumb on this street and in its mansions.

Their silence echoes down the centuries. Even in my grandfather's library, I do not need to strain my ears to hear their muteness.

M'lord enters the highest-minded in appearance of all the mansions on this dry and massive street, while his fly and horse are led to the echoing mews behind the buildings. Up the winding stony staircase of the house he proceeds. He has already taken off his mask; he had done so in the fly. In the lighted halls and staircase, he reveals a long, broad face, pale, with spreading brown sideburns, and eyes a strange shade of green, blue and grey-yellow. His thin lips and nostrils accentuate the length and breadth of his aristocratic face.

Now, slowly, he divests himself of his attendants: the massive coachman at the door, the doorman in the hall, the cook and housekeeper, who hesitantly enquired if M'lord wished… and was discarded with a gesture, on the stairs. He climbs up the cold marble steps, he walks past the portraits of ancestors, such stolid faces, subtle mirrors of his, with the certainty of a man who knows all the shadows around him, until he reaches a heavy door, a door so massive and padlocked that it stands out even in this mansion.

With great care, M'lord draws out a bunch of three keys from a secret pocket in his waistcoat; with precision, he unlocks each of the three locks on this massive door; with a practised movement in the darkness to which the groaning door has admitted him, he finds a candle and lights it. Then he lights another candle and another, each candle appearing to magically reproduce itself all over the room, for it is full of mirrors and glass cases. With what pride and scientific interest M'lord now looks around this room of a thousand and one flames and surveys its precious hoard of skulls: long skulls and short skulls, skulls of bone and cast skulls, skulls as smooth as marble and skulls knobbly as old oak, small skulls and big skulls, skulls on tables and skulls in glass showcases, all labelled and catalogued. And here we stand, by him, in this massive house wrapped in the fog of a London night, admitted to a temple that few outside the London Society of Phrenology have been admitted to, allowed to gaze on the great scientific project of M'lord, his indelible contribution to the glory of his race and family name, his proposed Theatre of Phrenological Specimen. Above all, the theatre would be his answer, not to those who scoffed at head reading, for they had long been answered by Daniel Bell and Dr Gall and Johann Spurzheim and H.C. Watson if they only cared to listen (or read), but his answer to the followers of that Scottish upstart, George Combe, who had, M'lord was convinced, done as much to harm phrenology as to champion it. With the finished Theatre of Phrenological

Specimen, M'lord would stop the mouths of the Combians in the London Society of Phrenology, and see the mark of defeat stamped on the effeminate features of that Captain William T. Meadows who had, since his return from India with his reprieved thug Amir Ali, taken society by such storm.

4

[WILLIAM T. MEADOWS, NOTES ON A THUG: CHARACTER AND CIRCUMSTANCES, 1840]

'No, sahib, I have no hesitation in relating the full account of my life, for, as you say, you intend it for the delectation of your own people, and for their education as to the ways and beliefs of the benighted people of Hindoostan. I came to you when you lay in bed at the Firangi hospital in Patna, and many a dusty mile had I walked to get there, for word had gone out as far as Gaya and Phansa that in your illness you wished to hear the account of a real Thug, perhaps even a famous Thug, the full murderous account on condition of a full pardon, and if necessary, were the approver untainted by blood himself, you would take him with you to Firangheestan, the better to inscribe his tale and cause it to be printed on the miraculous machines you have in that land. And so it has transpired, for here I am, your devoted servant, in London, the city of cities, having served you for twelve months now, first in Hindoostan and then during the passage over the Black Waters, and I have told you all about the atrocious rites of my race, so that now all I have left to narrate is the story of my own life, which you say will be the last and shortest chapter of your book.

'Life, sahib, is dear to everyone; to preserve mine, which was forfeited by the act of denouncing all my old confederates and revealing to you the nature and number of their heinous crimes, which I beheld and helped in, but only as a lookout, sahib, only as a young boy taken along by older men, I serve you now and hasten to tell you all you wish to hear. But unlike so many other approvers, I came to you on my own, and in my face and in my voice, and wonderfully from my skull, as you still lay recovering in Patna, you read, with the acuity that all sahibs are blessed with, the truth of my narrative. For others had come to you before me, attracted by the word in the bazaar that you had promised a large reward, and you had driven them away as braggarts and liars. But something in my narrative, and I still wonder at the wisdom of Solomon that sahibs possess, made you listen and recognize that what I said was nothing but the truth...'

'It is indeed true, Amir Ali,' said I, 'but it was not the wisdom of Solomon that I exercised; it was the guidance of Reason, which is a God unknown to your race, for when the others came and spoke their lying stories to my face, all I did was listen, and Reason told me not to believe them.'

'But sahib, surely it takes a blessed being to hear a God, even if the name of that God is neither one of the hundred names of Allah, nor one of the million names for Bhowanee, and surely sahib is blessed to hear the voice of his God...'

'Alas, Amir Ali,' I replied, 'I despair of making you understand, for you who grew up among men not afraid of killing other men, nay, having practised that crime as other people practise an art, you have learnt from the selfsame men to frighten yourself with painted dolls and empty Arabic words. Reason is not a tyrannical God like Allah, or a bloodthirsty demon like Bhowanee; Reason does not speak in my ears but gives me ears to listen with. For some came and told me of the murders they had committed or participated in, and I asked them about the cult of Thugee and they feigned ignorance or gave differing explanations, and hence I knew they were dissembling, for Reason told me that in the land of Hindoostan all is built on the scaffold of superstitious faith. And others came and spoke of being Thugs and of the cult of Thugee, but claimed to have wandered into that murderous profession. They maintained that they had once been farmers, before the drought burnt all their crops, or that their fathers were carpenters or weavers, and Reason told me they lied because in the land of Hindoostan sons follow in the footsteps of their fathers as surely as the mango tree grows out of the stone of a mango, and a cat gives birth to kittens.'

'Forsooth, sahib, but to an ignorant man like me, this is the veritable wisdom of Solomon, for we Thugs are master inveiglers, and know how to make a man look at the stars the better to pass the knotted scarf around his neck, and we are master scouts, watching out for passing witnesses to our murders and able to throw dust in the eyes of the wayfarer, but all this is nothing compared to the wisdom of your God, Mighty Reason, who makes material truths out of insubstantial words, and teaches you to verify them by reading the skulls of men, which you did after hearing me out on the first occasion in that hospital in Patna. Truly, sahib...'

'Enough, Amir Ali,' said I. 'There are matters your race cannot comprehend, or not yet, and perhaps it is best so. Let us not waste time; proceed with the story of your life.'

'Forgive me, sahib. I will not tarry any more in regions you know so much better than my deluded intellect can ever comprehend; I shall proceed, like an arrow shot from the bow, straight to the target of my tale. My first memory, though somewhat dim as all memories of childhood are to the likes of us, is that of kites in the sky...'

'Kites, Amir Ali? Birds?'

'Oh no, sahib, kites of paper and wood, which we used to fly like children sometimes do in parks in London, the mother of cities, the jewel of the empire...'

'And what was the significance of that, Amir Ali?'

'Significance, sahib? Oh, I see what you mean. Being a superstitious race, sahib, we flew those kites in honour of our Gods and Goddesses, and it was then that I first heard the name of Bhowanee, the guardian deity of Thugs, both Muslim and Hindu...'

5

Jaanam,

There used to be kites in the air, pinned against the grey-blue skies brushed with the white whisk of clouds. Kites of many colours. Red, blue, yellow, two-coloured, multi-coloured. We had names for each kind. Kites with tails and kites without. Sometimes suspended in the breeze, almost immobile, a window in the sky. Sometimes dipping and twisting and turning, impelled by the wind, or manipulated by the flyer in the field or on the roof, in his bid to reach the string of another kite and cut it. And then the shout would go up, woh katee, kat gayee re, giree, giree, giree, gireeee and we, the young boys and girls, would rush to catch the drifting kite, the kite that was now helpless without the guidance of the string that moored it to earth.

I had always admired Hamid Bhai's ability to guess where the cut kite would alight, just as I admired his capacity to hold his breath for so long during our games of kabaddi.

'Mind over matter, Amir,' he would say to me, laughing. 'What's bigger: the brain or the buffalo?' But then, he was a few years older than I was and I suppose his seniority was a factor in my hero worship. That, of course, was before Hamid Bhai was sent to Patna.

We started flying kites around Dussehra and kept flying them till Holi the next year, all of us, Hindus and Muslims of various sects and castes. If there was religion involved in this flimsy hoisting of paper in the air, it had long slipped from our memory. But of course, my moon-faced one, that is not something I mentioned to our mutual and, I must add, gracious employer, Kaptaan Wali Mian Khet-Khaliyaan, as we used to call him (behind his back) in Hindustan, or Captain William T. Meadows, as he is known here. I discovered, a long time ago, even before I offered him my stories and was pressed into his service, that truth and credibility are two different things most of the time.

Mustapha Chacha was wrong about truth. I never met a man who was wrong so often, but always because he was too right for this world of ours. His wrongness was a sign – though I did not realize this until it was too late – of a greater disorder in the scheme of things. He was wrong because truth and credibility might well be beyond reconciliation in our world. But I am anticipating myself; these are thoughts that came to me only gradually and with time.

To begin with, it was one of the things Mustapha Chacha preached to us: the need to reconcile truth and credibility in our lives. Perhaps preach is not the right word. He did not really preach; he would be pulling the strings of his kite as he spoke, manoeuvring it with practised ease along the invisible tunnels that the wind always makes in the sky.

Mustapha Chacha – I have mentioned his name to you before, and you have not raised an eyebrow at its difference from the names you are used to. You are the first and only person in London who has not accosted me with the first two questions of the catechism, one uttered – What is your name? – and the second – Who gave you that name? – in their expression when I speak my full name: Syed Mohammed Amir Ali.

I owe my knowledge of the catechism to Mustapha Chacha. He had prepared me thoroughly for the future, just as he had prepared himself. And he was convinced that, for better or for worse, the Firang were part of the future of Hindustan. Look at us, he would tell me as he tugged at the kite strings, for generations our family has held on to our ancestral lands by the simple expedient of passing it on to the eldest son, in lieu of some financial compensation at times, while the other sons, if any, sought service with the ruling powers. In the past, these were the Mughals, the Nawab of Awadh and others, and our family shed much blood and sweat in their service, as soldiers or clerks. But your father, God give him peace, who was he serving when he was killed? Who, indeed, but the Firang Company Bahadur forces? And your father, God bless him, was a prescient man: he knew the sun now rose from the west. So, my little nephew, the lamp of our family, if you want to face the future, look west into the rising sun.

Little good it did him though, this facing of a new future, the diligence with which he, in his youth, worked as a munshi before the death of his father called him back to the land, and the way in which he set himself to learn the customs and language of the Firangs. But that, jaanam, explains why I can speak fluently with you, far more fluently than

Kaptaan Meadows suspects, while you do not understand a word of any of my languages.

Come to think of it, you cannot even read your own alphabets (which I can decipher with some effort), let alone this cursive Farsi script in which I write my letters to you, letters which I might some day translate for you, letters that remind me of all that I have left behind. For, jaanam, I do not know who I write these letters for, if not for you to whom they are addressed. Perhaps no one will read out these letters to you; perhaps no one will read them at all.

And yet I am driven to write them, stealing a candle-end from the Kaptaan's kitchen under the eagle-eye of Nelly Clennam, the housekeeper and cook, who dislikes me more and more each passing day as familiarity dulls her initial terror of my past. Scribbling away in the murk of the scullery, I wish, perhaps, to leave an account of myself in words other than the ones Kaptaan Meadows uses in his notebook, the carefully inscribed pages that he intends to turn into a book about the infamous institution of thugee and my fledgling career in what he calls 'ritual murder'.

Because, my dear, I was not, I am not what the Kaptaan wants me to be – I am not Amir Ali, the Thug.

6

If graveyards are places of absolute repose, then this place is not absolutely a graveyard. For late as it is and foggy, shadows move from gravestone to gravestone, from a marble angel, wings fixed in flight, to a plain sandstone crucifix, from a grave with elaborate lines and floral tributes to one with only a name and a date. There are far more graves like this one than graves with floral tributes and fine lines for, like the streets outside, this is a crowded graveyard, a busy graveyard, and often an anonymous graveyard. It is a graveyard that spills its secrets, so that a heavy downpour leaves a harvest of bones and skulls in the sludge, and gravediggers sometimes shovel through a rotten coffin in a bid to find an eternal resting place for the freshly dead.

The shadows pause in front of this plain, taciturn gravestone, this resting place with only a name and a date. There are two shadows; one of them carries a lantern which, at certain angles, multiplies the two into a hundred stealthy shades. And then there is a fierce whispering between the two, louder in the crowded emptiness of the graveyard than it would have been on the streets outside.

'Are you sure?'

'This is it, John May, I tell you. Here. Here. Look, the earth is still fresh...'

'Damn you, Shields. If you have got it wrong again, I swear I will bury you in this grave.'

'Run down by the mail, he was. Cross my heart, John May. Bowled over like ninepins. Carted over from Portugal Street and buried only this afternoon...'

It is believed in this neighbourhood that the unquiet dead walk at night in the graveyard, for the ground here is too cluttered, dug and disturbed to ensure eternal rest. But the dead do not shiver, as these two shadows do at times, when a gust cuts through the still night. Moreover, the hooded lantern that one of them carries hints at the need the living have for light. The heavy burlap bag the other one unburdens tinkles with metallic sounds that attest to the hunger the living have for all – iron in the hands, iron in the heart – that is in excess of the frail mortality of flesh. Slowly, warily, the two shadows take out the instruments of the trade they will practise tonight: a spade, a pickaxe, an iron bar, ropes, a small saw, some sacks. Taking turns, they start digging up the earth on the fresh pauper's grave.

It takes time, but they work doggedly, skilfully. They are careful, because even though the watchman has drunk himself to sleep in a neighbouring pub, only a few yards and the darkness and fog separate the graveyard from the backs of the houses on Clement's Lane. They are poor houses, falling to pieces, slimy and stinking, and they are inhabited by poor people, falling to pieces, but both the shadows know that it is such people – not the wholesome rich – who are likely to charge to the rescue of one of their like, finally fallen to pieces, being dug out of eternal rest by body-snatchers, resurrectionists, lifters, grabs. So they dig carefully, only occasionally stopping to exchange labours and to curse: Why did they plant the devil so deep?… Damn the body bugs, do they have to be out even at night?… Lord, it stinks!

Finally, they reach the coffin, a flimsy affair, easily wrenched open with the iron bar. One of them – the one who is often cursed and does not curse back in reply – jumps into the grave and passes the rope around the corpse. Then he climbs back up and helps his accomplice haul the body out.

His accomplice is not impressed with the corpse. He drops the rope as if it has singed his hands. 'Damn it,' he says. 'Damn you.'

'But John May,' the other replies, 'it is a well-preserved Thing. Look. Look at the arms.' He bends down and wrenches open the jaws of the dead man with his thick, stubby fingers. 'Look,' he adds, 'a perfect set of grinders. Those teeth alone will fetch two guineas.'

'Who cares for grinders, you fool? It is the skull that matters.'

'And what is wrong with it, John May, if I may ask? I have not seen a better skull in my life. Even the hair is clean and unmatted. Will fetch at least...'

John May curses under his breath. 'It will have to do,' he says finally. 'You take the body – I will expect five guineas as my share, mind you, at least five – and I will take the head.'

'I get to keep all I get over five? Everything over? Your word on it, John May?' Shields rubs his hands, perhaps to keep them warm, or perhaps he is gloating in anticipation of the money that will come his way once the Thing is sold to any one of London's medical schools or seventeen private anatomy schools.

'Yes, damn you. Get on with the saw. Don't stand yapping till dawn; it is getting colder.'

And so, in that empty crowded graveyard, shrouded in fog, smelling of decay, a muffled grating sound is heard as the head of the corpse is separated from its body. Then Shields, a short, powerful man, bundles the body into a sack and carries it out to a waiting cart. John May carries the head in a smaller bag, still cursing the dead man for having such a smooth, normal skull. Will have to do though, he mutters. M'lord will be upset, but something is better than nothing. Then John May sees the possibility of humour in the sentence and reformulates it, emitting the choked grunt that passes for a laugh with him: A Thing is better than nothing.

Soon the sun will be out and the shadows will disperse. Soon someone will discover the open grave and the missing body. Soon a pen-pusher such as Daniel Oates will come to describe the scene for his broadsheet, an artist will sketch the gaping hole for some one-dime pamphlet. Soon the marketplace will buzz with the news and the drawing rooms thrill with the knowledge of the crime. For a few hours at least, the dead man will be missed more than he ever was in his lifetime.

7

Things change, and do not. I recall, around the time I discovered the notes of Amir Ali, reading my first report – or the first one that I fully understood and hence recall – of a riot between Hindus and Muslims. The news report, as was the custom, did not use descriptions like 'Hindu' or 'Muslim'; instead, it employed the supposedly safer euphemism of 'one community' and 'another community' when describing the bodies discovered in charred houses, the amputated limbs recovered from railway tracks. The writer, surely with the best of intentions, tried to clean the bones of the atrocity of flesh and skin and gore, of the passions and anger and bitterness which hung from it like a rat in the claws of a crow. But it was to no avail. My Hindu classmates were convinced that the victims of the riot were Hindus; my Muslim classmates as convinced that the victims were all, and only, Muslims.

No, it is not easy to clean the bone of all that accretes to it: skin, flesh, tissue. Bone is as stubborn and possessive as books in a private, shuttered, small-town library. But John May has a system. In his home on the fringes of East London, he has worked out a scientific routine that he follows every time with characteristic diligence: after locking the door on his children and his wife, he first scalps the head, taking the hair off as cleanly as any mythical Red Indian on the warpath. Because the hair, if undamaged and lush enough, can be sold separately. Nothing goes to waste if one is prudent, and John May is a careful, prudent man. There is no nonsense about him.

There is no nonsense about him now as he unlatches the broken gate leading to the small barren plot in front of his two-bedroom house in an alley of East London that does not yet have a fixed name. All the houses here are alike: a kitchen attached to a closet-like scullery and a drawing-dining room on the ground floor, and two rooms, one hardly bigger than a cupboard, upstairs. Outside, in the backyard, there is a shed that functions as a toilet. Behind the backyard, there are a few more houses: this is where East London starts petering out into expanses of miasma and sickness, into bare fields and marshes.

John May can hear his family – wife and three children – in the drawing-dining room. His wife must be laying the plates for dinner. She knows her husband's routine and respects it. She is a good woman, though somewhat inclined to melancholia.

John May walks purposefully across to the small kitchen. There is a broth bubbling on the stove. But the kitchen smells less of food and more of formaldehyde. When John May opens the locked door to the scullery, the smell of formaldehyde and sulphate grows stronger. John May lights a couple of candles and takes them to the scullery. He closes the door behind him. He closes it with a loud enough bang to intimate to his wife that he is working. She will have to delay dinner. No one interrupts John May in the scullery. No one but John May enters the scullery. And no one eats in the family until John May sits at the head of the table.

Inside the scullery, John May looks at the head: it still lies on the dark-stained wooden shelf where he had deposited it last night. This will take time. He cannot do much now. Death needs time to ripen into art. All he can do is strip off the rotting skin and flesh, make two holes in the skull where the eyes used to be, and start to empty the contents with a selective use of acids and chemicals, knife and scalpel. Later, when the skull has been cleaned and emptied, he will have to let it soak in an aqueous chemical solution for some time, before drying and treating it.

In his many professions since the day when, at the age of fifteen, he ran away from a violent and mostly unemployed father and an alcoholic mother in Liverpool, John May has tried his hands at various skills. True, they have been mostly in a rather unspecified capacity. He has been an errand boy rather than the waiter; he has been the butcher's help rather than a butcher; he has been a lawyer's clerk rather than a lawyer. Sometimes John May is amazed at his success: in less than thirty years, he has not only a family but a house, and some money saved up. What is more, he can read and write.

He remembers his various professions and jobs (at least from the time he turned eighteen and became aware of his own thoughts; became a man, as he puts it) in terms of what he had when he went into it and what he had when he left it. As a rule, he has come out of each profession a richer man. He is a self-made man, that he is, and he takes no nonsense. Well, most of the time. There were a few occasions when a profession seemed to be a complete waste. For example, when at the age of twenty-one, he worked for a taxidermist in Leeds. It paid little, and left him with a smell in his nostrils that deprived him of sleep for days. When he gave up the position after two years and left for

London, where he was finally headed, thank heavens, he could only think of the experience as a dead loss, a complete write-off in the narrow account book of life. For he had not even saved money in that position; he would have had nothing to show for those two years if he had not made off with some of the taxidermist's recent work. And yet now, years later, even that experience was coming in useful.

As John May slowly peels and slices the rotting skin off the skull, he wonders if M'lord would have continued to employ him without the skills he had picked up at the taxidermist's. For John May, while he can do nothing but admire someone in M'lord's position, is not blind to the fact that M'lord is unlikely to prepare his phrenological specimens himself. And there are few who can do it as well and as quickly as John May.

For, thinks John May, slicing and drilling away, preparing a skull as a phrenological specimen is much simpler than stuffing an animal. Take the skin, for instance. With an animal, the skin has to be taken off carefully, with minimum incisions. After all, it has to be put back on a stuffed animal, and show as few flaws as possible. But here, well, here you can hack it off as you wish, as long as the skull is not damaged. And once the brain has been dissolved and emptied, you can colour the skull exactly the right 'natural' shade. This too, John May learned from that miserly, brutish old taxidermist in Leeds, for stuffed animals need to look natural: marble eyes, hide paint, fin and fishtail colours... He had his version of skull paint, and that was his secret, for it enabled him to prepare the skulls for exhibit more quickly than nature would permit.

But now, John May is done for the evening. The acid will need time to work. He needs to wash his hands and join his hungry family for dinner. There is a time for everything, and this skull will have to await John May's procedures the following morning. He walks into the kitchen and locks the scullery door behind him. His wife and children get nightmares if they see a skull. John May considers this a sign of weakness and is faintly disappointed, not in his wife and daughter (for they are women), but in his two sons. He does not believe in such things as ghosts: he is a no-nonsense man, a self-made man.

Outside, the wind picks up; it fumbles with the chimney cowls, spins the weathercocks, bangs loose shutters all over East London.

8

[WILLIAM T. MEADOWS, NOTES ON A THUG: CHARACTER AND CIRCUMSTANCES, 1840]

'Bhowanee is a many-armed goddess, sahib. A mischievous devil to you, for you are favoured by your God of Reason, who enables you to read men like books. But to us – to me too, before you shed on me some of the illumination of your greater God – she is the mother of the world, protectress and patroness of our order. All this you know, Kaptaan Sahib, for I have already narrated the tale of my order to you. I will not tarry here, nor repeat myself, but proceed with my own story, the story of how I became a Thug.

'When I was about twelve or thirteen, my father came up to me and my mother and said, it is time. At this, my mother looked both sad and proud. I knew my father went out for "trade" with his friends, sometimes for months on end. And I understood that this time, I would be taken along, like my older cousins were when they approached adulthood. Imagine, sahib, the pride in my ignorant young heart, which swelled at the thought of being accepted as a man amongst men.

'The next morning – it was in early February – my father and two other jemadaars, who led the gangs of Thugs, assembled with lesser members in the village maidan. All three gangs – for I learnt that my father was a jemadaar too – were to depart in different directions, but before that the ceremonies of initiation and embarkation had to be performed.

'Of the two, the former was simpler and closer to what I was accustomed. Verses were read out from the Holy Quran and then a Hindu pundit applied vermillion from the plate of offerings to Goddess Bhowanee to my forehead. A bit of consecrated molasses was brought from the temple of the Goddess and placed on my tongue. I swallowed its brown sweetness amid much murmuring of approval and invocation of deities, Muslim and Hindu.

'I was now a member of the gang, though I did not yet know the purpose of my initiation. Then my father carried the consecrated kudalee-pickaxe to the field and walked the entire length, holding a lota brimming with water, suspended from his mouth by a string. Whether the water spilled or did not spill was an augury of the success of our enterprise; every jemadaar performed this ritual before embarking on an expedition. Were the lota to fall, it was said, nothing would avert the death of the jemadaar in that year, or at the furthest in the year following, and the expedition would be doomed to great losses. But, sahib, I never saw a lota fall – and yet I saw so many deaths, such huge losses in my years as a Thug.

'That day, sahib, my father had only good omens: he walked the entire length without a drop of water spilling from his lota. The other jemadaars spilled a little, but not enough to cause any worry to their gang members. Our gang members though, were elated with my father's performance: the clear blue sky rang with their cheers. And we set out that very moment, they in pursuit of the career they had practised for years, I to a new life, a life that I had eagerly anticipated – sahib, I cannot convey to you how eagerly one anticipates adulthood and initiation into the profession of one's forefathers in the deluded lands of Hindoostan! Alas, in my joy, I could not even have begun to imagine the life I was being initiated into...'

'And yet, Amir Ali,' said I musingly, 'would you have hesitated if you knew what lay in wait for you beyond the dust-shrouded miles, along the narrow roads and travel-tracks on which you had embarked? Would you have hesitated to embrace the dictates of the bloodthirsty religion of Bhowanee, to walk in the steps of your father as he had walked in the steps of his father, and so on and so forth to the misty ends of time in Hindoostan?'

'Forsooth, sahib. Forsooth. You know how it is.'

9

Jaanam,

I never knew my father. I was a few months old when he died, and I was brought up by Mustapha Chacha and his wife. Even my mother I only have faint recollections of, for she was carried off by fever and delirium four years after my father's death. But Mustapha Chacha and Chachijaan and their two sons, one three years older than me and the other eight years younger, were my family. I never felt the lack of my parents, and when I finally left to be apprenticed to a babu in Patna at the age of fifteen, following in the footsteps of my older cousin Hamid Bhai – for Mustapha Chacha could sense which way the wind of progress was blowing, and in any case our ancestral lands were not enough to comfortably sustain more than one family – I felt more lonely than I ever had.

Perhaps more lonely than I have felt in London because here, on the second day of my arrival with Kaptaan Meadows, I met you, and... Oh, what can I say, jaanam, about meeting you? It was almost half a year ago: how time flies! The weather was more or less like it is these days, a bit colder then, because it was early spring – I remember distinctly that your Queen had not yet been crowned – and I was still not used to the climate. I remember that when you walked into the kitchen, I mistook you for a visitor and not a servant, and addressed you as such. Later, after you had laughed at my mistake and corrected me, I saw that your clothes were threadbare and dirty, and wondered why I had not noticed them earlier. But truly, jaanam, the moment you walked in, all I could see was your face, which you always manage to scrub clean, and your dark brown hair, tied into a neat bun. And I got my laugh at you too, for you assumed that I was a rich nobleman from 'Persia', and were disabused of it only when you returned to the house the next day and asked Nelly Clennam, the cook, who, with her instinctive dislike of me, informed you that I was only a 'paid servant' and had been a murderous 'thug' in India, and that it was a danger to all servants, God preserve honest people, and not least to her – for she was a decent woman and had always been, so help me God – to have thugs and murderers living in the houses of gentle *folks like the Captain but then it is well known that going abroad puts strange ideas in the minds of people and though it was not her position, or habit, to utter a word against her employer, it would be said by many that to harbour a nigger, lordey, a cannibal in the kitchen was not only a danger but an act verging on the unchristian... I remember you recounting the introduction as a breathless monologue to me in Nelly's voice – you are a gifted mimic, jaanam – and for days I burst out laughing (much to Nelly's horror, I dare say) whenever I came across her.*

But all that seems such a long time ago. Our initial hesitation in addressing each other, your surprise at my English, your interest in all that I had seen out in the wide world which fascinates you, the first walk that we took in crowded London, the first time, only a few weeks ago, when you took me to visit your aunt and the opium den – though you call it by a polite name, just as you do not fully acknowledge that what I take occasionally is a variety of opium too; no, it is not just an 'Oriental medicine', as you prefer to call it. It was in that den that the wizened old woman raised you and it is there you still return to sleep on the nights when you do not seek shelter in one of the houses you clean. I remember that you were both proud and ashamed of your background: you had to show the place to me, you are too proud to deny it, but you also had to excuse it by giving it a different name. And I could see the relief in your eyes when I told you about the various names of the lotus flower, surely the most beautiful and sacred of flowers in India, and how the most common and esteemed name for it is 'that which grows in the mud'. Intoxicated by your smile, I had applied the description to you and confessed that I was secretly writing a series of letters addressed to you, letters to keep a record of what had happened and what was happening to me.

At which you said, but then you will have to teach me to read first. Alas, I had replied, even if I taught you to read your own language, it would be of no use to you – for I am writing to you in Farsi, one of my languages. You grew thoughtful and asked me, how do you address me in your language? And I replied, honestly: jaanam. Is that 'Jenny' in your language, you asked. No, I said, it sounds like it, but it means 'my precious' or 'my life'. I had blurted it out in a moment of bravado, and I was already regretting it, for you went quiet for a second, and then you laughed and said, I should slap your face, you... you thug. But you said it with a twinkle in your eye and a few moments later, for the first time, under a gas lamp swarming with insects, we held hands. It was then that you asked me to tell you more about the places I had known in the past – my village, my province and, of course, Patna.

But what can I tell you of Patna, jaanam? It is a place you had never heard of. And yet, there was a time when in all of Asia and perhaps beyond, you would have been laughed at if you said you had not heard of Patna. It would be like someone here, in London, claiming not to have heard of Paris or Rome. Patna was a city of a thousand gardens, a hundred schools, but they are all gone. Now it is simply a provincial headquarter, sustained by the presence of the Company, its bureaucrats and its soldiers, its shipping from the ghats. But this is not shipping on a grand scale. The docks in Patna do not harbour brigantines, bulkats or schooners; it is cluttered with small boats, dinghies, baulias and woolocks. Sometimes a larger craft belonging to some trading company casts anchor to pick up a load of opium or girmitiyas. But by and large, Patna is nothing but a minor stop on the Ganges, its broad banks lined with wheat or rice to the north and west of the city and with poppy flowers to the east.

No, I will leave Patna out of my story. It lies there, unremarkable. Next to an impassive Ganges across which the wind blows slowly, sometimes with the smell of wild flowers and sometimes the stink of human refuse and dead bodies. In the monsoon, the Ganges swells and inundates most of Patna. Even this is hardly remarked upon. In the winter, mists seep across the banks and fold the two-storey buildings in their embrace. No one speaks of Patna with love: people only speak of places they have left or the places they are going to.

I did not know where I was going. So I spoke of the place I had left: our ancestral lands in the village, tilled by Mustapha Chacha and his youngest son Shahid, with occasional labour hired by the season. The other clerks in the babu's office came from similar places. They knew what I spoke of. Hamid Bhai himself had now moved to a lawyer's office as a munshi. He was married and lived with his wife's family, in a small house in Maruganj, while I shared two rooms near the Chowk with five other apprentices. Hamid Bhai had two children, but he came to see me almost every other evening, at least until he started being sent out of town on business by the lawyer. And always our conversation turned to the lands in our ancestral village. It was not just that we had grown up on those paltry acres, eaten the crops they yielded, drunk the milk of cows pastured there. That land was in our blood; for generations we had watered it with our sweat. But it was also on our minds, for we knew the difficulties of Mustapha Chacha.

Did I say our ancestral lands were not enough to sustain more than one family? Would that it was our sole problem! For then, perhaps, I would not be the thug that Kaptaan Meadows wants me to be, and Mustapha Chacha and his family – my family – would still be alive. For you see, jaanam, our ancestral lands, like everything from the past, were both a blessing and a curse.

10

'I must say that I am disappointed, sir. Extremely disappointed. The subject here is deficient in the size and strength of the cervical vertebrae, which you have expertly preserved. The organ of Conscientiousness, as the upper and forward parts of the parietal bone indicate, is also small. This combination, lack of Firmness and Conscientiousness, places the subject exactly where, as you have informed me, he died: in the workhouse. And while it is true that this, this Thing, is a highly developed example of such characteristics, it is also true – need I remind you, sir? – that you have already brought me at least two such specimens. I must say that my museum does not need any more like this one, and if you cannot find me better examples, I am sorry to say, my man, I will have to dispense with your services.'

John May has never heard M'lord sound so angry. True, his lordship does not look angry: his mask – a different one this time – hides his expression. He does not even raise his voice in anger. His gestures and the volume of his voice are deceptive: he appears to be holding forth on a pleasant topic to a friend or a colleague. And yet, John May knows his cold choice of words suggests glowing anger. This, John May thinks with approval and admiration, is how the nobility get angry. They do not rant or shout like the riffraff do. They do not grow red in the face like the mob. And yet, their anger cuts into you like a thin steel blade.

John May looks into the eyes of the stuffed fish, observing it for the first time in this private parlour of the Prize of War public-house, a small part of him remarking on the shoddiness of the work, the transparency of the colours painted on the fins. The skull, on the other hand, which he had unwrapped and quickly wrapped again for M'lord moments ago, is a superior specimen of work. Despite the rush to prepare it, all art, all colouring is invisible. It appears just a skull, somehow clean, unstained and dry, something skulls never are in nature. John May feels a slight twinge of resentment at M'lord's lack of attention to the finesse of his craft, but he also knows that M'lord is right. It is the third such skull he has sold to him in a year. But finding different kinds of skulls is difficult. John May has, over a couple of years, supplied roughly thirty different types of skulls to M'lord. He feels that all of London, no, all of England, does not contain much more variety. The only really exceptional skull he can think of at the moment sits on the old woman who runs that disgusting opium den, and she is nowhere close to death.

'M'lord,' he says in a placatory tone. 'M'lord, I always do my best in your service. But at the moment this city does not seem to contain anything else.'

'In that case, my man,' says M'lord, standing up, putting on his gloves and picking up the wrapped skull in one fluent, habitual movement, 'you have nothing more to offer me.'

The potted plants and stuffed animals in the room suddenly seem to have stranded John May in a jungle: he is lost. His greatest source of income is on its way out of the door. He runs after M'lord, tugging at the gentleman's sleeve like a common beggar. 'M'lord, M'lord, if you give me time, I will provide you other specimens... rare ones, M'lord.'

M'lord shakes him off without stopping in his stride, and hisses: 'Two weeks then. Two weeks from this date. Leave your message in the usual way if you have something to offer me. And, sir, this is your last chance. Your last chance, sir.'

11

The one-armed bartender, sweating as profusely as ever and using the same rag to wipe his forehead and the glasses, pushes two glasses of rum hot towards John May and Shields. John May, contrary to custom, makes no effort to pay, forcing Shields to fish out a few coins and put them on the counter, grumbling under his breath.

The bartender looks at the couple with malicious irony. 'His Lordship left in a dudgeon, didn't he?' he remarks to no one in particular.

'Blast his bloody Lordship,' mutters John May. He is surprised that the bartender has noticed. He drains his rum hot in one gulp, and takes a few seconds to stifle a cough as his eyes mist over.

The bartender laughs and moves on to other customers in the stifling, smoky room. Shields sits, stolid and unmoved, waiting for the inevitable outburst from John May. And it comes. John May starts off by making fun of Shields, calling him names just short of giving offence, and then proceeds to espouse a platform of radical socialism, almost suggesting that people like M'lord ought to be treated the way 'those frigging Frogs' treated their royalty in 1789. After five minutes of this, John May calms down, orders a round of beer and cocks an eyebrow at Shields, who has not said a word to interrupt the outburst.

'So, my friend,' says John May, 'it looks like we are out of business.'

Shields looks at him, sipping his beer.

'Do you understand, my obdurate friend?' John May likes using cultivated words at times, especially on people like Shields who are mostly incapable of understanding a word of more than six letters. 'Do you get it? No more purchases, no more Things.'

'But surely, John May,' replies Shields slowly, as if the effort of thinking is sufficient to slur his speech, 'surely there are other places. Things are still in demand. The vivisectionists, the...'

John May makes a gesture of repugnance and irritation. 'Pennies,' he barks, 'pennies.' And then he stops. He remembers that Shields has no idea how much M'lord pays for the skulls. Shields is only a resurrectionist, a common stealer of dead bodies from graveyards, to be sold to surgeons and scientists and students. It is an increasingly risky business, especially after the troubles over the Italian boy, and it still pays well. But it does not pay a fraction of what M'lord pays John May for the skulls, especially in the beginning, when the specimens were always of a new 'type'. John May cannot reveal this to Shields;

he has not shared his extra profits with Shields. He returns to his beer.

12

But the beer is not enough to drown John May's thoughts. His mind keeps going back to the money he has made, the money he could still make. All he needs is a remarkable skull. And there are a few walking around in London. For instance, the beggar outside Hyde Park, or the lascar he has occasionally seen selling tracts, or that old woman... Each has an exceptionally interesting skull: deformed, ridged, extraordinary, fascinating to men of science. Unfortunately, the skulls sit on living shoulders, shoulders that give no sign of going under, of being killed by disease or age or accident.

Accident.

The word gives John May pause for thought. London is a place of accidents. They happen all the time: workers falling off scaffoldings, children run down by carriages, women getting crushed between coal wagons, men falling into sewer holes, explosions, drownings, houses collapsing as if they were balloons pricked by an invisible pin. Why, when was it, not more than a few years ago, certainly, when a respectable woman, her babe in her arms, fell through the rotten floor of a privy and drowned in the filth underneath. Accidents are what happen most often in London.

But John May dismisses the thought. It is a temptation. But surely it is wrong.

13

Two beers later, John May is less sure about the wrongness of his idea. He thinks of the old woman in the opium den: what is her entire life but a continuous accident? Could one even pity such a person, a woman who lives by prostituting herself to lascars and Chinamen, by selling opium in a pigsty? A woman who can hardly be understood when she speaks? Is she a real woman? Is she even truly human? Would it be a crime in the eyes of God or man, if something were to happen to such a woman? Or would it be a service to society – and, of course, to M'lord's science?

Not that M'lord would want to know. Yes, John May is convinced of that. M'lord would take the skulls as long as he did not know how they were procured. Why else did he hide behind a mask? May knows enough of the rich and the cultivated to be certain of this. But Shields, now Shields is another matter. Shields will need to be sounded out.

'Another round,' shouts John May to the bartender, thumping his empty mug on the table. 'Another round of the same for me and my good friend here.'

14

[William T. Meadows, Notes on a Thug: Character and Circumstances, 1840]

'The three gangs decided to go in different directions, sahib, having agreed to meet after six months. This was the usual process. We took what was perhaps the best route – to Patna, and from there through Allahabad to Benaras, a route much travelled by pilgrims as well as traders. And just two days later, I was initiated into the intricacies of my new profession.

'It was a humid afternoon, hotter than the season warranted. I remember this clearly. Perhaps because it was the kind of weather that frays tempers, that brings people into conflict, causes arguments. The kind of weather that makes mosquito bites itch for longer, that attracts flies to your eyes. Perhaps if the weather had not been what it was, we would not have found our first victim so soon. Who knows, sahib, for lacking your great God of Reason, we can only comprehend the ways of Allah or Bhowanee with dread and suspicion, always fearing that what we know is not enough. As it happened, we were still outside Patna when one of our sothaees returned with news.'

'Sothaees, Amir All?' I enquired, pausing from jotting down his words.

'O sahib, excuse my oversight, for benighted that I am, I lack the forethought to avoid getting carried away by my own disturbing tale, every bit of which stands in front of me as vivid as a person in broad daylight. Perhaps sahib, you do not recall this strange word, sothaee, from when I explained to you the functions of the members of the gang: sothaees are inveiglers, they are members sent out in advance to scout around, identify victims, if possible smell out their weaknesses and plans, befriend them, lead them to us or us to them. So, Kaptaan Sahib, one of our sothaees returned, bearing news of a merchant and his son who were travelling with two menservants; the party appeared to be rich and vulnerable. By the time we caught up with them, we were in Patna, near the shops about the Jama Masjid, most of them closing, now that night had fallen. But this night was not cool and clear as nights usually are at that time of year. It was oppressive and humid.

'Perhaps this was the reason why, when we reached the merchant and his party, who were travelling in a smart horse-driven buggy, with another horse, saddled for riding, tied to it, we found him engrossed in an argument with a driver who was obstructing the road with his bullock cart. There was a group of young men sitting on the cart, probably returning from or going to some marriage party, and in high if not slightly inebriated spirits. Perhaps, had the night been milder, the two groups would not have got into an argument.

'When we reached the merchant, he was being intimidated by the greater number of his opponents who, being locals, though of a lower class, were pressing their advantage more than perhaps good breeding allowed.

'Into that fray, my father rode his horse. We had decided that the best horse in our group would be used by my father, who assumed the role of a nobleman from Oudh on his way to Benaras on business, while the others, mostly on foot, would pretend to be his companions and servants. We already knew that the merchant was from Calcutta and on his way to Benaras: such information is what the sothaees are sent to inveigle.

'The appearance of our larger party cowed down the men in the bullock cart, and soon they unblocked the road and let us and the merchant's party proceed to the mughal sarai further ahead from the mosque. The merchant was already taken with the cultured language and bearing of my father, and appreciative of his support during the fracas with the bullock-cart lot. After spending the night in the same sarai and after revealing, by accident, that we were also headed for Benaras, it was not difficult to get the merchant and his party to join us on the journey.

'And thus we proceeded for two more nights, sahib, heading for Allahabad, on our way to Benaras. My father, Allah pardon him his crimes, was always a careful man. Some members of the gang used to complain about it. But the graver minds knew that his care and planning saved them much trouble – for, unlike many other gangs, we never ended up running a risk by killing someone who turned out to have only a donkey and two rupees in a bundle.

'Perhaps, on the second night, my father would have given the signal for the merchant and his party to be disposed of. By then, the merchant had come to trust us. He and his son would come into our camp for the evening meal, leaving his servant with the horses in their camp, and he would let his sword lie at a distance from him. But that night, after we had set up camp, one of the sothaees came with information that a contingent of the Company Bahadur's sepoys was camping just a few yards further down the road. My father judged this to be a risk, though there were those who said that any real Thug could take care of a man without a single sound escaping his lips. Still, we waited for the third night.

'It was a cold night. We lit a bonfire, not far from a grove of palm trees in a desolate, barren field, just off the road. The merchant and his son came to join us as usual. I thank you, Ali Sahib, he told my father, for accompanying me all this way from that unsainted town of Patna. Truly there is enjoyment in the society of gentlemen who have seen the world, and more so when one is in such desolate parts.

'And thus the conversation continued, the merchant and his son being so used to our company by now that they did not grow suspicious of, or even notice, that three or four of my father's companions were sitting closer to them than usual.

'And the hospitality you have meted out to me and my son, Ali

Sahib, the merchant continued. That, if I may say so, is the mark of a true gentleman. Never have I travelled with a greater feeling of safety, with less need to be watchful. With you, O gracious host, I know I will be taken care of.

'Ay, growled an old Thug who was sitting next to me, behind my father. You will be taken care of. We will see to that.

'How, I almost asked him, for, sahib, I was still only vaguely aware of the details of my new profession. It was then that I noticed that both the men sitting behind the merchant and his son were holding gamchas in their hands, the scarves with which bhutottoes throttle their victims.

'My father and a couple of his older companions occupied the merchant and his son in gracious conversation all through the meal. Then, having washed our hands with a little water from the surahi, we settled back in our places, and my father raised his voice and ordered for the hookah and tobacco to be brought: tambaku lao, he shouted loudly. This was the signal.

'Quicker than thought, the thugs with the gamchas who sat behind the merchant and his son, the bhutottoes who specialized in this business, threw their scarves around their victims' necks. In an instant, the merchant and his son were on their backs, struggling in the agonies of death. Taajoob, sahib, not a sound escaped them, nothing but an indistinct gurgling. I knew that their servants had met a similar, silent fate a few metres away in the darkness. How easy it is, sahib, to snuff out a life; how easy it is to kill a human being!

'Under those palm trees, in that barren piece of land, we buried the four bodies, after having slit their bellies open so that the gases of decay building up in them would not explode and disturb the loose earth of their shallow grave. As we walked away the next morning, I looked back, sahib, and already, from a little distance, there was nothing extraordinary to distinguish that piece of brown land from the barrenness all around it, those nameless stretches of straggly weeds and no irrigation, the lands where the writ of Allah and Bhowanee runs, the lands denuded of the grace of your God of Reason, sahib.'

15

Jaanam,

Yes, a blessing and a curse, that's what our ancestral lands were to us. A blessing, for there were not many who had land of their own, and once we had vast stretches, given to one of our ancestors as a jagir by Emperor Akbar. The jagir lands have since been divided and subdivided with each contending generation, despite Chacha's claim that in the past, only the eldest son inherited the land – a claim that was true, I suppose, only for the last two or three generations, when siblings got along better than was the custom. For, surely the original jagir must have been bigger: what we possessed was not substantial enough to be a gift from an emperor, but of course no one had a copy of the original jagirnama, though we had other records of ownership.

And yet, by local standards, what my father and Mustapha Chacha inherited was substantial. It would have enabled us to live a life of fullness, if not abundance and ease. But, alas, my love, we could cultivate only a quarter of the land we had inherited. Oh, we had the papers to those plots all right, for all they were worth, but Mirza Habibullah, a much richer man who was related to us, or whose forefathers had been to ours so far back in time that I for one never understood the connection, this rich and powerful relation had laid claim to all our lands. Most of it he had occupied by force, and even the quarter that we cultivated was repeatedly claimed by him. Every planting season, his men would divert our water channels or block them; every harvest season his cattle would be accidentally herded into our fields.

Mustapha Chacha had the respect of many in the village and I think that was the only thing that protected us from the wrath of Mirza Habibullah and his henchmen. For Mirza Habibullah was a powerful man, one of the richest farmers in the village, a person who aspired to set himself up as more than a landlord, which probably explained his appropriation of the title, Mirza.

What angered him the most was that Mustapha Chacha defied him instead of coming to a compromise, perhaps conceding him ownership rights in return for the right to continue farming the land. I think that would have been acceptable to Mirza Habibullah: he already owned most of the land, and the bit that we cultivated would not have added much to his wealth in any case. But Mustapha Chacha was a man of principles, and he would never agree to being browbeaten; he would never resort to subterfuge, or cower in front of superior might. This was what he taught his sons and me too, but his life taught me another lesson – would that my youngest cousin, Shahid, had learnt the lesson too. For jaanam, the bending doob-grass survives the storm; the upright palm breaks like a twig in this world of ours.

There were other reasons for Habibullah's enmity. We knew his father and uncles had feuded with our grandfather. We also knew that on at least two or three occasions, Mustapha Chacha had worsted Mirza Habibullah in the eyes of the village – once at the village panchayat.

I remember the occasion of the panchayat. A servant in the house of Habibullah's brother, who was a rich farmer, just like Habibullah, and like him, a fat man with a sparse hennaed beard and no moustache, had been accused of stealing an expensive necklace. The servant, Haldi Ram, and his family were reputed to be honest people, and despite threats and beatings, Haldi Ram continued to proclaim his innocence. The matter was brought before the village panchayat, which had assembled, as was the custom, under the peepal tree in the village square. Most of the village had turned up too, quite a few siding with Haldi Ram and his family despite their low-caste status. However, Habibullah, who had recently had himself chosen sarpanch, was convinced that Haldi Ram, a villainous-looking, pockmarked man – faces can deceive as much as words – was the guilty party. The interrogation that followed was so one-sided as to get members of Habibullah's party twirling their whiskers in satisfaction. But then Mustapha Chacha interfered.

Do not misunderstand me, jaanam; Mustapha Chacha was not a man who opposed people out of dislike or a desire for prestige. He was a studious, religious man, regular in his prayers, and he was a member of the panchayat only because every villager, except Habibullah and his henchmen, wanted him there. If you had met him, I am sure you too would have seen him as the villagers saw him: a man hardened and leathery with work, with deep lines etched on his face, but seldom without a smile on his lips or a twinkle in his dark eyes. What he exuded was both a love for knowledge and a tolerance for the weaknesses of others – the two characteristics that he believed were enjoined upon all Muslims. He would not interfere in other people's affairs unless he was driven by a higher purpose. I think he was moved to interfere in this case because he genuinely believed in the innocence of Haldi Ram, having known his family for years. But perhaps there was also the desire – what Kaptaan Meadows might call 'scientific curiosity' – to apply his learning to a concrete situation.

This then, jaanam, is what he suggested, and his suggestion was accepted after a vigorous debate in which Habibullah's objections were discarded by the other members of the panchayat. It was an old and time-tested method to ascertain the truth of a statement in such situations, a method that was used, Mustapha Chacha said, in the Mughal courts of the past. This is how it went, my love:

First, Mustapha Chacha had the servants from the house brought to the panchayat square. There were five in all, and it was clear that one of them, though not necessarily Haldi Ram, had stolen the necklace. After soaking a quantity of rice in cold water and drying it in the sun, which does not take long in the glorious sunlight of my land, jaanam, he weighed rice equal to the weight of a rupee on a pair of scales. He arranged five such weights of rice. Then calling the five servants, including Haldi Ram, to him, he told them to swear by their gods and on the heads of their near and dear ones that they had not stolen the necklace, and that they did not know who had done so. When the oath had been taken, and Mustapha Chacha had impressed its solemnity on the gathering once again, he asked each of the five servants to extend their right hand, palm upward. On each man's palm, he placed a weight of the soaked and dried rice. Each man was told to hold the rice in his palm, not allowing any grain to drop, until all five had been served in a similar manner. Then, after repeating their oath again, they were made to sit down with a plantain leaf in front of them. Mustapha Chacha then said in a solemn voice: Some person among you has taken a false oath. But God, who is everywhere, is among us too. Let every man put his portion of rice into his mouth, and having chewed it, let him, when instructed, spit it out upon the plantain leaf before him. When this consecrated rice comes out from the mouth of the false, it will be different from the rice from the mouth of the honest and true.

And so it was done, jaanam: from four of the mouths, including that of Haldi Ram, the chewed rice came out much like milk and water, and from the fifth it came out almost like dry sand, fine as powder. Then Mustapha Chacha said: He who is the thief, or knows of the identity of the thief, from his false mouth the rice has come out dry and stricken; from the mouths of those who are innocent, it has come forth wet and well chewed.

Even though Habibullah grumbled, the panchayat sent, as agreed upon earlier, men to ransack the quarters of the servant who was now considered guilty, having been indicted by the consecrated rice. Even before the men returned with the recovered necklace, the servant had broken down and confessed.

Great was the rejoicing in the village, jaanam, not least in Haldi Ram's family and community, and the reputation of my uncle as a learned and devout man was further enhanced, though it was not a reputation Mustapha Chacha ever courted. That evening, when he joined us at the dastakhan for dinner, we asked him about the significance of the event, the means by which he had charmed the rice. He smiled and replied: The greatest charms reside in the human mind, my children. A guilty man will always find it impossible to chew – his gullet will be dry, his saliva meagre. God is not *our servant: he does not run about and do our errands, but he gives us arms, and minds, with which to do them. Yes, jaanam, now you know why I revere this man, this man of truth and vision who, finally, could not save himself or his family from destruction. For, my love, it is not only the greatest charms that reside in the human heart. So does the foulest evil. And when that heart belongs to the rich and powerful, like Mirza Habibullah, well then, jaanam, you should never cease to look over your shoulder. Never.*

16

[WILLIAM T. MEADOWS, NOTES ON A THUG: CHARACTER AND CIRCUMSTANCES, 1840]

'And thus, sahib, did my first year as a thug come to an end. How many did we kill that year? Close to seventy! And yet, I had no blood on my hands. Was it my reluctance or the vestiges of good sense in my father? Whatever the reason, for those five months, I was only trained to be a scout and camp follower. Even though some gang members criticized my father for it, and particularly so, the man who was next in command, Mirza Habibullah, my father never made me commit a murder. I returned to our village with my hands untainted by blood. But the second year, I knew, would be different. Alas, sahib, I had no idea just how different.

'Strangely, I do not recall how the lota ceremony went that year: did my father spill a few drops, which went unnoticed? Or did the partridge, for us Thugs a bird of omen, call from the wrong side of the fields? Or was the sacred kudalee not properly consecrated? Something must have happened, sahib, for we all, not least my gentle if misguided father, paid for the oversight. Strange are the ways of providence!'

'Surely, Amir Ali,' said I, 'surely providence cannot be blamed for meting out just deserts to such a horrible set of miscreants as you. What is the Thug's life but a preying upon those weaker than him? Crueller than the tiger, craftier than the fox, with less scruples than a hyena is a Thug. It is a wonder that providence has allowed your ancient vocation to flourish for so long!'

'I acknowledge, O Kaptaan Sahib, the justice of your criticism, for I have been exposed, however fleetingly, to the wondrous rays of your God of Reason, and I stand reformed of the evil ways of my ancestral order. But had you made this criticism to my father or his companions, they would have answered you thus: Are you English not passionately fond of sporting? A lion, a wolf, an elephant rouses your passion for destruction – in its pursuit you risk body and limb. How much higher game is a Thug's, and how much more fair, for man is pitted against man, not against a dumb, bewildered beast. And are you not fond of the battles and wars by which you win a town here and a market there? How much less bloody is the occupation of a Thug!'

'Enough, Amir Ali, evil thoughts are not meant to be repeated. Enough.'

'Forgive me, sahib. You are right, as always. I was carried away by my recollection of what befell my father in my second year out with him. It happened not far from Patna, for that year too we took the same route as in the previous year. This time, we started our bloody business early into the trip. On the very night that we embarked, we fell in with a family – an elderly man, his wife and their ten-year-old son (you will recall the bodies, sahib) – who were also headed for Patna. Though my father was against it – for the man was obviously a mullah, bearded and holy in his demeanour and voice, the dark mark of regular prayer creased into the middle of his forehead, and we had not even left the region around our village – my father's companions were impatient to begin and they garrotted all three and buried them in that place next to the neem tree from which your men later recovered the bodies. Then we set off, though not without an argument.

'It is a practice among Thugs not to take from their victims anything that is alive, be it a child or a pet, if it cannot be sold immediately. If we do not kill all that is alive, we abandon it, taking only coins and jewellery and such items. It is true, sahib, that Thugs take horses and such beasts to sell, but we are careful even with horses of pedigree, because they can be easily identified. This time, however, Habibullah, my father's main chela, took a fancy to a parrot that belonged to the murdered holy man. It could recite entire surahs from the Quran. My father tried to talk him out of it, but Habibullah, as you know, sahib, was a proud man and not willing to listen. He kept the parrot in its cage, and that proved to be my father's undoing.

'For, in the bazaars of Jehanabad the very next day, the parrot was identified as belonging to the head maulavi of the Nawab of Saleempur, and my father and two of his companions were arrested by the nawab's men. How could it have been otherwise? Are there many parrots who repeat, in the tone of an old man, the surahs of the Quran? The rest of us, even Habibullah, managed to melt into the crowd, but sahib, you can imagine my sorrow and terror as I beheld, hidden in the crowd, my father being marched away in manacles to imprisonment and death. Then, sahib, I again had doubts about my profession, and it was a bad time for such doubts.

'For now Habibullah was in charge, and he made it clear that he expected me to throttle the first victim we met after leaving

Patna. He had long been angry at my father for not forcing me into the real business of our profession, and he proclaimed, with no thought of remorse for what had befallen me, that the rules of Thugee demanded that I be fully inducted into the order by offering a life to Bhowanee as sacrifice.'

'Strange are the hearts of men, Amir Ali,' said I, 'and perchance they grow stranger in a land of so many hidden rites and superstitions as the ancient country of Hindoostan.'

17

Jaanam,

How strange this place is, this London of yours.

Now that my account to Kaptaan Meadows is drawing to a close, he does not call me to his library for days. This leaves me with a lot of free time, for the servants in the kitchen, unlike you, have never taken to me. I am never allowed into the kitchen if they can help it; my place is in the scullery. And they look positively relieved when I leave the house for a ramble in the city.

They are strangely alike, these houses of polite society and, as a much exhibited thug, I have been taken to quite a few. More than you, I suspect, my love, for you once told me that Kaptaan Meadows' house is the grandest home you have ever worked in, while I, I must confess, have been taken by the Kaptaan to much grander houses. They are all segregated in the same way: drawing room, parlour, dining room, morning room, kitchen, pantry, scullery... And it is in the bare scullery, on its hard, damp floor, that there is space for the likes of us: the thug from nowhere, the charwoman from somewhere. The better servants sleep in the kitchen or pantry, don't they? Or, in some cases, they have rooms in the attic. Though you, of course, seldom sleep in any of the houses – despite, I hear, occasional invitations by the men, master or servants. You mostly return to your aunt who lives in the rookery, which even the Kaptaan's servants seem to dread. You are wise not to tell them that you sleep there. You took me there a few times, though I do not think I would be able to find it again, so circuitous and crowded were the routes and side alleys by which you led me. And yet, I knew by the smell that the place was nothing but an opium den even before I entered, though you insist on calling it an 'eating place'.

Opium is something I am sensitive to; for me, it is not an addiction, but a medicine. Perhaps in one of these letters I will tell you how I came to cultivate the habit, though what I take is the dry akbari opium which has been eaten as a medicine and relaxant in India for ages, not the kind that your countrymen smoke. And not only in the opium dens, jaanam; you would be surprised by how often the sweet smell of opium has assailed me in the houses of society.

But this city of yours, jaanam, that is what I want to write about. Like these polite houses, your city is deeply segregated, much more than any city I saw in my land. I have been walking in your city regularly, and I have also discovered its drawing rooms and kitchens. Behind each drawing room, a scullery, a lavatory, or worse. Behind Westminster, the Devil's Acre, through which they are now ploughing a new road, for what better way is there to remove a populace or open up a land than to force new routes through it? Perhaps, jaanam, the trains that have started running to this city, and the new roads being built or projected by royal commissions are meant simply to substitute places like your aunt's den and Qui Hy's dhaba with something safer and nicer.

Qui Hy's dhaba, now, that is a place Kaptaan Meadows and even his household servants have never heard of: it is in one of the mouldering quarters of the Mint. When I was first taken to it by January Monday – who is a West Indian, jaanam, not an Indian as you told me – I thought it would be run by a Chinese man. It was a strange house, narrower than the other houses on that street, though those were no broader than a dozen paces themselves, and the front door did not open into a lobby. It opened directly into a room, which must have been a shop in the past.

I entered, expecting to be accosted by an old, whiskered Chinaman. But the place turned out to be run by an ayah, who is known as Qui Hy, or Koi Hai, which was the call she responded to in the family that brought her over to London almost twenty years ago. Or is it because in Company parlance 'Koi Hai' was what, as Mustapha Chacha told us, those British officers and traders were called who had been in India long enough to become 'someone'? Because Ayah Qui Hy is 'someone' in those crooks and crannies of London in which you may find asleep, a dozen to the floor, lascars and ex-slaves, ayahs and prostitutes of the poorest sort, gypsies and stowaways, urchins and pickpockets. People know her. And she knows people.

Will this save her from the fate that is perhaps even now being designed for her in some careless, powerful quarter? For Mustapha Chacha knew people too, and they knew him, yes, jaanam, even loved and respected him. But did it avail him at that final moment when the henchmen of Mirza Habibullah raised their lathis and spears and settled an old score in the traditional way?

My apprenticeship in Patna was coming to a close when word came from the village, in a worryingly roundabout manner, that Mustapha Chacha required our presence back home. I immediately went to Hamid Bhai's house, but Bhabhi told me that he was out on business. Hamid Bhai had risen in the ranks of the clerks who worked for the lawyer he was attached to, and now the lawyer sent him to get affidavits, petitions, etc. from adjoining courts, kacheris and thanas. He could be away for days. So I proceeded to the village alone.

It took a day and a night before I came in sight of the village. Part of the journey I had accomplished on bullock carts and buggies, begging or buying a ride when I could, and part on foot. It was morning: I had started walking with the first light of the sun. Something had worried me all night. It was not the first time I or Hamid Bhai had been called back: There were regular disputes over water channels with Habibullah's people, and we were called back for strength and support. Still, I had bad dreams throughout that night. I set out, as I have written, jaanam, at the break of dawn.

How peaceful it is, the break of dawn, in the villages of India. You would have no idea of it, jaanam, for here the fog and the buildings obscure the sun and the sky. But that morning, my second morning on the road, the sky stretched above me, a grey-blue washed by streaks of white cloud, those to the east tinged with the colour of the rising sun. Birds sang. Now that I was close to my village, I could identify each birdsong: the sibilant cheee-ee of the shoubeegi, the scolding observations of the myna, the chit-chit-chit of the baya, the soft cooing of the wood-dove, the shocking beast-screech of the peacock. A jackal, late from foraging on the outskirts of some village, slunk past on the mud road. A couple of peacocks sat on a low branch, watching me pass.

My part of India is not lush green wilderness, as you like to picture India. No, jaanam, it has been cultivated far too long to be the jungle that you imagine. But there are trees, sometimes twisted and deprived, sometimes wide and majestic. Sometimes there are patches of lush wilderness, sometimes barren, straggly land or a brown hillock, and everywhere there are more animals and birds than I can name. There are semi-arid stretches at times, and then there are rivulets and suddenly, across a brown mound, the gleam of a broad river, descending perhaps from the mighty Himalayas four hundred miles away, or flowing into the Ganga or the Jamuna further on.

I walked on, and by the time I caught sight of the twin-hillocks that marked the passage to our village, the beauty of the morning had almost erased my misgivings. But nature, jaanam, can be as misleading as art.

A kilometre from my village, still hidden behind brown hillocks, at the final turning of the road which would bring the village and its fields into view, I was hailed by a shout. It was the first vague indication that something was seriously wrong, for no one knew the time of my arrival. I was stopped by two young men, whom, after a moment of alarm that had me fingering the dagger hidden under my kurta, I recognized as the sons of Haldi Ram. Haldi Ram and his community, being low caste, resided in a hamlet just outside the main village. Could it be a coincidence that the two boys had run into me, perhaps having gone a little too far to relieve themselves this morning? But no, that was not the case. The men of the family had taken turns, all through the night, to keep an eye on this road, for they knew that I or Hamid

Bhai would be coming down it sometime. Something very bad had happened the previous evening, and I had to be warned of it. More than that the boys would not say. They requested that I accompany them to their hamlet, instead of first going to Mustapha Chacha's home in the village.

You might not realize, jaanam, how worried I was by then. No, I had no reason to distrust the boys of the clan of Haldi Ram. He and his family had worked for mine when we needed extra help in the fields. I knew they were honest people, and grateful to Mustapha Chacha for various minor favours, not least the matter of that theft. But the invitation to first go to their hamlet was disturbing – not least because Haldi Ram was very conscious of his low-caste status, and though the Muslims of the village did not observe the rituals of caste purification, he would not easily assume the authority to invite any respectable member of the village into his lowly hamlet. But here he was now, running up to me, followed by other members of the family, all carrying lathis, and with much courtesy but no further information, he ushered me into the village. It was done in a way that made it clear that he did not want my arrival to be widely broadcast.

How can I narrate to you, jaanam, the events of that early morning? I lack the words, and I can hardly explain to you the love and reverence that I bore towards Mustapha Chacha and his wife. Remember, my love, I was an orphan, like you, and I had been brought up by them.

Perhaps you will understand my feelings for them if you think of your own feelings for your aunt. I have seen that you love your old aunt in your own way; though she runs an opium den in the rookery, which you would not have her do, it was she who brought you up when your mother was deported. Or perhaps you will not understand my feelings, for you have had your share of fights and disagreements with your aunt, and I, strangely, do not recall one harsh word from Mustapha Chacha or Chachijaan. Sometimes they scolded their sons; sometimes they had disagreements with Hamid Bhai; between me and them, there was nothing but an unbroken stream of understanding and love. I could not have imagined better parents. No, jaanam, even parents could not have been as good to me as they were, for one needs to strain against the leash of parenting sooner or later, and parents do resent, if only in part, the fact that children, especially sons, grow into lives of their own.

Even today, scribbling these words as I kneel beside a single candle in the scullery, I can feel my eyes fill with tears of sorrow and frustration when I think of that morning. Aren't there moments when you wish time could be wound back, that you could change one thing, just one thing, in the past? How often, after listening to Haldi Ram that morning, have I wished the same!

Haldi Ram was frightened. I could see it in his face, in his unusually dilated eyes, his occasional stutter, the tense manner in which he clutched his lathi. And so were the other members of the community: they were all frightened. Almost all of them were outside, crowded around the khaat on which they had seated me. Of course, I was the only person sitting on the khaat. Haldi Ram and an older man who, I knew, was their headman, squatted on their haunches in front of me. The others, men, women and children, stood, faces strangely impassive but postures fraught with tension. Haldi Ram's wife brought me chai; I was in no mood to eat or drink but I accepted it as I thought my refusal would be seen as a recognition of their low caste and Mustapha Chacha had always maintained that both Islam and humanity – 'insaniyat' was a word he relished – refused to recognize such divisions between human beings. It was only when I had sipped a bit of the tea that Haldi Ram commenced his explanation. His words are still stamped on my memory, and I could write them down verbatim but for the fact that the language he spoke was not the language I write in and the language I write in is not legible to you, jaanam.

Forgive us, Amir babu, said Haldi Ram. Forgive us for interrupting your journey, not even providing you with a decent breakfast, for what can we poor people serve to a gentleman like you, son of the noble Syed Zahid Ali sahib, nephew of the learned and gracious Mustapha Ali sahib.

Small, wizened, much darker than I am, with a tiny, thin moustache, reddish eyes and a pockmarked face, Haldi Ram was a hard worker and a harder drinker, but he was also a cautious man. My heart in my mouth, I had to make the appropriate noises until he got to the matter that was troubling him. But for once Haldi Ram's vernacular eloquence failed him. As soon as he started giving me an account of 'the sacrilege that took place yesterday', he broke down and started to cry like a baby. I was worried now. Haldi Ram did not cry easily; he came from a long line of impoverished peasants who had borne more than most people, suffered more, lost more, and tears did not come easily to his eyes.

The headman took up the narrative and this, jaanam, with some interpolations and exclamations from me (which I will leave out), is what they said:

Headman: Forgive him, Amir babu. His soul is burdened by the many kindnesses of Mustapha sahib, kindnesses he can never repay in this lifetime.

(At this, some of the women in the crowd started weeping too. But the way they wept was disturbing. These were women who usually wept in a public manner, deriving the only relief sometimes available to them from an extravagant explosion of grief. But this time, they were sobbing into their pallus, stifling their wails.)

Headman: It is not right to let our sorrow prevent you from learning, as soon as possible, what I can see you are anxious to know.

Haldi Ram: It is my duty, the least I can do...Headman: It happened yesterday, Amir babu. Three of our boys, children of eight or nine, who were working in the adjoining field, saw it, though they were careful enough to avoid being seen.

Haldi Ram: We think it had to do with one of your uncle's cows getting into Mirza Habibullah's fields of mustard. At least, that is what the boys heard him claim. In any case, the Mirza came with his men and started harvesting the crop in a part of Mustapha sahib's fields. It was to compensate for the mustard cropped by the cow, he claimed. Mustapha sahib and Shahid babu ran to stop it, but this time it appears that Mirza Habibullah and his men were prepared to go further than they had in the past...

Headman (spitting on the ground in disgust): Habibullah has been doing this to us and to the Yadavs and Jollahs as well. But I never thought he would do it to a Syed, and that too a gentleman of Mustapha sahib's piety and learning...

Haldi Ram: But that is why he dared, because he knew that Mustapha sahib and his family would not stoop to such roughness, such coarseness.

Headman: I think you can guess what happened, Amir babu. Habibullah's men attacked your uncle and cousin and started beating them with lathis. They fought back but they were outnumbered.

Haldi Ram: And that was not all, Amir babu. How we wish it had ended there! How I wish...

Headman: Your Chachijaan ran out to stop the men and, we think, she was hit on the head by mistake. She seems to have died on the spot.

Haldi Ram: Calm yourself, Amir babu. Listen: there is more, there is more...

Headman: One of our boys had already run to fetch us. The others were watching from hiding, for they could do nothing against Habibullah and his henchmen. They thought the tragedy was over now. Your uncle had collected his wife in his arms and was rocking her back and forth.

Haldi Ram: The boys say that Habibullah, may he rot in hell, was shocked and frightened. He approached your uncle and suggested, in his blustering way, that they should let the matter drop and his men would help carry the body back.

Headman: But you know your uncle, Amir babu. Never was a man with more honesty and less subterfuge born in this village. He refused the offer. A lesser man would have pretended to accept it. But no, not your uncle, Amir babu, not that sainted man... Some things, he told Habibullah, cannot be forgotten, because they affect not the man you are or the man I am, but all of humanity...

Haldi Ram: Habibullah heard a threat in those words, Amir babu; the mean always consider wisdom a threat. Habibullah knew that he could not allow your uncle to take the matter to the panchayat. He turned and rode away, but his men, as if by his order, fell upon your uncle and Shahid babu. We were running towards the spot then. We were still half a kos away, but we could see what was happening. Your uncle had not expected such a premeditated crime from Habibullah and his men. He realized this only when they stabbed Shahid babu, who was standing by his side. Then your uncle fought like the brave man he was. He snatched a lathi from one of his assailants and defended himself. But alas, there were about twenty of them and he was alone. By the time we reached the spot, he had been stabbed and beaten to death. I... I...

Headman: There were only seven of us, Amir babu. And we had only a couple of lathis between us; we are not fighting men. But this Haldi Ram, this tiny Haldi Ram, would have thrown himself on Habibullah's henchmen and clawed their eyes out had I and the others not held him back by force.

Haldi Ram: I wish I had died there. I wish I had died with that noble man...

Headman: Don't be a fool, Haldi Ram. No, Amir babu, no, do not stand up. Hold him, boys. Yes, yes, hold him, hold him down. Do not let him run into the village and get himself killed. Habibullah's men are waiting for him. He has gone too far this time to stop... Listen, Amir babu. Listen to me, for the sake of my white hair, for your uncle's sake. Habibullah had the bodies carted to the outskirts of his property, and he has buried all three in one grave next to the abandoned well, the one below the neem tree. He has proclaimed: No one digs in my land without my permission. If anyone wants to dig here, let him beg my permission first. He wants you and Hamid babu to accept his power, and if you refuse to do so, if you take him on, his men have been instructed to kill you. Listen to me, Amir babu, calm down. Do not get yourself killed...

They held me down, jaanam; they tied me to the khaat until I promised not to run off in a rash bid to avenge my family. Those good men who had stayed awake all night to save me and Hamid Bhai. Had they not intercepted me and held me until my fit of anger and ranting subsided, I would not be writing this unreadable, never-to-be-sent letter to you. If it were not for those half-starved, half-naked men and women, people we considered dirty and uncultured, perhaps I would have lost that faith in humankind which Mustapha Chacha instilled in us and which, at times, I feel is still in danger of slipping away.

We say in our parts that a tiger never attacks a human being until his first taste of human blood. And once a tiger has tasted human blood, he never attacks anything else. It is like that with the powerful: once they have tasted blood, they feast more and more upon the weak. Perhaps it was the same with Habibullah: over the years his atrocities had been increasing; a labourer whipped here, a tribal woman abducted there, and it had finally led to this, the premeditated murder of his only rival in the village. Or perhaps, as the headman suggested, it was not like that. Perhaps a minor dispute of the sort that his family often had with mine went out of hand, a thoughtless blow proved fatal, and Habibullah and his henchmen were left with no choice but to finish the job.

Whatever it was, there they now lay, hastily buried under loose earth in the lands of Habibullah, not even accorded a decent funeral.

I knew I did not have the strength to accost Habibullah or recover the bodies. But I also knew that once my cousin Hamid Bhai, in many ways as straightforward and innocent of deception as his father, arrived, we would have to try – and sacrifice our lives in the process. Revenge I had nothing against, for revenge is the last resort for those whom the law fails. But to lose your life in the process, that, jaanam, seemed unnecessary. And yet, what else could I do?

18

Sometimes, reading those books in my grandfather's library, I would wander out to the small veranda attached to it. There, the plaster on the walls was peeling; lines of industrious ants crowded the corners of the floor, cobwebs netted the corners above. I would sit in the shade and look out: an ageing garden and a driveway covered with reddish gravel. Sunlight, bright and warm. Birds twittering. A gecko on the wall or a lizard, bobbing its red head, scuttling across the driveway. Sitting there, I would read about the damp, dark streets of London in Dickens or Collins. I could never imagine them. What would darkness and cold like that entail? Would birds sing in a place so bleak? If I imagined it, I would imagine it as a late evening in my hometown – and I would sense the imprecision of imagining it as a wide sky full of flitting bats, as walls on which geckoes stalked insects under low-watt bulbs. But I never had that problem with the characters in the books. Even when I could not hear them speak their many dialects, I always saw them with their recognizable defects and demands, their human frailties and inhuman strengths. I saw the way they walked, the way they stood, at times, even the way they thought. Or so I felt.

And so, when the time came, I had little trouble seeing the man Shields brought with him. He was angular and one-eyed; the black patch that covered his bad eye imparted to him a rather forbidding look. Not surprisingly, he was introduced to John May as One-eyed Jack, which, May intuited, was just the latest in a series of names that had been worn, like borrowed or stolen clothes, by this gaunt man. He did not enquire about his real name. And that was just as well, for One-eyed Jack did not always remember the name he had been christened with – or, at least, was liable to offer different versions on different occasions.

They had agreed to meet under the clock at Charing Cross, May preferring to stay away from the Prize of War out of a vague sense of precaution. If this One-eyed Jack did not prove to be 'game for anything', as Shields had billed him, at least John May would not feel exposed on home territory. He could buy him a drop or two and sound him out in one of the neighbouring taverns, or better still, walk with him a bit and, if the conversation was worth it, stop at a cheap place somewhere else, perhaps the Great Mogul on Drury Lane.

One-eyed Jack did look like he was capable of undertaking all and everything, but John May was doubtful of his capacity to execute anything. Even this early in the afternoon, Jack reeked of alcohol, which appeared to have spilled down the threadbare long-coat of a vaguely naval cut from the previous century that he sported over slightly more fashionable trousers, both obviously procured at a rebate from the thieves' quarter of Saffron Hill and Field Lane. There was a kind of languor in his gait that May correctly associated with opium. But he was deferential, which John May appreciated, he addressed Shields as 'sir' and May as 'guv'nor'. And he was a big man, obviously born and brought up in the countryside and not on the streets of London, a shoulder taller than Shields, some inches taller than May, though most of him was skin on bones, hanging loose like clothes on a scarecrow.

John May walked the two into the crowd that milled around Charing Cross, dislodging his coat corners from the grip of an old hag who had seen him looking at her: he had got into the habit of looking at the skulls of the poor and the strange. This woman had a perfectly normal skull though, with a great head of tangled hair, swarming with vermin. She tagged after them, pleading, 'Husban's laid with fever an I've four small chil'ren at 'ome, won't yer give a poor woman a 'ap'ny, sir? Only a 'ap'ny for a poor woman as ain't 'ad a bit of bread between 'er teeth since 'esty mornin'...'

Could one even talk, let alone plot, in this crowd, this roaring vortex in the heart of London, wondered John May. Or perhaps this was exactly where one could plot, so rife was the air with voices and sounds, the bustle of horses and omnibuses, the ladies and gentlemen trying their best to walk in bubbles through the milling crowd, the foreigners with their myriad tongues, the country squires riding in from Cumberland or Westmorland, the servants, grooms and lackeys running about, the waiters in the taverns shouting their orders, the potboys, beggars, lascars, hawkers, tinkers, gypsies, that omnipresent West Indian blackie wrapped in his strange garment, made of the rigging and sails of ships, who sang and sold handwritten songs signed 'January Monday'... Who would, who could overhear in the midst of this din?

At the moment though, John May was letting One-eyed Jack talk. Egged on occasionally by Shields, Jack was telling May about his previous jobs, trying to impress on him both his reliability and his willingness to do 'anything', two capacities that were difficult to conjoin. Jack's voice sounded almost educated, but it was loud and harsh, like a policeman's; it appeared he had done everything, from sailing to serving to 'dog-stealing'. The latter, he explained, consisted of working with a woman.

'This is how it's done, guv'nor,' boomed One-eyed Jack, keeping easy pace with Sheilds and John May despite the aura of alcohol emanating from him. 'The woman looks for a mug, any drunken or stupid sorta fellow. She stops him in the street and talks to him, encouraging him to get familiar like. When he does so, she relieves him of his money or jewellery, and is usually not caught, y'know. If he notices and makes a noise, her bully comes up and knocks him down, exclaiming, "What you talking to me good wife for?" I worked as a bully for six years, guv'nor, and I always knocked down my man fair and square.'

'But not always, as I gather from your lost eye,' quipped John May dryly.

'Oh, guv'nor, I knocked him down alright, y'know, but there was three of his friends in the crowd. I knocked down one of them too, but then I was stabbed in the eye with the sharp end of an umbrella...'

Shields was looking at John May with a satisfied expression on his face. His beady eyes seemed to say, I told you this is our man for the job.

For between them, Shields and John May had agreed that there was a job to be done. And that it would require three people: two for the main task, and one as lookout.

19

Amir Ali passes John May and his companions on Charles Street. They do not know him and he does not know them yet. He is on his way back from the phrenology meeting to which Captain Meadows had taken him, and he is walking fast because he is dressed in an Indian manner, with a turban and a flashy cummerbund over his kurta and angarkha. He is feeling a little cold; it is the wrong costume for the climate, no matter what the season. But more than that, he is afraid of being mobbed by urchins and drunks. He never dresses in rich Indian clothes when out in the city on his own, preferring to dress in the pyjamas and shirts worn by many of the lascars he had met during his voyage to England. He had slept below decks with the lascars and other lowly sailors, the skipper of the ship not allowing any 'mixed breed or nigger servants, other than ayahs' in attendance on the higher decks after nightfall. Except for the three nights that Captain Meadows lay hallucinating with fever: no one else had wanted to spend the nights in his cabin for fear of infection and miasma.

On landing in London, Amir had discovered that Indian dresses invited needless attention – sometimes flattering attention, from the beggars and riffraff who trailed him under the impression that he was a prince or nabob. And sometimes more caustic attention from urchins, pickpockets and, once, a group of drunken youths who besieged and berated Amir Ali for being an 'Oriental despot' who kept women like cattle in his harem.

But Captain Meadows insists on dressing up Amir Ali as a 'real Indian on the occasions when he displays him at dinner parties, luncheons, or meetings of various societies. Actually, thinks Amir Ali, the dresses the Kaptaan had procured before they sailed from Calcutta were far more elaborate and rich than anything he had ever worn before, and they had a distinctive Awadhi cut to them, a style not common in his village or in the regions around it.

Usually, Captain Meadows lets Amir ride back to the house with him on such occasions, sitting next to the coachman, but today the Captain had to stay longer for a debate. And as it was the third time that Amir had been taken to the imposing new building of the much-endowed London Society of Phrenology, Meadows was certain that he would be able to find his way back. In any case, the Captain was aware that Amir spent longer hours in the city each passing week, and as the ex-Thug was not exactly in his employment, there was no reason to prevent or resent it as long as he was available, when required, to finish the narrative of his life. Captain Meadows hoped that the notes he had been taking would, indirectly and cautiously, for he could not afford to openly antagonize the powerful, illustrate and defend his liberal position on phrenology and related matters.

Phrenology – now that is something Amir Ali does not really understand. Though it is not altogether alien to him: even in the village they had sayings like, if your feet are big, you are a farmer; if your head is big, you are a leader. That made some sense, for sometimes experience did bear it out. But the minute distinctions that the Kaptaan and his colleagues make and argue over, the fixed relations that they establish, Amir can only...

'Jahaajbhai, jahaajbhai,' comes the shout from the other side of the street. He stops and looks, but cannot see beyond a foot or two into the dense throng of humanity, coaches and cabs. Then he hears the voice again, speaking in Hindustani, 'Wait, wait, jahaajbhai, wait a minute.'

Amir had made friends with some of the lascars on the ship that brought him and Captain Meadows to England and sometimes they referred to him as they referred to other lascars on the ship: as a 'ship-brother'. Amir knows that it is a designation that matters to the lascars; many of them consider a jahaajbhai in the light of a real brother, and are willing to stand by him to the last. But the ship that brought Amir to London about a year ago was scheduled to sail back, via Cape Town, within a fortnight. As far as he knows, all the lascars are back in Calcutta by now.

Then, dodging between the wheels of coaches and horses' hooves, pivoting elegantly to avoid getting entangled in the petticoats of women or the canes of men, there comes a walking advertisement: a tall beanpole of a man, with a greying, forked beard, sandwiched between two boards, one hanging in front of him and one behind, both advertising a pantomime. A tall, misshapen hat sits on his balding head, with a large cardboard hand (advertising the same pantomime) jutting out of it like a feather in a cap. There are so many boardmen in this part of London, advertising everything under the sun, getting tickled in the nose or spattered with mud by practical jokers, that Amir would have walked on if the walking advertisement had not, with difficulty, for he is truly tied to the boards, shouted again, 'Oho, Amirbhai, jahaajbhai, oh you look like a prince, nawabzada!'

It is then that recognition dawns on Amir. Only one of the lascars, in an ironic acknowledgement of Amir's purer Urdu and better education, called him 'nawabzada', or for that matter, addressed him solely in Urdu.

'Gunga!' exclaims Amir. 'What are you doing here? I thought you were all going back to Calcutta...'

'So we were, so we were, nawabzada, until that dog-turd of a skipper took a recount and realized that there were six more than he required. So he discharged all six of us, the pig; he kept slimy Fakru's larger gang of lascars and put me and my men on the pilot's boat to the wharf and sailed off...'

Amir has heard similar stories. The ports of Europe are full of lascars who had been signed up in Asia or Africa and discharged in Europe. The lucky ones find employment on a ship sailing back to their part of the world, the less lucky set sail for other parts, and the unlucky ones linger on at the docks, some of them as helpless as fish on dry land, the others drifting, like Gunga, in and out of various jobs. But most gangs of lascars stick together, even on land, with a tenacity that is surprising in men who by and large do not come from the same place, belong to the same religion or speak the same language.

Gunga's band, Amir recalls, contained seven men, three from Bihar and Bengal, one Malay, one Chinese and two Arabs, all of them managing to communicate with the help of some kind of pidgin: two of them, the Chinese and one of the Arabs, had died on the way to England, leaving Gunga with five companions and placing him at the disadvantage of having too small a gang of lascars to bargain with. For the lascars mostly board as a gang, working and cooking together, considering themselves bound by ties closer than that of blood.

Gunga, however, is ebullient as ever: 'But look at you, nawabzada, you have been adopted by the Queen of England!'

'Appearances are deceptive, brother. I am still in the employment of the Kaptaan.'

'Kaptaan Khet-Khaliyaan? Don't tell me! I thought he was to free you in a few days, once you had told him about your days as a Thug…'

'Almost, Gunga. We are almost done. I am looking around now, for other opportunities.'

'But you told us the Kaptaan had promised you a passage back…'

'He has, brother. And he will keep his word: he is a man of principles. But I do not wish to go back.'

'Not go back? Are you ill, brother? What's wrong? What son-of-a-pig in his right mind would want to stay here, in this land of cold and rain, this city of the half-empty stomach and the unexpected kick?'

Amir shakes his head. Gunga is about to say something, but a figure in the crowd catches his attention. He moves away.

'I have to run, jahaajbhai. I can see a policeman headed this way, and they usually push us boardmen off the pavements. When can we meet again? The others would want to see you too…'

'Qui Hy's place, in the afternoon, three days from now?'

'Mai's place? Qui Hy's?'

Amir nods, but Gunga is already twisting, turning, dancing his way through the crowd. A lanky man, he is strangely graceful in his movements, and there is still in him, even on land, the motion of someone used to scampering up the lines of a ship. He has the reputation of being one of the best foretop men who ever sailed the seas, dancing up and down the ratlines, glued to the ropes without the least effort on his part, always perfectly balanced and always with a joyous shout, though the joy in his voice is seldom reflected in his eyes, which are brown and hard, accustomed to seeing too much.

The policeman walks past in his blue frockcoat. Solid and dour, he eyes Amir Ali ambivalently, unable to choose between his natural deference for rich clothing and a native suspicion of foreigners. At the last moment, he tips his hat to Amir, and Amir reciprocates with a low, very Oriental, very ornamental bow.

20

They are huddled in a corner of the Great Mogul, with its elaborate and clearly fake pretensions to an exotic royalty, a place better ventilated and hence less warm than the Prize of War. John May is still sipping his first beer, but both Shields and One-eyed Jack are on their third, since the drinks are on May. It is a relief to see that the extra beers have not affected Jack's demeanour in any obvious way: his languor has neither increased nor decreased. John May gives Shields the signal they had agreed on, and Shields broaches the subject.

'You have worked as a resurrectionist, haven't you, Jack?' Shields asks.

'Yes, sir, that I have. Two years running: supplied King's College too. Top quality Things. Whatever Jack does, he does well, sir.'

'How would you like to get back into the business?'

'Ain't the same, guv'nor,' replies Jack, addressing John May now, as if he has guessed that Shields is asking questions on his behalf. 'Too much danger, now, guv'nor, and less money. The Italian boy affair was bad for the business, y'know. Trust the rich to get all upset like about a rosy-cheeked Latino; had he been a London potboy, no one would have noticed and the police wouldn't never have begunned hopping about...'

'What if it paid twice what you think, Jacky,' says Shields.

'Ah, sir, that would be 'nother matter.'

'And what if it paid four times more, if only one got the right Thing?'

'Freshly buried, y'mean?'

'Yes, Jacky. Or, shall we say, buried with some help from you.'

'Nah, that is a thought, that is.'

'Isn't it, Jacky? Four times more, say. In ready silver.'

'That is a thought. It sure is, guv'nor.'

'Perhaps another ale will help you think about it, Jack,' says John May.

'That it might, guv'nor. It just might.'

21

Much to Captain Meadows' barely hidden annoyance, in the draped and curtained 'lecture hall' of the London Society of Phrenology, a large neoclassical room adorned with plaster casts of skulls on dark wooden pedestals, Lord Batterstone was in full flow and an audience of thirty-nine men and five women were captivated by his eloquence. One of the drawbacks of the increasing prestige of the Society had been this: they had moved from meetings at inns to their own premises. Captain Meadows wondered with a bitter smile if Lord Batterstone would have demeaned himself to the extent of delivering his harangue in a public place; here, he was thundering away, mesmerizing his audience with the sheer audacity of his decibels.

'Gentlemen, it is not my purpose to defend the Mosaic estimate of creation: my faith is not a blade of leaf that can be blown into perdition by the revised accountancy of years.' The right hon'ble Lord Batterstone paused for a second and looked at his notes. He was not wearing a mask here. He did not need to wear a mask in this company. But just as the mask never hid his authority so that, unbidden, John May always called him M'lord, his bare face, slightly podgy but noble in its dimensions, high-cheeked and full-jowled, attested to the inherited prestige of his family name. He raised that heavy noble face to his audience and continued: 'Nor will I dispute the whispering few among us who suggest that man owes his origins to an unknown tadpole hatched in the misty swamps of the past.'

Lord Batterstone waited for the smiles and mutters to subside.

'These are matters in which theology and science have decided to look at different aspects of the same experiment: where science sees the steps leading to the temple of creation, theology sees the full resplendent temple. I am a man of science though unlike some, it has merely strengthened my faith in God and His Son. I am a man of science and I do not want to examine issues, like the Mosaic estimate of creation or the amphibian ancestors of man, which are either the realm of religion or not susceptible to practical observation and analytical reasoning. However, when some of you – following the insinuations of

Combe and talking of man in the same breath as animals – go on to suggest on the analogy of botany that there is little difference between the skulls of animals and men, and even less between those of the races and nations of men, then, gentlemen, I have to raise my voice and remind you that what you claim runs counter to scientific evidence. As Watson has noted, evolution in the realms of geology and botany does not, I say, does not (thumping the podium for emphasis) prove evolution in the human species. And even Combe, who obdurately, irreligiously and unscientifically placed man at the end of a chain of animals, conceded that whatever the state of the body of man, his brain is unquestionably the workmanship of God. If so, is God's workmanship so uncertain and so fickle that we cannot distinguish between the skull of an ape and that of a man except in the degree to which a certain faculty is present? Is God's workmanship so slight that we can distinguish between the various races and classes only on the basis of wrinkles on the face and the turn of lips? Everything we know of nature and God militates against such an assumption.'

Long pause for effect, and a sip from the glass of watered-down white wine in front of him.

'But then, the question is implied in some of our circles, is the skull of a Negro or a Chinaman the same as the skull of a Caucasian except in degree? Has the Caucasian simply developed from other forms of man, perchance sharing an ancestor with the lowly Negro? I have, gentlemen, two objections to this contention. First, to make the Caucasian a child of the Negro or some other race, is to blur the essential difference between the races, and forget the lessons of history, which records Greek and Roman antiquity as the cradle of every civilization, as well as the lessons of biology, which reveals a slow degradation of the species, the ill characteristics of the father being strengthened in the son in direct proportion to the loss of vitality that comes with time to both man and civilizations. Second, our science of phrenology – of whose scientific truth not one of us has any doubt (pause for the confirmatory shaking of heads to subside) – our science of phrenology argues against the assumption that the Chinaman or the Negro is almost a Caucasian, failing only in degree. There is a difference in the size of the brain and the organic quality of the body, with which the brain must inevitably correspond. We know that a piece of wrought iron is tougher than a piece of cast iron of the same size: why should we suppose that both will cut as deeply if fashioned into a sword?'

Longer pause, in which thumps of support were mixed with a few murmurs of dissent, the loudest from Captain Meadows.

'Moreover, gentlemen, we phrenologists know that organs and faculties do not operate in isolation: one faculty is tempered by another. Forsooth, there is no organ for murder, but indeed, there is a faculty intended to impart energy, force and effectiveness in character and action. In races such as the Red Indian, where these faculties are not restrained by firmness, conscientiousness, ideality and by the more conservative powers of the mind, or where they are accentuated by the faculties of destructiveness and acquisitiveness, as in the Negro, we need not look for an organ for murder before adducing that the individual concerned will be, or is, a murderer.'

Was this a reference to his exhibition earlier today of Amir Ali, wondered Captain Meadows. Should he object? But no, the reference was too oblique, and an objection would sound churlish. But why did he find Lord Batterstone's ideas so hard to accept? They did not contain many differences, perhaps nothing beyond Batterstone's belief in the final irreducibility of difference and his related conviction that character had to be read from the skull and not from 'incidental' attributes like eyebrows and ears. And why was it so hard for Lord Batterstone to countenance any opposition in that area? Was it, thought Meadows, because of Lord Batterstone's blue blood, his aristocratic pedigree, while Meadows himself, being only a middle-class gentleman, having risen over the past three generations through trade, found it as difficult to accept a world not capable of progress, evolution, movement towards a greater sharing, a sameness of peoples?

He brought himself back to M'lord's speech. 'The brain in texture, size and configuration reflects the soul, whose seat it is. And as the brain is the means by which we may recognize the shadowy workings of our eternal soul, so is the cranium a reflection of the brain. On its bony casement may be read, in universal forms and particular elevations, in folds and depressions, a correct and indisputable outline of the moral character and intellectual propensities of that man. But just as God did not give the same soul to all men (more murmurs of dissent here, which made Captain Meadows hopeful) – some are saved and some are not and some, it is argued, do not have souls – just as God did not create all beings equal, it stands to reason that the marks on the skull are as permanent as souls and not liable to be erased by education, or wealth.'

Pause, again, as Lord Batterstone prepared to end his speech.

'It is indisputable, at least in scientific circles, that the brain is the organ of the mind and that each faculty of the mind has its special organ in the brain. The contention that the brain functions in a general way can be dismissed with the help of practical experiments as well as, and more importantly, by analogical reasoning. Throughout nature, each function has devoted to itself a particular organ. Sight has the eye; digestion, the stomach. It may be further observed that wherever the function is compound, the organ is correspondingly so, as in the case of the tongue, which has a nerve that subserves the sense of feeling and another that conveys the sense of taste. In short, ladies and gentlemen, in the entire human frame there is, as far as we know, not a single instance of one nerve performing two functions, or of two nerves performing the same function. Why is it then, as the honourable Captain Meadows has suggested, though not said in so many words, why is it, gentlemen, that Nature, so consistent in all matters, should break her established mould when it comes to that bony casement which is the record of the brain and in which is seated, like God Almighty on his throne in Heaven, that divine spark, the eternal soul of man?

'As I have already said, it is true that there is no organ of murder, but there is a faculty intended to impart force and effectiveness in character and action which, when large, active and not restrained by the more conservative powers of the mind, may, nay, *will* inevitably lead to murder. While it is true, as the honourable Captain has argued, that every faculty of the human mind may be strengthened by judicious culture or weakened by disuse, it is also true that in some men, and in some races, the balance of countervailing faculties is so uneven that their faculty for force, unrestrained by their puny organs of ideality and conscientiousness, predisposes them towards violence and bloodshed. In that sense, gentlemen, one may consider a highly developed organ for force in the Caucasian brain almost the equivalent of an organ for murder in a certain kind of Asiatic or Negroid cranium: it will inevitably cause this Asiatic or Negroid man to commit murder, though it might not have the same result in the case of the Caucasian, whose brain most excels in the countervailing special organs of ideality, conscientiousness, amativeness and mirthfulness.'

Lord Batterstone's trademark gesture of draining his glass of wine and pushing it away: end of speech. His noble face lit up by the sincerity of his convictions, the purity of his heart and blood. A moment of silence. Then thunderous applause from almost everyone except Captain Meadows and the Captain's two staunch supporters, Mrs Grayper and her daughter, the lovely Mary. Meadows wondered what they would tell Major Grayper when he joined the three of them for dinner at the Grayper residence later that evening. He was looking forward to the dinner, as he always looked forward to his moments with Mary, but he could not help feeling that the steely Major Grayper, with those piercing grey eyes and pursed lips, tight in thought and suspicion, would side with Lord Batterstone.

22

Night has fallen when the three men walk into the opium den. The woman who runs it recognizes one of them as the man who had tossed her a coin just for messing up her hair when she – the old woman chuckles – had been preparing herself for more, much more than that. She does not like him but he obviously has money, and she likes money. Oh, she loves money, much more than her niece Jenny, who should be coming back soon, wants her to. But Jenny, thinks the old woman, Jenny has ideas. She is a nice girl, an affectionate, hard-working girl, but she has ideas, and she will get into trouble because of them. Like gambolling around with that Indian prince she has brought to this place twice already. Not that the old woman has anything against Indians and Chinese and suchlike, they pay more readily than the English do, but whoever heard of a charwoman and servant gambolling with a prince!

She bestirs herself for the new guests – there are three men already lying in an opiate daze in her den – and prepares a pipe for them. But only one of them, the tall wasted one with an eye-patch and the slow gestures of someone long acquainted with opium, accepts the pipe and pulls on it with appreciation. She is surprised. But they pay double what anyone would and she does not complain. What she does not like is the way they keep staring at her and looking around her den. Could they be policemen? But no, nothing she does is seriously illegal, and would a policeman come in and smoke? Still, perhaps she should ask around a little, find out if others had reported the presence of such men in their places too.

The men leave in fifteen minutes, and when they push aside the flap that serves as the curtain of the door, they almost run into the young woman coming in. Her clothes are dirty and she smells of sweat and dust, but she is uncommonly pretty, with straight, well-formed limbs and high cheekbones, long hair done up in a clean bun; the men notice her. They are also too sober a group and at least John May is too well-dressed for this place; she notices them too, if only in passing.

'Oy Jenny, yer back,' says the old woman in a voice, like her life, of bits and pieces, saving and borrowing and patching and hoarding.'An' ain't no Injun prince wi' yer, m'gul? Wuz't 'is granpa the Great Mogul they ses just upped and died in Inja?'

She chortles at her own joke and starts hustling the customers out, for she knows that Jenny does not like to see too much evidence of her trade, and it is time for the aunt and daughter to retire for the night. It has been nineteen or twenty years now, she recalls, that they have been sharing these smelly, dank quarters; ever since Jenny's mother first handed her the girl, then a baby of four, or was it three, before being taken to Newgate and from there to that upside-down place, the land of black swans, Australia. That is where she must have died, for they never heard of, or from her, again.

23

Mrs Grayper and Mary withdrew for a few moments, as was proper, and the men moved to the parlour fireplace to smoke. Carried away by the conversation and Mary's presence, Captain Meadows had drunk and eaten more than he should have, and he welcomed the opportunity to stand up and smoke a pipe. Major Grayper never smoked a pipe; it was one of his idiosyncrasies: he lit his trademark cigar, studying its end for almost a minute before biting it off instead of using a clipper. The men puffed in silence, Meadows reclining against the fireplace, the Major sitting in his favourite armchair in one corner of the room.

The two men were used to such silences between them: they

preferred them to discussions which were likely to go awry. For, while they were polite and courteous to a fault – the Major because it was the wish of his wife who considered Meadows a good catch for her daughter, and Captain Meadows for the sake of Mary – the two men seldom agreed on anything.

It was a sign of the high esteem in which he was held by his peers that, despite Lieutenant-Colonel Charles Rowan's and Richard Mayne's total agreement with Sir Robert Peel on the issue of not employing gentlemen of the retired officer class, Major Grayper had been made a superintendent in the new force. He was known to be one of the most successful Metropolitan police superintendents in the land, once praised by Sir Peel in person and reportedly admired even by the famous private investigator, Mr Seaton Holmes, but he was also known as a man who did not give criminals, or anyone, a second chance. No, Major Grayper did not hold much hope for those who had failed even once. One life, one chance. You needed to be the Son of God to raise the dead, and even He did not raise them from death twice, did He?

It was only when Mary and Mrs Grayper returned to join the men that the conversation resumed. And it resumed on the topic that had engrossed the three, under the Major's bemused gaze, through most of dinner: Captain Meadows' pet, the thug he had brought from India and whose tale he was transcribing. Major Grayper sat back, his eyes half closed, and listened to the women enthuse about the thug, Mr Ali as his wife called him, who, it appeared, had been displayed yet again to the gathering at that society of phrenology his wife and Captain Meadows kept asking him to subscribe to. Major Grayper had nothing against phrenology, but he did not need to feel the skull of a man to know whether he was a criminal: you could tell from any scoundrel's background, language, gait, clothes, eyes, from so many things. Criminality always revealed itself: only the blind refused to see it.

'It impresses me, Captain,' his wife said, gasping a little as she often did these days when she got excited or exerted herself, the way you underline the possibilities of the science not as an instrument of condemnation but as a corrective, a possibility, and I suppose this is what Lord Batterstone cannot accept.'

'There is a lot that Lord Batterstone cannot accept, Mama.' Mary laughed, her yellow hair rippling like her laughter in the firelight.

'No, Mary, I think what he finds most difficult is exactly this. In Captain Meadows' hands, Mr Ali is proof of what a proper study of character can be used for, how it can be employed to redeem a person, perhaps even an entire race. But for Lord Batterstone, everything has to remain the way it is, people cannot be changed.'

'That is mostly true, missus: people cannot be changed,' ventured the Major, eyes still half-lidded, voice slightly sardonic.

'Oh, how can you say so, Papa!'

The Major poured himself some brandy and swirled it thoughtfully around in the frail glass.

'I will tell you a story, Mary. You were still a child then, perhaps twelve or thirteen, and I had just joined the Metropolitan force, after retiring early from the army. It was my first case: a couple, a venerable old couple living in retirement in the countryside, were discovered murdered in their beds. Suspicion revolved around their footman, who was missing, along with much of the silver. Everyone was surprised, therefore, when I recovered the silver from the London abode of an Indian nigger, who had left the old couple's employ five years earlier. It made my name, and people wondered how I was able to find the culprit, a man who had not been seen in those parts for five years. But I worked on two simple principles: those of precedence and elimination. I went through the list of servants and checked the two, the Indian nigger and a woman with a police record (who turned out to be innocent), who were most likely to have committed the crime. I eliminated the footman as a possible suspect because his background was impeccable: he was a solid Welsh serving-man. It later turned out that he had gone to visit an ailing sister in Bangor. If I were you, Captain, I would listen to your housekeeper and not keep that thug in the house. Leopards and spots, you know, leopards and spots...'

Captain Meadows looked irked and was about to remonstrate when the tea was brought in and Mrs Grayper took advantage of the interruption to veer the conversation into safer areas. She disagreed only slightly with the Major, who was an admirable man in every way, if a bit unforgiving with people of less moral character than himself. But she also had Mary's future in mind. Thug or no thug, with some luck Mary would be married and settled like her older sister – only in a much grander house – before next year. It was time. Her sister had married at a younger age but then, Mary was pretty and Mrs Grayper knew that beauty could be its own burden.

24

[William T. meadows, Notes on a Thug: Character and Circumstances, 1840]

'Imagine the state of my mind, Kaptaan Sahib. I had just lost my father. Deceived and fallacious though he may have been in the eyes of the All-Seeing God of Reason, he was a loving father, and my eyes were not yet dry of the tears shed at his fate – at least imprisonment, perhaps even death – when Mirza Habibullah began contemplating our next victim. And this time he was determined that I would have a hand in the killing.

'The sun had dipped below the horizon. It was an orange orb, tinged a strange shade for the time of year, and on any other evening we would have noticed it and expected a change in the weather. But on that evening we were too distracted, I and my few companions, by the tragedy that had befallen us. Mirza Habibullah and his companions, on the other hand, clearly relished the free rein that the imprisonment of my father had handed them.

'We had set up camp not many miles outside our village, for we had retreated after the arrests, initially with a view to flee if they were followed by further investigation. That, sahib, would have been the case if the Company Bahadur's soldiers had been involved. But when we realized that the arrests did not go beyond the scope of the Nawab of Saleempur's private force, Habibullah breathed a sigh of relief and decided to proceed with the expedition.

'Do you remember that evening, sahib? It was just a day before I came to you. There was a freak storm that night, about three hours of lightning and thunder, and a downpour of the sort that occurs during the monsoon. Palm trees were uprooted in the region, some huts unroofed. We had to seek shelter in a neighbouring hamlet. But even as we sat there in one of the better huts, hearing the storm rage outside, Habibullah raged against my father and me.

'We had been smoking. Habibullah, like so many others, often laced his tobacco with bhaang. As the smoke got to his head, he started denigrating my father for his lack of enterprise – he claimed that we had, over the years, let at least a hundred victims escape because my father had been too cautious. And to be too cautious is to lack faith in Bhowanee, he added. His men nodded in approval, for strange to say, sahib, even some of those who had sided with my father in the past had gone over to Habibullah now. Above all, he accused my father of breaking the rules of Thugee, most recently by initiating me into the order and then letting a whole year lapse without ordering me to kill my first human being. I should have been made a bhutotto much earlier, he argued, and most of the others sided with him.'

'And why was that so, Amir Ali,' I interposed.

'O Kaptaan Sahib, need I answer, for you are sagacious and have the God of Reason to guide you,' quoth Amir Ali, the Thug.

'Was it then because your father was one of the bhutottoes, the men trained to despatch the victims of Thugee, and a leader of the order too?' asked I in reply.

'Forsooth, sahib, great is your wisdom. How well you know that in the deluded lands of Hindoostan, the son has to follow in the footsteps of the father: this is why Habibullah and most of his companions put the blame of the tragedy which had befallen my father solely on his own acts of omission. They reasoned, if one may ascribe such an august word to their muddled thinking, that Bhowanee had grown angry with him. For, most of us believed, sahib, that it is only when the great and terrible

Goddess Bhowanee turns against a Thug that the law catches up with him.

'All this will stop under me, Amir, said Habibullah to me, brushing back his hair and fixing me with a stare, his bushy eyebrows joined together in a frown. Under me, we will all do what our order and the rules established by our protectoress, the Goddess Bhowanee, enjoin us to do. And the first victim we take will be despatched by you.

'Perhaps if this had been said to me a year ago, I would have been thrilled by the honour. But my year in the order had filled me with doubts, and the arrest of my father had left me particularly vulnerable to these doubts. If there was one thing I did not want to do, or imagine, at that moment, it was the murder of another human being, for my thoughts were filled with premonitions of the fate being suffered by my father. For all I knew, he might have been condemned to death too, at the ends of the gallows. I had, and still have, no knowledge of my dear father's fate, for, as you know, sahib, I quit those regions soon after I came to you, and when you enquired of the Nawab of Saleempur, he claimed, with the slyness of all native potentates, to have no knowledge of the matter.

'However great my horror at the act being forced upon me, I knew I could not display it to the gathering, especially to Mirza Habibullah. I feigned excitement and willingness. I knew I had at most twenty-four hours before our "hunt" began again. For the storm that night had left the roads wet and difficult to traverse: there would be very few travellers the next day. I knew from my experience of such storms that Habibullah and most of the Thugs would spend the day in camp or in the hamlet. Only the sothaees, the scouts, would go out, to look around, join other camps, select possible victims.

'The next morning I joined the sothaees, much to Habibullah's delight. Look, he shouted, the young prince wants to select his own victim. That is good, son of Ali Jemadaar, that is good, he said to me. By Allah, Bhowanee will be pleased.

'But the only thing I really wanted was to be free of my companions for a few hours, so that I could think clearly. I would have run away, but I knew that Habibullah and his friends would track me down and punish me, that they would harass my family back in the village. I had to think my way out of the fate confronting me. I walked the few kilometres back to the weekly market, hoping that in the bustle of the haat I would meet someone who could help find a solution to my problem. It was, in any case, the best station for a sothaee, for what we do most of all is listen, overhear, collect and sieve the tiny grains of information and gossip that float around the marketplace. And, for once, sahib, providence took pity on me. Perhaps your great God of Reason had decided to watch over me, having perceived in my faltering steps some indication that I could walk, if guided by those who knew better, on the road to redemption. For it was in the haat that I heard of you, O Kaptaan Sahib, and of your quest.'

25

Jaanam,

Haldi Ram and the Headman did not let me go until I had promised them, by swearing on everything sacred to me, that I would not do anything rash to avenge my uncle and his family. I have no recollection of how long it took. The morning turned into afternoon and the afternoon into evening before the thoughts raging through my mind subsided, and I began taking stock of the situation in a somewhat calm manner.

What I remember most is how I first became aware of my own thoughts, of having woken from a fever, from a delirium of vengefulness and anger into something resembling the person that I used to be. Perhaps they had drugged the tea I had been served: later on – for in those days I was not used to opium – I recognized in the dreams of that night some of the figures and images invoked by that medicinal drug. If so, opium has been my companion in misery long before I chose it for comfort and forgetfulness during my passage to your land.

Isn't it strange, jaanam, that in my wrath (and perhaps because I was drugged) I had become blind to the place? When my anger subsided, what I noticed first was the smell of the village, which was largely the smell of cowdung cakes plastered all over the walls of the hut in which I had been given shelter. With that smell, the enormity of the situation returned to me: for the fact that I was there at all denoted a great wrong in the ordering of the normal structures of the village, and I could not simply hope to walk away and right that wrong with a word of accusation or a gesture of bravery.

That evening, for my protection, Haldi Ram insisted that, if I did not mind, I should sleep in their village. I agreed: it was too late to go back to Patna, and this low-caste part of the village, at some distance from the upper-caste sections, was the last place where anyone would look for me, should Habibullah get wind of my arrival.

I knew that Haldi Ram and the headman still had their scouts on the road leading to the village, so as to intercept

Hamid Bhai if he followed me there as well. But I was certain Hamid Bhai would be away on business for at least a few days. Now that I was calmer, I was trying to devise a method by which I could avenge Mustapha Chacha and his family without confronting Habibullah either physically, which was bound to be a failure, or legally, which Hamid Bhai would insist on and which was even less likely to succeed, for Mirza Habibullah had the wealth to buy lawyers and also henchmen to intimidate witnesses, poor and vulnerable as these were in any case.

Early that night, however, I insisted on being shown the mound under which my family lay buried. It was, as I think I have already written, near a straggly neem tree that grew over an abandoned well, just inside the extensive fields of Habibullah, not far from the main road leading to Patna. It marked the outskirts of the fields that belonged to our village. We stole up to the place, because Haldi Ram insisted on it, and it was a good thing we did – for Habibullah had stationed a few of his men by the grave even at night. Obviously, they had instructions to prevent the bodies from being recovered. Having committed the murders, pre-planned or not, Habibullah knew that he had to bluster his way out of it, and it was part of his bluster, if not part of his twisted nature, to bury his enemies without the proper rituals, in a place where even the fatiha could not be said over them. I stood there, hidden, looking at the mound, and I would have stood there all night if Haldi Ram had not tugged at my sleeve and said, Let's go back now. There is a storm brewing.

The storm broke while we were returning from the grave. It was unseasonal. Lightning streaked the dark heavens, thunder reverberated across the land. Large drops, heavy as pebbles, fell on us, and as we sprinted for the village, a river of rain descended from the clouds. I had to force myself to run with them, for a part of me felt no desire to do anything, and a part of me was dead, and it hardly mattered whether I got drenched or drowned. It continued to pour for three hours.

And in some ways, jaanam, it gave me the answer I had been searching for. Because when I woke up the next morning, after a night of fretful sleep, the horizon had changed perceptibly: a palm tree had been uprooted, branches wrenched off the tamarind tree outside the hamlet, the thatch over some huts had been blown away. But the grass by the road and in the fields was wavy and green, unaffected by the storm. It was then that I knew the way out: I had to be like the grass. And I remembered the gossip that I had heard in Patna. It was one of those tales that often circulated, about the craziness of the Firangs who were taking over our land, their strange ideas and ways. This time it was about one Captain Meadows, who was convalescing in the Company hospital in Patna, on his way back to his country.

26

My grandmother's whitewashed house, before it gradually emptied of things and people and then, surprisingly, of memories, used to contain the usual quota of family servants. One of them was the family ayah, a woman from Punjab who had somehow ended up in Bihar. This was against the usual trajectory: usually it was impoverished Biharis who left for affluent Punjab. But this large, fair, somewhat manipulative woman with her Punjabi Urdu had brought us up, the children who, after a few years in the house, left for other places, bigger cities, foreign countries, sometimes with a few books from my grandfather's library for company or as a memento. When I write of Qui Hy, I inevitably think of her. And because of this superimposition of persons, I can see Qui Hy more clearly than I manage to imagine Amir Ali, whom I have met only through some Farsi notes: his own words both define Amir Ali and remove him from my grasp. Language is always slippery, but Qui Hy exists in flesh and blood in my mind, and my memories. I do not need her words to see her. And I see her now, in her house that is known as a dhaba, surrounded by Amir Ali and his random friends and acquaintances.

Qui Hy is a large, short woman, broad-faced and big-bosomed, and when she laughs, every bit of her – cheek, jowl, chin, bosom, stomach, shoulder – seems to shake as if an earthquake has occurred in the centre of her being. She does not utter a sound, though: she laughs silently.

And that was what she did now. She laughed silently but heartily at Karim's account of his brush with an English prostitute, as she folded a paan and handed it to Gunga. Karim was describing the prostitute's attributes, which had been advertised in a printed booklet, and much of the humour was in his droll interjections, mostly in Hindustani, between the descriptions: 'Nancy has a good deal of vivacity (if plied with sufficient gin, interjected Karim, before continuing to read from the booklet) and a pretty face (when seen in the dark), she has a pleasing aquiline nose (and quite a lot of it), excellent teeth (though not too many), she does not much care to give her company to anybody whose person is not in some measure pleasing to her (without they make it well worth her while)…' Karim was, or had pretensions of being from an aristocratic family, and his mannerisms and language were accordingly elaborate: his gestures, like his alphabets, for he wrote a fine hand, came adorned with curlicues and effete flourishes. This, for the gathering of mostly illiterate or semi-literate Indians in Qui Hy's dhaba, naturally increased the humour of his many narratives about his encounters with various kinds of women in London.

Qui Hy's place was known, at least among the Indians who lived in the attics, abandoned houses, overpriced rented rooms, docks and street corners of London, as the only place where one could get, at any time of the year, a proper, well-folded paan. She would, if you paid enough, tuck a kernel of akbari opium into it for you – the solid akbari opium which was as hard to come by as betel leaves in London – but she never allowed any kind of opium to be smoked in her premises. It could only be eaten, in the traditional Indian way, in her dhaba.

The only person who could smoke opium was her Irish husband, an ex-sailor and soldier who had lost the will to exert himself somewhere in India. There were rumours that he had made a fortune through some undiscovered crime or that he had abandoned his ship or regiment, but it was hard to reconcile these with the old man who lay supine on his bed, except when he danced around the room to some mysterious tune in his head. It was known for certain that he had inherited the place and, it was said, married Qui Hy when she was abandoned on the streets of London by the family that had brought her to England. She was in her early twenties then, and the Irish man perhaps closer to fifty. Now, he was an old man, racked by mysterious bouts of pain which would subside only when a treacly drop of chandu opium was placed in the clay bulb of his bamboo pipe and roasted into sweet smoke over the flame of a candle. Qui Hy would repair into the room that he occupied inside and prepare his pipe for him.

The advertisement read out, Karim, with Gunga and Tuanku, the Malay, went back to their jargon, which Amir could barely comprehend. The others in the room, three men and one woman – a dark and wiry ayah from Madras – were only vaguely familiar to Amir.

The two candles sputtered as someone opened the door. It was Fetcher – not Fletcher, as he was known to insist, but Fetcher. They had been saying it to him since the age of two or three, when he began running errands on the streets of London: ere boy, fetch that for me, boy. Fetch im. Fetch er.

Like a trained dog, he had fetched and carried his way into adolescence, squirrelling over fences and walls like other street Arabs at the sight of a bobby, a thin dark-skinned boy with a cheeky, gap-toothed grin, some of his teeth victims of various accidents and fights. He always carried a leather water bag, which he called his chagoul: it seldom contained water. Speaking his own version of English, mixed with words from a dozen languages, and living as often in the tunnels and sewers of London as on its streets, Fetcher boasted that he knew more shortcuts, below, in and over the city, than anyone else. It was a boast borne out by his ability to materialize in a surprisingly short time from any faraway spot.

Behind Fetcher walked in a woman Amir had seen only occasionally on the streets: from her attire, he knew she was what Jenny would have called a 'tinkler'. Elf locks bristled under the rim of her hat, her gypsy complexion passing for European in this room of Asians, though on the streets she would have been called 'black as a crock'. The room tensed with her entry but Fetcher reassured them by describing her as a friend. An' wha's more, babulog, her's gonna read you yer fremtid.'

'No one reads me my future, boy,' said Qui Hy.

'What about you, Karim?' nudged Gunga. 'Don't you want to know if the next white whore you approach will let you between her legs or kick you away like the last one did?'

'Kick me away? No woman, white, black or purple, kicks Maharaja Karim Shah away!'

At this Gunga and Tuanku dissolved into laughter, interspersed with swear words and back-slapping.

But all of them let the gypsy read their palms, all but Qui Hy, who refused, and her Irish husband, who remained as usual in his room. The gypsy did her mumbo-jumbo well and came up with standard answers: promising a passage home to one and a great voyage to another, health to some, wealth to others, disease and recovery, a major joy or a minor sorrow. Just like any tonsured palm-reader in India, thought Amir. That is, until she came to Amir's palm. She grasped it like she had grasped the palms of the others, but then she frowned. She held his hand tighter, spat on his palm and rubbed vigorously. Then she peered again and let his hand drop.

'What?' asked Gunga on Amir's behalf. The room was suddenly quiet, pervaded by the smell of tobacco and paan, and a trace of opium from the room occupied by Qui Hy's husband.

The gypsy woman shook her head.

Amir insisted. I want to know, he said, though he only half believed in such things. Mustapha Chacha had taught him not to believe in prophesies – they were both illogical and unIslamic, he had believed. But Amir had grown up among villagers who feared omens and signs.

The gypsy looked at him and said, 'Nothing.'

'Nothing?' echoed Gunga and Amir together. Even Qui Hy looked interested now.

'Nothing,' the gypsy repeated, 'there is nothing.'

Fetcher sensed the shadow of fear fall on the room and he hastened to shoo the gypsy away. 'Off with yer,' he said, giving her a coin, 'off'n buy yersel' some al-kuhl.'

But the gypsy's abrupt prophesy had left a burden hanging in the atmosphere, and first Amir, then Gunga and the others slipped away in ones and twos into the evening gloom, leaving Qui Hy alone with her husband. She hummed a Punjabi song as she cleaned up after them. Once she interrupted herself to snort and say, 'Palm-reading, ha! That man Fetcher's nothing but a baby-fool.'

27

Jenny carried the brush and the pail, cold water slopping in it, from room to room, floor to floor, spotting the grease from the candles and removing it with a hard scrub. Then she returned to the scullery to dissolve a bar of soap, shredded for the purpose, in two gallons of hot water. She carried this bucket of dissolved soap, a bucket of fresh water and a third bucket of vinegar around the rooms, scouring the floor first with the soapy water, then sponging it with vinegar and finally wiping it with water and drying it. The entire process took time and it left her aching in the arms, though she was used to hard work. But she had promised Nelly Clennam, Captain Meadows' housekeeper-cook, that she would finish the job today, no matter how long it took, so that tomorrow the house could be prepared for the grand dinner the day after. Nelly was in a tizzy over the dinner: nothing like it had taken place since before the Captain had left for India, and that was years ago. Since his return, he had not shown any inclination to invite more than two or three people over for dinner, and these were usually members of his society who spent more time examining Amir Ali's skull than they did appreciating the cook's efforts. But this time it was different: a dozen guests were expected, and all the servants knew that it had to do with the Captain's wooing of that lovely young lady, Miss Mary Grayper.

It was getting late, and Jenny still had to stop in the house of the Collinses, two kilometres away, where she helped their maid do the dishes for the day: it was one of the many places where she helped out, being paid in cash or kind. After that she had to negotiate the dark streets back to her aunt's den in the rookery. Jenny was not afraid of the dark and the streets – she was capable of looking after herself – but lately there had been all kinds of news of murders and hauntings, and something like fear had slithered its way into her mind. She felt a sense of foreboding. If only Amir were around, filling the house with his brooding but calm presence, perhaps catching her for a kiss or a fumble in a dark corner. But today he had left early – probably for Qui Hy's place – and he was yet to return.

28

John May thinks of wearing a mask. But he finally abandons the idea: it would attract too much attention; he does not have a fly to fetch him, like M'lord. Instead, he wears a low-brimmed hat. Shields wears his usual cap and One-eyed Jack has turned up bareheaded as usual, still clad in the clothes he wore when May first met him. Now that night has fallen, Shields is visibly nervous, but May is glad to see that Jack goes about in his usual languorous, garrulous manner, unaffected by the prospect of what they are about to undertake, twirling his heavy wooden cudgel with ease. As for May, he has made up his mind that this is necessary, even desirable – and he is a man who does not have qualms about what needs to be done. In any case, unlike Shields, he does not believe in ghosts.

The streets of the rookery are never deserted, but tonight they seem particularly crowded. John May knows it is just his imagination, but Shields resents the people on the streets and once makes as if to kick an urchin who gets in his way. May restrains him in time; he does not want to attract attention. As it is, there are no gaslights in the area; the little light that falls on the garbage-strewn streets comes from behind shutters and windows.

The three men reach the opium den a little before midnight. They want to get there early enough to be allowed inside, but late enough to be seen by as few customers as possible. They are lucky. There is only one customer, a white-bearded lascar who was also there the first night, May remembers; the night he lost his temper and kicked the Chinaman. They will have to wait for him to leave.

The old woman with her knotted skull welcomes them and prepares their pipes. John May and Shields merely pretend to smoke – both belong to the intermediate working classes which, unlike the upper class and the lowest classes, seldom indulge in opium – but One-eyed Jack takes to the preparation with an alacrity that indicates prior and wide exposure. May just hopes that Jack does not get so high as to become useless; they need to be in their senses, all three of them, for the work they have set out to do. If only the lascar would leave now…

But the lascar is drugged and half-asleep on the dirty bed. May tries to poke and prod him, but he only smiles dreamily and sidles out of reach.

Perhaps, thinks May, the blasted nigger can be bribed to leave. Will he remember it tomorrow? It seems unlikely. In any case, who would ask him – and even if somebody does, he is unlikely to disclose to others that he is one of the last people to have seen the old woman alive. Suspicion is more likely to accrete to him. John May is sure the lascar will be careful not to mention that he was in the opium den that night. Perhaps a coin offered surreptitiously will give them the few minutes they need. Ten minutes at the most; maybe only five.

May shuffles closer to the white-bearded lascar, who makes vague apologetic noises.

29

Amir Ali walks up the avenue leading to the Captain's house. It is late, almost midnight, and he knows that Nelly the cook will protest at his coming back at this hour, perhaps even complain to the Captain tomorrow. He wishes he could let himself in without anyone knowing but of course, none of the servants would trust him with a key. But as he reaches the house, he sees the Captain's coach draw up – evidently, the Captain was out too – and Amir tries to slip in without being noticed. But it is hard to evade the eagle eyes of Nelly, who greets him with a snide remark: 'If you are looking for that girl Jenny, she left an hour ago after asking for you. Where were you, murdering poor gentlefolk on the streets?' Amir wishes her goodnight and walks inside, followed by a loud mutter: 'Lordey! Thugs, murderers, cannibals – this city is no place for a decent woman; thuggism on the streets, no wonder…' One day, he thinks, he will be tempted to take a bite of Nelly's plump red cheeks.

30

It goes well. The lascar accepts the proffered coin and shuffles off to the street. Two minutes later, when the old woman indicates that it is almost midnight and she will soon close shop, One-eyed Jack, no worse for the opium he has smoked, stuns her with a neat blow of his cudgel, inflicted, as stipulated by John May, not on the crown but lower down, on the neck. Then, in less than five minutes, while John May stands by the door, Shields and Jack throttle the woman and saw off her head.

John May likes Jack. The man goes about his tasks with less emotion than any of them. May trembles despite himself as the old woman is throttled and decapitated, though he can only sense the struggle in the murk of the smelly, cluttered room. Shields curses and evokes both God and the Devil. But Jack works with the precision and apathy of a man slicing a carrot.

Everything has gone according to plan. It is only when the three leave the den and walk through the narrow alley connecting the building to the street, the valuable head in a bag carried by Jack, that the first and only bit of bad luck comes their way. They brush past a young woman who hustles past them, barely glancing in their direction, but May recognizes her as the pretty woman they had met while leaving the old woman's den the last time.

A minute later, there is the sound of a woman screaming. The murder has been discovered sooner than they expected it to be. But the men are already some distance away; they increase their pace. At that moment, a dog comes sniffing at the bag carried by One-eyed Jack. Jack laughs and delivers a lusty whack with his cudgel. The yelping of the dog erases the woman's screams behind them and sets dogs howling in street after street.

31

Nelly the cook was flustered, and bossier than ever. It was difficult to be housekeeper, cook and shadow butler rolled into one. For Captain Meadows' household did not contain a butler or a proper housekeeper: Alec, the only other manservant, apart from that blackamoor Thug, the good Lord preserve us, doubled as butler and coach driver, and Nelly had to make do with two giggling, inept girls from the provinces as housemaid and kitchen help. Then there were the occasional part-time servants, such as Jenny, but they could not be employed for an occasion such as this.

Nelly could recollect the time when Captain Meadows' parents were still alive: things used to be different then. Not that the Captain was not a thorough gentleman. Nelly had seen him grow into manhood and she knew he had a heart of gold. Perhaps his heart was too good, too ready to trust people, including niggers and cannibals. But he had been living alone for years, much of the time in places like India where, Nelly was sure, butlers and dinners could not be what they ought to be. He had assumed loose manners; he let Nelly take care of the household and confined himself to his books and library. This had become the practice, more so after his return from India. When Johnson, the old butler, retired, Nelly had written to the Captain – he was still in India those days – asking him if she should look for a replacement. But he had postponed the decision, and on his return, when Nelly brought up the matter again, he had said, But Mrs Clennam, what do I require that you and Alec cannot get me? It was a flattering answer, but it did mean a diminishment in the status of the household: Nelly was sure the Captain's parents would never have condoned a house without a butler. It was a pity, for the Captain had recently inherited money – which had enabled him to quit seeking his fortune in India – and he could surely afford to live in greater style than his parents.

But then, Nelly could see it happening all around her: noble old houses were letting go of the fine distinctions that had maintained them; everywhere there was a bit of slippage, an element of decay. It was the times, sighed Nelly. Look at the turkey she had been boiling. It should have been ready ten minutes ago, but it was still tough. And the butcher had said it was in its juicy prime. No butcher would have tricked her in the past. No butcher could have tricked her; her eyes, it must be said, were not what they used to be.

Despite Nelly's dissatisfaction, all was close to perfection. The tablecloth matched the 'Turkey' carpet and fuchsine curtains. The Captain left such matters, not only on these occasions but in general, to Nelly's tastes, and Nelly was a diligent student of upper middle-class fashion. It was a dark, sober room, full of mahogany furniture, with an impressive multifaceted sideboard and arabesque patterns on the wallpaper. A wide mirror was placed over the mantel.

The girls had laid the table well. Of course, it had all been done under Nelly's eagle eye. The cutlery and crystal evenly arranged, the hare soup, cotellettes à la maintenon, oyster patties and oyster sauce already placed, as they should be, on the table. The course to follow, once the guests were seated, would be boiled turkey and mashed potatoes, with stewed sea-kale. This would be followed by... Nelly went through the list in her mind, inhaling the smells of cooking that wafted in from the kitchen.

It was late. Nelly knew it was fashionable to eat late these days, but, lordey, this late? In the past, the guests would have been seated at the table at four or even earlier. Now, well, it was almost six, and the Captain had instructed her not to serve dinner before six. The guests were still in the drawing room, engaged in what sounded like an animated debate over that heathen, the thug. Why did the Captain have to call him in today of all days, on the day when Nelly hoped he would propose to the lovely Miss Mary?

32

The conversation in the drawing room was animated. It flowed almost tangibly, like the smoke in the narrow passages of air permitted by the objects that inhabited the room: a profusion of candlesticks (despite the glowing Argand lamp) and mirrors, clocks, Staffordshire figures, paintings, prints, engravings, drapery, ceramics and wax fruit, an aquarium, books, ferncases – a strange combination of the bachelor's touch and that of an older woman which, the Major knew, had to be attributed to the cook. Mary, with her delicate sense of balance and harmony, would probably have a few things to say to both. He laughed inwardly.

Conversations did get animated, thought Major Grayper, drawing on his foul-smelling cigar, whenever Meadows brought out that joker in his pack, the thug from India. There he stood, a criminal by the look of him; he had a low, cunning appearance, though he was not as dark as the Major had expected him to be, more like a gypsy than a nigger. He was dressed in resplendent Oriental robes, something the Major would never have permitted, and he even spoke English. His head, which had just been callipered and commented on for perhaps the hundredth time by Captain Meadows, was almost a perfect oval, smooth, with dark, half-curling hair, and he had a small, carefully clipped and waxed moustache with pointy ends.

The Captain had been narrating the thug's history to the company and had illustrated some phrenological points by measuring his skull with thread, scale and calliper. He had been helped in his endeavour by Daniel Oates, the journalist, who –

with the exception of Mary, who was ensconced in a Wolsey easy chair at a ladylike distance from the thug – was the only other person in the gathering who had studied phrenology. The Major had read half a book or two, one by that chap Dr Andrew Combe who was perennially being quoted in Meadows' circle, but he had desisted from following that branch of knowledge any further. It was not that Major Grayper disagreed with phrenology; he simply found it superfluous. If you knew anything about a man's background and if you could observe him for a few moments, you could instantly place him within the criminal class or outside it. This man was marked not only by his murderous history but also by his wild cascade of hair and the way his eyes darted about every so often, as if he were hiding something. The eye, they say, is the lamp of the body. Major Grayper could never trust this Amir Ali. He said as much, after the thug had been asked to leave the company.

'And all should cry, Beware! Beware! His flashing eyes, his floating hair,' quoted Mary, mischief in her bright blue eyes.

'Mary,' remonstrated her mother half-seriously, but Captain Meadows simply laughed. So did the other young men and women in the room, all but Daniel Oates, who frowned in confusion, or was it irritation?

People like Meadows were well-meaning but naïve, thought Major Grayper. If they had not been so naïve, he himself, and people like him, would have less unpleasantness to deal with. Why, just this morning, the matter at the opium den...

33

The Major was an admirable person but he had no sense of timing, thought Nelly. Did he have to bring up the subject just as the saddles of mutton were being served? She had laboured so hard to get them right. And now she could see the ladies toying with the meat on their plates and even most of the men had lost their appetite. Only Daniel Oates was tucking away, but that man was always hungry, and the Captain, God bless him, was doing dutiful justice to her cooking.

The Major, of course, had not slowed down, even after providing a macabre account of the latest murder he had been called upon to solve this morning. A decrepit crone in some opium den in the rookery who had been discovered with her head, no, not just chopped off, but missing. Yes, the Major repeated, missing, and it was yet to be recovered. Then he provided a rather graphic account of the scene and suggested, with a gleam in his eyes, that the woman might be the victim of some madman, perhaps imported into the land from the colonies. Oh, how he was going on and on, encouraged by questions from Mr Oates, that greedy, gory pen-pusher!

Nelly prayed they would stop this tasteless talk before she signalled the girls to clear the table and bring in the cabinet pudding and the Jaune Mange. She had spent hours and hours on them, days, in fact, on the Jaune Mange, measuring out the boiling water and isinglass one day, mixing in the right quantities of sweet wine, lemon (with peel), loaf sugar and yolks of eggs the next, and finally boiling and stirring and straining it all into moulds today. It would be so unfair, so… so heathenish to let an unknown headless woman, and that too from the rookery, spoil her precious efforts.

34

The head stares at John May. He has locked himself into the room in which he works. He has roared at his children. He has slapped his wife. He has banished them from this part of the house. He has entered and left the room half a dozen times today. But the head just sits there, its locks stiff and snaky with blood, its eyes still staring, the coarse lips, the knotty skull, all of it a growing presence, minute by minute, a presence that takes over the room, his house, his very soul, sucking them all in. He wishes he were Shields, who must be drowning his horror and fear in some tavern. He wishes he were One-eyed Jack, incapable of any feeling that does not pertain to his own animal appetites. But he is not; he is John May, provider, self-made man, rational worker, ex-taxidermist, ex-resurrectionist, now murderer.

He does not believe in ghosts, but he is haunted by the eyes of this woman. He has to tear them out. He has to strip her skin, dissolve her brains, clear the skull until it becomes the extraordinary museum specimen demanded by M'lord. With every cut of the knife, every drop of chemical, he will sear his own soul. And it will have to be done in secret. Even M'lord, the prime mover of his actions, will pretend not to know how he procured this splendid skull. Skull number 50. Or skull number 550. How many does M'lord already have; how many people has he employed to procure such samples, people like John May?

And has any of them gone as far as John May has? It is a good thing he does not believe in ghosts. It is a good thing that he has stuffed animals. It is good that he knows how much more beastly than animals a human being can be. Like that Thing there, staring at him. That head, that skull, that Thing that belongs to a white woman who was as depraved, as obscene, as any nigger or lascar. More perhaps. Surely, more. Why should he, John May, self-made man, be afraid of that ugly bolus of skin, flesh, blood, hair and bone? Why should he let it turn him to stone?

35

Amir Ali retires to his 'room', the scullery, as soon as he is dismissed from the polite company in the drawing room. It is a bare room with a tiled floor, a counter, a sink and a copper for the laundry. Unlike many other sculleries, it has a small fireplace too. It is also used less often than the other sculleries that Amir has seen, as Captain Meadows' house is rather large and has a pantry in which the pans and dishes are washed.

Because it is hardly in use, and has its own supply of water and a fireplace, the scullery was imposed on Amir Ali by Nelly, though only after some resistance from the Captain, who first offered him one of the servant rooms in the attic. But Nelly was adamant. It is bad enough to have him hulking in the scullery next to the kitchen all day, Amir Ali overheard her telling the Captain; she does not want her nights disturbed by the knowledge that he is sleeping on the same floor as her and the young girls who are, after all, her wards in a manner of speaking.

The fire in the little fireplace has burnt low and the room is chilly, despite the warm smell of cooking from the kitchen. By now Amir has become used to the overbearing smells of London houses, especially around the kitchen: the odours, he feels, are stronger and more basic – burnt meat, boiled vegetables – than in respectable houses in his village, which are open to the cleansing air, purified by agarbattis.

In the little light afforded by the fire, which is augmented by a candle stub, Amir sits writing in his journal. He is penning one of the letters that he has been writing to Jenny in the elaborate and silenced strokes of cursive Farsi. The letters she will not, cannot read. The letters which, more than a century later, across continents and seas, will be read, with some difficulty and assistance, by a teenager in his grandfather's library in a whitewashed house. Jaanam, he begins.

36

Jaanam,

There are days when I wait for you, sometimes outside, sometimes in the scullery. The kitchen I avoid, for I have no desire to increase the ill-will that Nelly bears towards me. It is not that I am afraid for myself, I am more afraid for you: Nelly is no fool, I think she has noticed that we like each other, though she may not have imagined more, so alien am I to her and her world. Still, I do not want her to inflict on you the cruelties and indignities which, if it were not for the Captain, she would inflict on me.

As for me, I have only a few nights left in the Captain's house. I have completed the narrative that I have been providing him with and I could leave tomorrow, if I wished to. I have already arranged to rent a small place not far from Qui Hy's at the Mint. It is dilapidated and vermin-infested, but it is cheap and will provide me with enough space to allow Gunga and his jahaajbhais to join me. Now that Gunga has lost his job – he ran into trouble with some guild or union – I can hardly do anything else. I cannot let them stay on in that damp little room in the East End with so many others, at least three of them seriously ill. Even more seriously ill than Karim who, I fear, is slowly dying of consumption.

As you know, jaanam, I can afford to rent the house. The Captain is a man of his word. Not only has he paid me regularly for the months I have been with him, today he also paid me – as he had promised – for the voyage back. I have most of the money sewn into my English coat, the one you helped me buy from that pedlar on Chick Lane. The Captain has gone even further: he has given me a statement of character, vouching that I am an honest and reformed person and may be employed on his recommendation. How many people would do that? Not one of the men who probed my skull in the drawing room tonight; not one of the women who chirruped and exclaimed over me.

Over the months that I have spent with the Captain, I have grown fond of him. I concede that. And I dare say he has grown fond of me too. In some ways, we are so similar, we are people who have grown up with others and yet alone. There are moments when I feel guilty about the stories I have embroidered for him. No, I would not say I have lied to him, for I have told him what he wanted to hear, stitching together a colourful garment from the threads and patches of stories heard here and there, in my village and in Patna. I believe that we are lied to only to the extent that we want to believe in the lies.

In one sense, the barter was fair enough: He got his thug; I got my revenge. For, when I approached Captain Meadows in the Patna hospital, he did not just interrogate me and examine my skull, he also instructed the authorities to confirm my story. But my story was simple enough. The mound with the dead bodies was exactly where I had described it; Mirza Habibullah and his men just where I had said they would be.

Oh, the Company is efficient, jaanam; we all know that in India. It swooped on Habibullah and his men and rounded them up before they knew what had hit them. On being arrested and interrogated – and not just with words, jaanam – the men broke down and confessed to the murders. Of course, they attributed it to enmity and a feud over land. But I had already anticipated that. I had told the Captain that thugs, on being arrested, try to attribute the murders they have committed to mundane causes, as they expect to be let off more easily then. And neither the Captain, with his story to tell, nor the authorities, with their new crusade against thugs, were in the mood to believe the blustering Habibullah.

I am told that two of Habibullah's relatives and three of his henchmen were awarded the dreaded sentence of Kalapani, but Habibullah managed to get his sentence commuted to ten years in jail by paying his henchmen to lie about his involvement. I was never confronted with them. I pleaded terror of the gang, and the Company authorities only asked me for a signed statement. After that I was free to go – except that there was nowhere I could go. To return to the village might have embroiled Hamid Bhai and his family in the matter: it was best that no one fully discovered the role I had played in the arrest and prosecution of Habibullah. The Company worked in mysterious, incomprehensible ways, and it was safest to let the mystery remain undisturbed. So, when Captain Meadows offered me service and a free passage to England in lieu of my 'history', I accepted his offer.

But when I had spun him a story about Habibullah being a thug, I had not realized I was spinning myself into a web of my own making. Stories, true or false, are difficult to escape from, jaanam. Especially the stories we tell about ourselves. In some ways, all of us become what we pretend to be.

37

[William T. Meadows, Notes on a Thug: Character and Circumstances, 1840]

'I fear, O sahib, that I have wearied you with the minute relation of my history. But I have told all, and I have not concealed from you one thought, one feeling, much less any act which at this distance of time and place I can recall and that I feel may have a bearing on the moral of my history.'

With these words, Amir Ali, the Thug, ended his narration, the long account of which I have here presented to you, revered reader, in the hope that it would weary you as little as it wearied me. For man is such a beast of wonder that even in his mistakes, errors and lies, even in his darkest manifestations, even when he follows devilish rites and false gods, there is much to learn and even more to hope for. May this account, then, offer to you, indulgent reader, the story of the reclamation of not just one benighted heathen, but through him, evidence of the civilizing of entire cultures and nations. Nay, I would say more: the promise, so dear to any Christian heart, of salvation of the human soul, of mercy and redemption.

38

The gilded wooden cherub of the Prize of War is difficult to face alone. John May has dragged Shields along for moral support, and also because he does not want to carry the canvas bag containing the polished, gleaming, knotty skull of the old woman. It has taken him almost a week to prepare the skull, a week of sleeplessness.

Handing the Thing to M'lord is not any easier. He meets M'lord in the parlour of the house, as usual: a carpeted room with potted plants, cheap coloured prints of various queens and royal consorts, and a number of stuffed animals. The two foxes and the otter look particularly ravenous to John May. He feels alone and naked, raked by M'lord's eyes through the slits of a new mask, his guilt transparent to anyone who cares to look him in the eye. He wishes for a mask. He wishes he could bring Shields into the room, but that, of course, is not possible. He would lose M'lord's patronage in a second. M'lord likes to believe that the skulls materialize, cleaned and polished, in John May's hands out of nowhere, without the aid of any stratagem, accomplice, or even undue labour.

And M'lord does not see through John May this time either. In fact, he hardly sees John May. All he has eyes for is the skull. A superb specimen, he utters, as if in a trance. A superb example of the structural traces of depravity, my man; structural traces, not a minor matter of wrinkles and upturned lips that Combians like Captain Meadows fool around with. Look at the superciliary ridge, the narrow eyes, the indentures, ridges... You have done a good job, Mr May.

Carried away by M'lord's enraptured praise, John May volunteers another skull as distinctive, as precious to his Lordship's precise physical science as this one, and that too within a month – at a slightly higher price, if I may, sir. And M'lord accepts the price with a generous wave of his hand.

Now, sharing a beer with Shields, John May is both thrilled and worried by his offer. Unusual skulls are not altogether impossible to find in London. Difficult, true, but not impossible. He often comes across a gypsy here, a cockney there, whose skull would be welcome in M'lord's collection. The problem is that all these people are vigorously alive. They are not even old, like the woman in the opium den. And, give or take a few whores, it is difficult to justify their death on moral grounds: they might be niggers, they are poor, but these attributes are not really sins.

The pinched publican stands with his elbow on the counter and looks at the two.

'His Lordship didn't pay,' he observes to John May.

'Oh no, he did. He paid splendidly,' replies Shields, the half-drunk fool, before John May can kick him.

'Why so glum, then, my friend?' the barman asks John May.

There is something about barmen that makes you want to open up to them, thinks John May. Perhaps it is because they are good at echoing your words, sometimes even your thoughts. It is a little like going through a tunnel: one feels tempted to shout into it and hear one's voice echoing, changing shape and sound, and still remaining identifiable. John May resists the temptation.

He knows his soul is oppressed by the need to shout into some tunnel. But he also knows that there always are people listening at the other end of a tunnel. He wishes he could at least take his confusion out on Shields as he used to in the past, by swearing at the smaller man, running him down, even cuffing him on occasion. But the night in the den has changed all that: now he cannot afford to make an enemy of Shields; he has to be reasonably polite to the uncouth man, he has to ply him with drinks.

Luckily, the temptation of the tunnel-barman is removed due to a brawl that erupts in a far corner of the pub. By the time the barman and his helpers have coped with it, by tossing one side out and providing a round of free drinks to the other side, John May and Shields have moved to a corner table, out of reach of the barman.

They are soon joined by One-eyed Jack. This is the other consequence of that night of enterprise at the opium den: Jack has penetrated the more intimate corners of John May's existence; he seldom uses 'guv'nor' or 'sir' to address them now.

John May actually welcomes the gaunt man's company this evening; unlike Shields, who is not drunk enough to blur the horror of their acts that recent night, Jack is unperturbed, calm. Smelling of alcohol and opium, and dressed in worn hand-me-downs and a battered hat, his gingery hair falling on his shoulders in lanky lumps, Jack is probably the blind tunnel John May craves. After another drink, he broaches the topic indirectly.

'Some people say it is wrong to take a life,' John May says to the two.

Shields grows pale; he is still not drunk enough to be recklessly brave and blasphemous.

Jack does not even look up. 'Bloody Budderists,' he growls into his mug.

'Who?'

'Budderists. Hindoos. Them that don't eat meat, they say.'

'But what do you think, Jack?' John May asks him.

'Me?'

'You.'

'What do I think?'

'Yes.'

'I think... well, I think if God didn't want 'em slaughtered, he wouldn't've made 'em sheep.'

'That's a thought, isn't it, Shields,' replies John May.

'Sure is, sure is,' says Shields, drinking desperately and hoping that something will happen to break off the trail of this discussion. It does, for it is a Saturday evening. The publican hops on to the bar counter and bangs a pan for silence. It does not manage to curtail all the conversations in the room. Shut up, gentlemen, shut up, sirs, will you, the publican roars into the hubbub, banging harder with a ladle on the metal pan. Conversation subsides. It's time; it's time, announces the publican, and further conversation is made impossible by the loud singing of men as the 'free-and-easy' starts in the pub.

39

Major Grayper sat in the cooling room of a Turkish bath, assiduously jotting down and checking the points of the 'opium den beheading' case in a covered pocketbook. He looked up when Daniel Oates, in the Major's view a godforsaken hack who shared not only his acquaintance with Captain Meadows but, more sadly, also his club, lounged in and swung himself into an adjacent chair. He was cupping a drink in his hands and crumbs of bread adhered to his robe.

'Major,' he said by way of greeting.

'Mr Oates,' replied the Major, pausing in his careful collocation and correction of written clues. He always carried a pencil stub for this purpose: in his receptivity to facts and clues, the Major was as sensitive to the moment of inspiration as any airy poet.

'Am I not right, sir, in recollecting from our dinner some days ago at Captain Meadows' residence that you have been entrusted with the task of clearing up the opium den mystery?' Oates observed, after taking a sip of his drink.

'You recollect correctly, sir. Holborn falls within my jurisdiction.'

'It could not have been entrusted to more capable hands, if I may say so, Major.'

Major Grayper made a gesture of thanks and self-deprecation.

'You would not have a lead or two to offer the reading public, would you, Major?'

Major Grayper was prepared for this question. Oates had a reputation for writing perceptively and with much colour about the street life of London, but Major Grayper suspected that his stories were gathered at the club and garnished with a stroll down some East London street or, at the most, a nervous night in some place of licence. He had the answer ready: 'It is too early, sir.'

Oates smiled cloyingly, squiggling like an amoeba to fit his ungainly frame into the chair. 'That it is, Major. That it is. And yet, this afternoon in the club, there was a lively discussion of the matter.'

'I am sure there was, sir.'

'Yes, Major, I was there. It was actually something young William Byron let drop; he has just returned from Africa, you know. He suggested that the manner of the beheading indicates a heathenish rite, and of course there were men in the room who took to the idea: so many of them have been to different parts of the empire and have witnessed such sights. I must say, for someone like me, who has not travelled much farther than Paris, the tales were almost beyond belief... To think that one such savage might be here in our midst, perhaps walking next to us on the streets, dressed in the civilized garments of an Englishman.'

'I would not worry too much, if I were you, sir. The heathens we have here are no worse than our own criminal classes. It is unlikely that they would go about beheading people on a whim.'

'Perhaps, Major, perhaps, though I distinctly recall that you suggested otherwise at Captain Meadows' place. You know, I suppose you do, though to be honest I did not until it was brought to my notice, that there are natives in places like Burma (or is it Borneo or Brazil?), who chop off heads and shrink them to keep as talismans. Surely, sir, it could be a cult, as young William suggested. Someone like that thug our good friend Captain Meadows has imported into the land. I must confess that with his pointy moustache, flowing tresses and dark, shifty eyes, he looks the very part of a vindictive murderer, a practitioner of barbarous, unspeakable rites. It surprises me that the learned Captain harbours him in his house.'

To this the Major did not volunteer a response, for it was a feeling he shared. He had never liked the idea of his daughter Mary visiting a place that housed such a villainous-looking Moor, and one who openly confessed to being a 'reformed thug'. Reformed, my foot! The Major was not a missionary: he did not believe in reforming the criminal soul. He hoped that the Captain would keep his word and turn the thug out once his narrative had been completed.

40

Jaanam,

Three days ago, I moved out of the Captain's house. Now we will be able to meet without worrying about Nelly. I only wish the circumstances were not so sad for you. When I discovered at Qui Hy's – just a day before I moved out – that the headless woman that Captain Meadows' friends and guests had been talking about was your aunt, I ran all the way back to the Captain's house, hoping to find you there. But, of course, you had still not reported back to work. Nelly was complaining about it, about the unreliability of the working class, as though she belonged to some other strata of society. There was nothing I could tell her. I knew why you had disappeared but I had to be alone in my knowledge. Any association with the opium den murder would have been too much for Nelly: not even the Captain would have been able to talk her out of firing you. I remained quiet. But I was restless and Nelly noticed this; she looked at me strangely for the rest of the day.

The next day I waited again for you to return. When you had not come by noon, I could not bear it any longer. I left the house without telling Nelly, something she dislikes, and searched for you in every passing face.

The streets were crowded; it was late in the afternoon. I felt a desperate need to see you, and I ran in the direction of your aunt's home but I could not find it: there are places in this city where I still lose my bearings. By the time I had calmed down, it was almost evening and the air had grown chilly. The weather had taken a turn for the worse a few days ago, and winter – so dreaded by Gunga, Karim and all the other lascars I know – was creeping up.

I lingered on a path of cobbled stones near the Thames and then made my way back to the Captain's house. When I got there, Gunga and Karim were standing outside, and it was then I remembered that I had arranged to meet them there early in the evening. They were to help me cart my wooden trunk and an old cot, both of which the Captain had given me in one of his gruff gestures of generosity and affection, to my new lodgings in the Mint. All my possessions fit into that trunk.

I went up to see the Captain and take my leave. I was in a bit of a hurry, as we wanted to get the trunk and cot to my lodgings before it became dark: we had been told that the law forbade furniture being moved out of a house after dark. The Captain was in the library, reading as usual, and he did me the honour of asking me to sit down. Then, addressing me as Mr Ali, he expressed the hope that I would continue to sustain the good reputation and character that he had observed in me during our year or so together. I was touched by his address, but perhaps I appeared even more moved than I was, as I was still distraught over the news of your aunt's murder. When I took my leave, he shook my hand and wished me luck and a good voyage back. The Captain assumes that I will be returning to India. He loves to believe that everyone belongs somewhere and that people can always return to where they belong. It is a belief which, I suspect, has to do with wealth.

After that, conveying the trunk, balanced on the cot, to my new lodgings took us deep into the night. The place that I have, and which I hope you will visit as soon as you can, contains two rooms. I will be sharing them with Gunga and his boys, all of them, at least until you decide to join me. It was the least I could do with my money: Gunga and the four men left from his gang had been sleeping in a damp basement with a family of tinkers.

When we fell asleep, Gunga winked at me and said, Amir Bhai, I promise we will disappear as quietly as ghosts whenever your jaanam visits you.

I lay in bed, the Captain's cot, worrying about you and getting used to the noise from the streets – the Captain's house, as you know, is in a much quieter neighbourhood – until finally, I fell into a fitful sleep disturbed by nightmares. I do not remember my dreams like you do, jaanam, nor do I seek significance in them. Perhaps our dreams do indeed tell us something about our hours of wakefulness. That is probable. It may even be inevitable, for how can half of one's life be completely disconnected from the other half? And yet, how can we be certain of remembering what we dream, remembering it exactly and entirely? And if what we remember on waking up are only shards of images and sounds, as in my case, isn't the sense, the story we make of them, just an arbitrary shape that we impose on our nights after waking into the difference of the daylight?

41

Outside my grandfather's library, a different world pressed against the wrought-iron gates at the end of that driveway of red pebbles. I knew it was different even when I was a teenager as, preceded by the jangle of my grandmother's keys, I slowly unravelled the stories I am threading into a book here, unravelled them in Dickens, Collins and Mayhew as well as in smudged snippets of paper, a mouldy notebook in Farsi, and many other fragments of text and language that were to follow.

But even then, in my teenage, when I was less aware of the world within and the world without, I could sense the difference of those hands at the gate, those eyes on the streets. I could sense that they gazed at another horizon, or none – not like my eyes which, from my early years, had been forced by family tradition to focus on a career in engineering or medicine. It was then that I started realizing the privileged ease of my learning, haphazard as it was (having been picked up in the clutter of a provincial town), and the angle my learning made to their living. For, no matter how haphazardly, I could still afford to access life through books, while for them, books existed, if at all, only to make life possible, or easier. To earn a livelihood: two square meals a day, or a reputation. How many of them refrained from pushing themselves over the precipice of crime, and how many succumbed, who knows?

It was when I saw their world pressing against the wrought-iron gates of my reading that I began to see John May. Not understand him – for how could I claim to understand someone across such a stretch of space and time? – but to see him well enough to be able to write of him. It was then that I noticed how he changed from place to place, his voice when confronted with M'lord, his clothes when they passed through the layered streets of London. I saw his anger and pride, his desperation, his constant, cruel, courageous cunning crawl towards a precipice of his own making. John May. Never just John, never just May. Always John May.

John May was a man much used to figuring things out, thinking dispassionately and objectively, and acting finally in his own best interests. These, he believed, were the characteristics that distinguished the better classes from the worst. The lower classes tended to be hasty, emotional, impractical, imprudent; the higher classes deliberated, planned and acted calmly. Even their morality was restrained and practical. As John May picked his way up the hundreds of rungs leading from the puddle of the lower classes to the tower of the upper ones, he liked to believe – and not without reason – that his success was attributable to his ability to keep a cool head.

For instance, he never got completely drunk, unlike Shields, who was at that moment sitting head in hands, elbows on table, in a Haymarket café, lonely despite the company of John May. They had started meeting in different places to discuss their business, for John May did not want to risk the same bartender or waiter overhearing them twice. The café was full of elegantly dressed women and men in close proximity to each other, and it appeared very much the hub of society to John May. It was not the sort of café that had one spoon dangling by a dirty thread next to the counter, used by all patrons to stir in the sugar; in this café, each cup was served with its own spoon.

Shields was already quite drunk, though it was only late afternoon, the sunlight not much more than a rumour. John May had been plying him with expensive wine, for he had a proposal to make, and he knew that Shields' entrepreneurship was inversely proportionate to his sobriety. John May felt distinctly ill at ease in the plebeian company of Shields in this place of polished tables and glittering people, though perhaps, if he had known more of real society elsewhere, he would have felt at ease – for the cafés, casinos and supper-rooms of Haymarket were seldom frequented by the better set of men and women. The company around John May was, like John May himself, a shoddy replica of what existed elsewhere, at Mott's for instance, or in the Burlington Arcade.

But unfamiliar with the society he aspired towards, John May steeled himself and bought Shields another drink, hoping the charms of the place would render the man pliable to the proposal he had in mind. For John May had thought much about the rights and wrongs of the matter. He had thought dispassionately and coolly. He had thought as he imagined the better class of people would think. And, as soon as Shields was drunk enough, he would walk the man out and tell him about the Italian boy who could be seen with his performing white mice all over London, or perhaps the ancient lascar who sold tracts and sang psalms on a fiddle. Both had skulls of the most interesting shape.

42

Man Beheaded by Monster

Sketch by Daniel Oates

In a city as thriving and magnetic as Mother London, some crime and disorder is to be expected. And yet, what happened last night was a crime no Christian could have expected – or imagined. It was the sort of crime one only associates with other, hotter climes, with people reared on superstitions and barbarities, and not on the milk of human mercy that flows through Christian veins in the lands of civilization.

Mr Stanton, doing his midnight rounds in the notorious district of the Mint, was distracted into a dark alley by what sounded like a noise. Not daring to enter the murderous alley on his own, he whistled to a colleague who he knew was in the neighbourhood. The two policemen ventured resolutely into the alley, which was, as mentioned before, dark and foul and smelly, paved with filth and bordered by houses of a mean sort. Such was the filth in the alley that the two policemen, guided by the pale beams of a flickering lamp, almost failed to spot the crime on evidence. It was only when they were returning to the street that Mr Stanton's feet struck a musical instrument that let off such an alarm that hearts less stout than those of our resolute heroes would have suffered an immediate collapse.

Bending down before what appeared to be a pile of rubbish, Mr Stanton and his colleague, Mr Drew, retrieved a fiddle of the sort that is used by the gypsy musicians who cater to the public's taste for a lively tune on various streets of our fair city. Intrigued by their finding, the two men brought their lamp closer and discovered that the pile that they had taken for garbage was actually a man. On turning over the body, Mr Stanton could tell, by the evidence of the clothes and some tracts lying next to the man, that it was the body of a gypsy who has often been seen in these parts, selling Christian tracts and singing psalms in a passable accent to the accompaniment of a fiddle.

Mr Stanton and Mr Drew quickly discovered that the man was dead, and that he had obviously been murdered recently, as his body was still warm in the chill of the winter night. However, their horror was increased by the discovery that the man was lacking a head: yes, gentle reader, the man had been beheaded by the monster who had deprived him of life. Despite a search of the alley, the missing appendage was not recovered – which reminded at least this correspondent of the unsolved murder of an old woman in an opium den some weeks ago. In both cases, the bodies were, it appears, ceremonially decapitated.

That crimes take place in a teeming city is a matter of regret. But that such crimes should take place in Mother London is more than a matter of regret: it is a matter of alarm and condemnation. If the authorities have not yet woken up to the nature of these two crimes, then perhaps it is time they did so. We have a monster loose in this fair city: a cannibal who consumes the heads of his hapless victims.

43

Jaanam,

Time is such a cheat. The more importance you give it, the less you have of it. I could see it in the people around Captain Meadows: they were always looking at their pocket watches, tugging at their fobs, running from appointment to assignment, and they were always the people who had less time than anyone else. On the other hand, there are people in the villages, like my uncle Mustapha, or even people here, like your late aunt, who order their calendars more by the seasons than by the clock, and it is these people who have hours to spend. Time, jaanam, is not like money: it seems as though one needs to waste time in order to have more to spend.

In these weeks on my own, I have been both niggardly and a spendthrift with time. I hoard the hours that I spend with you with the intensity of a miser, and these are the hours that fly past most swiftly. The rest of the time, the hours and minutes go by slowly, as I walk the cobbled streets or sip chai with Qui Hy and Gunga, or try and find a profession for myself, or an enterprise into which I might put my savings with good chances of success.

Return has never struck me as an option. Would it have been an option if I had not met you? I doubt it. I fear that some people have no desire to return, for to return is to disturb a past which, whether good or bad, is better left well alone. So the only return I have in mind is the moments when you return to me.

Days pass, sometimes news comes and goes – news from nearby which concerns me (as that of the singing gypsy who was beheaded just a month ago, or the fire at Lloyd's Coffee House and at the Royal Exchange) and news from afar (gossip about a rebellion in Canada or the proposal for Jewish emancipation in Sweden, places and events that mean nothing to me) which keeps the city agog. Time passes, and I measure it by the frequency of your coming and going.

44

Qui Hy had her basket of garments and pockets next to her, and was stitching away diligently, earning some extra money even in her spare time, while listening to Karim ramble on, in the gossipy girly way he had, about the latest beheading. It was someone Karim knew vaguely, having once shared a street corner with him during a night of drunken stupor. Gunga nudged Amir at this, for the murder victim was a young boy – Greek or Italian – who lived off the streets of London by exhibiting a cage of performing white mice, and Karim was known to his friends for his penchant for young boys, whom he befriended with the utmost generosity.

Karim caught the gesture and cursed Gunga in mock seriousness, switching from Urdu to the lascar patois which Amir understood only vaguely. Then he returned to his flowery Urdu, which he spoke far more fluently than any of his jahaajbhais, and continued the narrative.

Evidently, the Italian boy had been discovered only late in the morning, his body discarded on one of the middens behind the slaughterhouses of Newgate market. The body must have lain there at least a couple of nights, for it was decomposing – its stink mingling with the smell of decomposing meat and bones discarded by the butchers of the market.

Amir had never been to the market, but he had heard about it from Jenny, who always spoke of it in terms of extreme revulsion. Some years ago, she had worked there as a porter: carrying everything from hides and Colchester baize to entire sheep, from shop to shop, sidestepping rivulets of bloody water on which floated large blobs of fat. Porterage was women's work in all such markets and Jenny had made good money, being young and strong enough to carry entire carcasses, running from shop to workhouse on the slippery, blood-and-water smeared paths of the market. But she had found the smell and work repulsive. It was this experience, she had told Amir, that had made her determined to work in polite houses, even if it meant longer hours and less pay. Of course, most of the houses she worked in, Amir knew, were hardly polite: they were the houses of tradesmen and poor gentry, who could not afford more than one full-time servant and had to depend on the services of part-timers like her. Captain Meadows' household was perhaps the only exception. And Jenny had lasted there simply because the Captain, with absent-minded generosity, had told Nelly to keep her on; Nelly had been far less willing to try out a young girl without any respectable recommendation and with the easy ways and accents, no matter how desperately camouflaged, 'of the streets'.

Karim continued his story. 'So, hazraan,' he said, 'the poor boy had been killed at least a night earlier and left on the midden, where he might have been foraging for some food for his mice. He must have been murdered some nights back, for bodies do not decompose in just twenty-four hours in this cold. The mice were discovered, all except one, dead and half-eaten in their cage, next to him. Evidently, some animal, a cat or a rat or a dog, had managed to get at them through the bars.'

'And your punch line, Karim?' said Qui Hy, stitching carefully in her chair.

'My punch line?'

'Your punch line, Karim, for you would not have given us such an intricate description if you did not have something shocking to say at the end of it,' Qui Hy added.

'Mai knows you well, bastard,' said Gunga in their patois.

'No head,' replied Karim.

'What?' Qui Hy paused in her stitching.'Again?'

'No head. Clean cut. Swish.' Karim drew a finger across his own neck to illustrate.

Qui Hy looked at Amir, who sat in a huddle, unnaturally still. She knew about Jenny's aunt. She shook her head, as if in warning or regret.

Karim continued, in his usual determinedly heartless manner, 'Though who would want the poor boy's head is anyone's guess. It was the most ugly skull I ever saw, the top of it that is. He used to keep it hidden under a cap. Such a fine-looking boy, gentle, with beautiful eyes and lips, but he had the skull of an ogre, as though a giant hand had twisted it out of shape.'

45

Jane Austen. My grandfather's library had its inevitable quota of Jane Austen. He could not have been what he was without those gilded, hardbound books.

Looking back, I feel vaguely disappointed with myself for taking to Austen like a gecko takes to the backs of cobwebbed paintings and portraits. Couldn't I see the distance between Austen's world of the gentry and mine, sense the loud silence of her servants and those gaps that were trips to plantations and colonies? Perhaps I could; perhaps I couldn't. But what I could see and hear were the muffled footsteps of her female characters, their satin voices that often covered an iron will. I had heard those sounds and voices. My grandmother's house was full of them. I knew them intimately, though in another language. It was in that ghostly resonance that I recognized the sound of Austen's world, which was, after all, not too different from how I came to imagine the Batterstones in their ancestral seat. How else would I have been able to enter that world? For even though my grandfather's house was not a fraction as grand as the Batterstone country seat and the twain were divided by gaping differences, I have no doubt there was also a similarity of prosperity, politeness, patience, persistence, patterns, paths.

Lady Batterstone walked down the path to the ancient landing place, carefully restored and maintained, by the muddy river. It was difficult to imagine that this narrow river, swaddled in dark rushes in the middle of the quiet countryside, wound all the way to noisy London, which her lawfully wedded husband must now be quitting to make his annual three-hour journey to the family-seat. He was supposed to join them for dinner tonight. Not that the family was around any more – both the boys were married and settled on their own estates. And not that she had been family to Lord Batterstone for at least twenty years now, no, not in anything other than words. Yet, this was a ritual they maintained: Lord Batterstone coming 'home' to his country mansion from his London residence for a fortnight every year, usually, but not always, in early summer. In the past, Lady Batterstone had reciprocated by visiting London for a week or two during the season. But it was four years since she had last been there and she did not miss either crowded London or her husband's large, spooky residence, filling slowly with skulls.

Appearances had to be maintained though. She had to play the charming hostess for a few days every year. She had to invite interesting or distinguished guests and throw an annual ball. Lord Batterstone would be there throughout, polite and cold. She would be there too, the perfect hostess despite the various minor ailments that plagued her, her rheumatism, her migraine, her aches. And, almost without realizing it, she would manage to include in the twenty or thirty guests who visited during the period, at least one person whom Lord Batterstone abhorred.

There was the sound of waves breaking as a small barge sailed past. The men on it raised their hats to Lady Batterstone, ceasing to row for a moment, and their barge floated like a light shadow on the dark waters of the river. Then a fish jumped, and there was the sound of a party – some of her guests – following her down the path.

She knew it was futile to hope for solitary moments during her weeks of fashionable hospitality. But she was relieved when the guests who stepped out from under the trees overshadowing the path turned out to be only that pale, serious young man, Captain Meadows, and Mary Grayper, the girl he was obviously wooing. Mrs Grayper followed at a discreet distance, complaining that the young people were walking too fast for an old woman like her, but Lady Batterstone had seen enough of mothers like Mrs Grayper to know that they always allowed their protected broods ample elbow room with a suitable bachelor. In any case, everyone knew that Mrs Grayper and Mary were angling for the Captain who, Lady Batterstone had heard, was eminently suitable, now that he had come into an unexpected legacy from a distant uncle, which enabled him to live a life of ease in the London house he had inherited from his parents.

Lady Batterstone had heard of Meadows' 'scientific' differences with her husband. In fact, the Graypers, whom the Batterstones knew very slightly, had been invited in order to enable and induce the Captain to come: neither the Graypers nor the Captain were in the Batterstones' league. Not that it bothered Lady Batterstone. She ignored such matters when she wanted to, just as she had forgotten, now that Captain Meadows was here, about the rumours of acrimonious debates between him and her husband. There was very little of note that Lady Batterstone did not eventually get to hear. London was far away, no doubt, but then, who would believe this narrow, muddy river flowed all the way to it?

She nodded to the men in the passing barge and moved to join her guests. The rest of the party would soon follow; unless, of course, the gods being merciful, they had decided to head for the new Chinese pavilion in the park.

46

Major Grayper had remained in the library of the huge Batterstone mansion. It was an impressive library. The Major had been to great houses in the past, but never to one of this stature. He was, though unwilling to show it, a bit overawed. He needed moments, now and then, to recover from the majesty of the place. And the library was the only place where he was assured of privacy: most of the other guests hardly ever used it, and neither did Lady Batterstone. Captain Meadows, he knew, might have been here, but that was the likelihood Mrs Grayper was resolutely guarding against. Men never propose in libraries, she had sagely pronounced on her way to the Batterstone mansion. Ever since she had received the unexpected invitation to spend a week at the Batterstone mansion and learned that the Captain had also been invited, Mrs Grayper had not only strained to induce the reticent Meadows to accept but was now plotting insidiously to throw her daughter and the Captain together in romantic, Arcadian surroundings, certainly not bleak, bookish ones.

So it was with a degree of surprise and mild irritation that the Major looked up when the door was flung open and a large man walked into the library. Eyes not used to the gloom of the library, it took the newcomer a few seconds before he noticed the Major at a desk. By then the Major had recognized the man as Lord Batterstone and hastened to greet him.

'Oh, I am sorry to have interrupted you. I just arrived and was told that everyone was out for a walk in the park,' said Lord Batterstone, shaking hands. He did not recognize the Major, for they had met only once or twice in the past, but he pretended he did. He was used to being greeted by complete strangers ensconced in his mansion as his guests, and often, by people he would never have invited himself. It would not surprise him, he laughed inwardly, to find that upstart Captain Meadows reclining in the armchair one summer!

But what was this man, Major whatsisname, babbling about? A garden walk, yes, yes, he knew that; a trip through their park to see the new pavilion that his lawfully wedded spouse had spent a minor fortune on just last year, yes, yes, he knew that too – though of course his smile and nods did not betray the irritation of his thoughts – his daughter, so, the Major had a daughter, called Mary, yes, what else, also out, with his wife, the Major's that is, of course, poor woman to have to put up with a man of military bearing and the wobbly talk of a dithering poet, his wife gone out too, with Mary, yes, who else, and what, what, Captain Meadows... Captain Meadows!

'They should be back anytime,' Major Grayper was saying.

Lord Batterstone gripped the edge of a reading table to steady himself.

'Captain Meadows,' he gasped.

'Oh yes, sir, he should be back soon too. I forgot that the two of you were acquainted.'

Acquainted. Yes, yes, you could call it that.

But Lord Batterstone could hardly enunciate those words. His throat was dry. He smiled weakly. Then he mumbled, 'You must excuse me, sir. I forgot to instruct my man about the baggage.'

And he rushed out of the library, leaving the good Major with serious doubts, not for the first time, about the mental health of members of the English aristocracy.

47

Lady Batterstone had, over the years, quite unintentionally of course, made Lord Batterstone eat shoulder to shoulder with people he would have crossed the street to avoid in London. But never had his Lordship taken the slightest notice of it. This time, however, he took her aside before dinner and instructed her to ensure that Captain Meadows was not seated next to him, or immediately opposite him. Where would you want him to be seated then, she asked, eyes wide with innocence. Anywhere, he retorted, his mask of imperturbable control slipping for a second, anywhere, but not too close to my chair.

When dinner commenced, Captain Meadows was seated on the same side of the table as Lord Batterstone, but so far away as to be almost invisible. Major Grayper had been placed opposite the Captain, and the rest of the company had been arranged with due respect to social status and gender.

Now, it is a matter sometimes observed by scientists and more often by clandestine lovers, that sound travels more freely than sight. Place a wall across sight and it is stymied, but sound seeps through bricks and stones. Sight, as cheating lovers know too well, cannot turn a corner but sound, ah, sound can find its way through labyrinths. While Captain Meadows was hardly visible to Lord Batterstone, the sound of his conversation, alas, could not be banished. Not that the Captain would have made much conversation, left to himself; the fact that Mary was so confident of success was attributable to this one flaw in Meadows' persona. A reasonably handsome man, eligible in various worldly ways, well-read and well-travelled, he lacked the sort of frilly language that would have bestowed on him the attribute of being 'charming'. But at this dinner he was seated opposite Major Grayper who, having smothered the feeble poet that Lord Batterstone had detected in his conversation in the library, was now discoursing with the efficiency and loudness of a man used to marching other men in straight lines and geometrical patterns.

At first, Lady Batterstone was relieved by Major Grayper's decisive interventions: they served, towards the fag end of the dinner, to knit together the conversation at the table. Until then, instead of ebbing evenly like a sated sea, the conversation had been eddying and twirling, collecting in pools around Lord Batterstone, where it gave out the pungent scent of science; around Lady Batterstone and her good friend Mrs Montmorency, it assumed the fragrance of gardens and nonchalant domesticity; around Mr Reginald B. Sangrail and the young men and women next to him, it emanated an odour composed of equal portions of the ballroom and the stable; and around Major Grayper, it often leapt into the acridity of law and order.

It was law and order that enabled the Major to thread the various other conversations at the table through the singular eye of his discourse. This was what he said, addressing Lord Batterstone first: 'If I may take up what you have said, that, sir, was exactly the point I was making to Captain Meadows here. As you put it, sir, and so admirably, human beings are made by divinity, and God does not play dice. Now I have often been asked – why, just this evening Mr Sangrail put the question to me – I have been asked if I know who might be behind the beheadings which, as you know, have plagued London over the past few months. With the necessary withering away of the Runners, we are left without a detective body that could spread its investigations over the whole of London, and hence I have been asked by my superiors to look into all such murders, regardless of the vicinity of their occurrence. With that grave responsibility come inevitable questions, such as the one Mr Sangrail posed to me: Do I know the identity of the murderer? Well, no, I replied, I do not know who, but there are signs. For God, as you said, sir, does not play dice: He leaves marks for us to read.'

Then, raising his voice to drown out the nasal treble of Reginald B. Sangrail, who was trying to slide into the more salubrious mud of races and foxhunts, the Major reworked the thread of conversation enmeshing Lady Batterstone and Mrs Montmorency through the eyes of his needle of Law and Order: 'Now, as anyone who has anything to do with the working orders knows, and as you have noted a moment ago, what the working classes desire and need is order. But it is not an order they can create on their own; it needs to be imposed on them with an iron hand. It is with them –' here the Major turned to Mr Sangrail and his circle, finally knitting them into his meta-conversation '– as it is with horses, that you need to ride with a firm hand. Kind, but firm. Kind, but firm. Now, sir (he turned his conversation to Lord Batterstone again), what I say is that I know what signs to look for: as soon as the culprit is found, he shall be identified by the signs.'

'That is to say, Major,' Mr Reginald B. Sangrail could not help interjecting, with an iota of relish, 'you have not found the culprit yet.'

'It is not the finding that is important, sir. It is the reading of signs – as in, what is that (lacking the word, he looked at Captain Meadows, who supplied it: 'phrenology')... yes, phrenology. Once you know how to read the skull, you have your man. Now, I know that this man is either a native from the colonies or a working man, perhaps Cockney, who has been abroad. And there are other signs: I simply have to look for the signs, and...'

The Major snapped his fingers to signify the ease of the prospective capture.

'But that, Major,' said the Captain in his quiet, studious way, 'that is where I beg to differ. The signs, the physical signs, are not enough: they can signify different things, depending on the man's background, experiences, and so forth.'

'Humph,' pronounced Lord Batterstone, finally entering the discussion, 'you mean to say, Captain, that God is a gambler.'

'Who can really know, sir?'

'That might be laudable freethinking in some London circles,

Captain, but you and I differ on the matter. We differ very much, sir. I cannot express to you how much we differ.'

'And yet, Lord Batterstone, I must defend my position. I am not dismissing the science, I am not dismissing the hand of divinity; I am simply suggesting that signs are not enough, that God does not provide easy answers. And in any case, how can we know enough about the brain of a man, encased as it is in its bony casement, to be able to judge him...'

(Lady Batterstone, wary now of the direction of the conversation, tried to intervene with a comment on one of the dishes, but was ignored by her lord.)

'By reading the bony casement, sir. I think that is what we do, don't we?'

'There, if I may say so, Lord Batterstone, a majority of our colleagues would disagree with you: the skull gives you indications, not answers. We need to look deeper.'

'You are wrong, sir, if I may say so. Indications, not answers! It is the mark of ignorance, if not disbelief, to attribute a failure to read the signs to the absence of signs. God has made the skull to fit the brain: if you read the covering, you read the content. It is as simple as that...'

The sea of conversation was heaving dangerously on the fragile table, shiny with silver and candles, and Lady Batterstone took the drastic action of ringing for dessert, even though some of the guests had not finished the food on their plates. Holding his pince-nez decisively in place, Mr Reginald B. Sangrail came to her rescue by turning the conversation, with uncharacteristic resolution (born of utter boredom with matters relating to science, law, order, and the working classes), to the ball that was going to be the highlight of the week.

48

Breakfast in his chamber. His butler entering, helping him into his slippers and gown, and leaving soundlessly. The maid placing the silver tray, as was the custom, on the table in front of a deep window seat. From there, Lord Batterstone could look out and see a sizeable portion of the terrace and the park, while consuming his breakfast slowly, between occasional glances at a book or newspaper that he seldom read in a consistent manner. Lord Batterstone had established this tradition simply in order to avoid his guests for as long as possible. If he could manage to avoid them until noon, he would feel capable of bearing their company into the evening if required.

Lord Batterstone was counting the days. After the ball next evening, he would be a free man for a year. And, if things went well, next year, he would be in Africa collecting scientific samples and not wasting his time with a bunch of social nincompoops, invited haphazardly and perhaps spitefully by his dear wife. He was grateful that Major whatsisname had been called back to London yesterday morning with news of yet another beheading – some beggar or prostitute found in an abandoned ruin – though he had, unfortunately, left his family and that insufferable Captain Meadows behind.

Beheadings, forsooth! When had London ever lacked beheadings?

49

Mary and Captain Meadows stood in the small pagoda in one corner of the landscaped parks that surrounded the mansion of their hosts. They were not thinking of beheadings. Or, at least, Mary was not; Meadows was a bit worried about the way talk in London rags had moved towards accounts of thugs. It was only a matter of time before someone pointed a finger at Amir Ali, he thought. The Captain was convinced of Amir's innocence, but he had his doubts about the authorities – despite the fact that the Major was in charge – and he did not trust the London mob. In any case, he hoped that Amir had availed of his discharge from the Captain's service to board the first ship going east.

But Mary did not allow the Captain to dwell on such thoughts. She had better things to fill his mind with: things to do with herself. She dropped a handkerchief, and when the Captain did not notice it drop, she pointed it out to him. Meadows gallantly stooped to retrieve the fabric from the bedewed grass.

'Oh, look,' said Mary.

Captain Meadows looked. There was a ladybird on the handkerchief.

'It is quite unusual,' began Captain Meadows.

'Isn't it beautiful,' Mary interrupted.

There was a slight pause before Captain Meadows could think of the right response. 'Not as beautiful as you, if I may say so.' But perhaps it was not the right response.

Mary frowned.

'Are you comparing me to a bug, Captain?' she asked with a perfect pout.

She watched him stutter and fumble and realized once again why it was taking her so long to reel him in: this highly eligible man, excellent in so many ways, simply lacked the social ease with which other young men besieged her at parties and balls. But Mary, though exceptionally pretty, was no fool. She was not looking for a beau, not any more; she was looking for a husband. And Captain Meadows had 'husband' written all over his pale, blushing face with its long sideburns and washed-out eyes. She relented and laughed.

The Captain looked incredibly relieved.

50

Jenny and Amir could not hold hands in the polite parts of the city. This was new, Qui Hy had told them: when she was young, no one had objected to a coloured woman walking hand in hand with a white man. Perhaps that was so, thought Amir, or perhaps it was simply because in his case, it was the woman who was white. He did know that he could walk with Jenny in the rougher neighbourhoods of the city, in the rookery, for instance. But in the polite parks and streets he had to walk behind her, or some man or the other would take offence on Jenny's behalf and shove him away with a word or a gesture.

This was less disturbing for Amir, who had long realized that all societies had their untouchables, than for Jenny. She felt obliged to protest on his behalf. On one occasion, it had led to a scuffle. It would have ended badly too, if the two white men who had objected did not speak with such a heavy American accent – this had inspired Jenny to accuse the two of being slavers, thus winning the sympathy of the crowd. Killers of Lovejoy, this isn't America, a voice from the crowd had shouted. The men had been shoved and booed away by the mob and Jenny and Amir were actually cheered and applauded when they resumed their walk. But now Amir pre-empted the possibility of unpleasantness by keeping a step behind Jenny in the fashionable avenues of London.

Having spent the afternoon at Hyde Park, watching squirrels quarrel with long-tailed tits in the uneasy company of people of the higher classes, they were now walking back to Amir's half-house. Amir relished these rare trips – for Jenny was always working – to parks or monuments. He was fascinated by the look of rapture with which Jenny pointed out the latest features of the place they visited – this time, it was the monumental entrance at Hyde Park Corner, which Jenny recalled being built when she was a child. But while she could point out all the new features, she was largely ignorant of the history of the parks and palaces. She would listen with a combination of disbelief and fascination when Amir supplied some of the missing history, culled from papers or gossip. This afternoon she had laughingly refused to believe Amir when he told her that the Serpentine was an artificial lake, created only a century ago.

In general, Jenny and Amir did not talk much. On the way back from Hyde Park, they admired the buildings and the dresses: Amir because he was still getting used to this city, Jenny because it was seldom that she had time to look at the houses she passed, the people she served.

As they walked towards the neighbourhood where Amir was renting a place, not very far from Qui Hy's dhaba, imperceptibly they drew closer to each other. As the streets got darker and dirtier, the houses more dilapidated, the invisible pressure of decorum that had kept them apart dissipated and they realized they were holding hands. Unlike her hair, which was carefully tended and protected even during her most difficult chores, Jenny's hands were hard and callused. If her hair, when she let it down for Amir, evoked a desire to protect, her hands seemed to proclaim a capacity to survive on their own, unprotected by anyone. It was this that Amir found most fascinating about Jenny: her vulnerability and her toughness.

They walked on together, hand in hand, in the growing darkness of this rough neighbourhood full of dogs and homeless people, of houses with broken shutters, of people with abandoned dreams; they walked on like any other couple down a street that had seen and borne so much that it felt no surprise at the sight of a young Asian man, dressed like a lascar, walking with a slightly older English maid. When the clouds parted and the moon was revealed as almost full, the two lovers felt alone in the slight fog, wrapped in themselves, though the street was still teeming with people, carts and horses, urchins and sellers, porters and burglars, lascars and gypsies, Malays and Moroccans, tinkers and beggars, drunks and prostitutes returning home or, in some cases, going to work.

51

If Amir and Jenny had not been so intent on each other, perhaps they would have noticed the 'Singing Salesman', January Monday, on one of the streets they passed on their way back to Amir's house. They would have known him. He was known by sight to many in London: his name purportedly taken from the month and day when he arrived in London on a ship from Jamaica.

Perhaps because he had already made enough money, at that moment, January was not singing the songs that he wrote on paper and sold to passers-by during the day. They were mostly hymns or ballads celebrating some English victory and hero, particularly Lord Nelson, and many people bought them out of patriotism or altruism, for they could not really take the texts seriously as poetry, though everyone agreed that the man sang handsomely. But then he was black, wasn't he, and the Negro race was good at singing and dancing, being closer to nature; it was at athletics, sports, literature and science that Negroes showed their inferiority.

So Amir would not have been exceptional in recognizing January Monday, wrapped in his sails and rigging, fashioned with stylish care if only one looked at them with different eyes. He was a fixture in these parts. But January knew Amir too, and perhaps if the two men had seen each other, he would have joined Amir and gone on to Qui Hy's or some other place. Had he done so, he might have escaped the fate that had been trailing him all evening, in the shape of three men, one of them one-eyed and armed with a cudgel. For January Monday was not only a gifted singer and poet, a man who had stitched himself into a future in an alien land; he was also a man with a deformed, indented skull.

52

Having cultivated a meagre moustache, I left Phansa for the first time. I had finished high school and there were no decent colleges in town. With a few other boys from my class, I went to Patna. We were not the best students, I must say: the best students were accepted by colleges in Delhi or by the various government-run medical and engineering colleges. Those who went to Patna were average students, unable to study 'science' in better places and not willing, due to family pressure or career expectations, to study Humanities.

Suddenly, from living in a large compound with sprawling houses – my grandfather's whitewashed one in the middle, flanked by the slightly smaller houses of his two sons – I had to live in a flat. The flat was only slightly bigger than the library in my grandfather's house. And I had to share it with three other boys, two of us in each of the two rooms. There was a kitchen with a grilled window, which looked out on the dirt-streaked walls of another building. There was a bathroom with a window covered with wire. The wire had rusted and a hole had been poked into it, for cigarette stubs to be thrown out; they littered the window ledge outside.

I felt constrained. I felt imposed upon, observed. But then I looked around, and all around me there were people living two to a room, four to a room. I had never realized life took so little. This constrained, corralled space, not my grandfather's spacious whitewashed house, was (I realized) closer to the common inheritance of humankind. When I try now to imagine Amir Ali, Gunga and his friends in London, I think of such rooms in places like Patna. How fine a thread – the silk of surviving – links them apart.

53

Gunga and his gang were as good as their word. For the third evening in a row, the moment they heard Jenny come in, they rolled up their blankets and, after a short conversation, sheepishly excused themselves, leaving the two-room half-house entirely to the young lovers. Jenny and Amir had no place but the half-house to be intimate in. Jenny was no longer living at her aunt's house: she could not afford to rent it alone and the landlord had foisted two other young women on her after her aunt's murder.

Amir used to feel uneasy on such occasions, for all the men – everyone except Gunga, who remained as he had always been, wiry, alert, indefatigable (despite having lost his job) – were showing the effects of being landlocked in a cold place. Karim, despite his tall stories about encounters with English and Irish women, was coughing much of the time and occasionally spat out blood. Even Tuanku, a tough, gnarled little man, was thinner and less ebullient than before. Amir knew that if it had not been for his house, they would have subsisted in some dilapidated room, damp and dark, sharing with others like them. He also knew that when they went out, they had few options regarding shelter: Qui Hy's dhaba was never open to anyone after midnight, and it was seldom that the gang had money for drinks in dockside pubs.

Sometimes, when Karim felt better, he sold biblical tracts on the streets: he had invested in a pile and he knew some English hymns. Amir had heard him on some of those occasions. He gave the same story to all the kind ladies and gentlemen who interrogated him. 'I was born in Calcutta and was Mussulman – but I Christian now. I have been in dis countree ten year. I come first as servant to a military officer, Englishman. I lived with him in Scotland six, seven mont. He left Scotland, saying he come back, but he not, and in a mont I hear he dead, and den I come to London. I wish very often return to my countree, where everything sheap, living sheap, rice sheap...'

He would follow this up with a hymn in his melodious voice, maintaining a conscious balance between the crispness of English intonation and the fluidity of Hindustani rhythms, pronouncing and mispronouncing the words in the way he knew he was expected to, and it would almost always charm the gentleman or lady into purchasing a tract. But with his consumption exacerbated by the recent winter cold, it was seldom that Karim had the energy or the voice for this livelihood now. Instead, he tagged along with the rest of his gang of jahaajbhais, pilfering, scavenging, grateful to Amir for providing them with a warm and free shelter. Only Gunga still went to the docks, looking for work on some departing ship.

Jenny had cleaned herself thoroughly for the visit to Amir's place – her hair still smelt of vinegar and she had put on a fresh, if threadbare, dress. Her only shawl – which she kept as carefully as her hair – was wrapped around her sturdy shoulders, over a plain dress that reached her ankles and had, despite the attentions of a darning needle, obviously seen better days. In the gloom of the sparsely furnished room, she took off her petticoats in a matter-of-fact way that Amir found fascinating: it combined the knowledge of the tawaifs he had known in Patna with the demureness of the girls from his village. He waited and watched as garment after garment was discarded, methodically, and in some cases folded away. Jenny seemed to reveal herself more and more with each gesture: the half smile that belonged to a shy girl, the measured movements of an experienced woman, the hair that cascaded down unreal as a dream, the slender work-hardened muscles of reality that her bare arms exposed... but when she came to the last garments, she bent and blew out the only candle in the room. She would have considered it improper to be seen fully naked. She was a woman used to seeing other women importuning from doorways, half hanging out from windows so that the pedestrian could look down and beyond their breasts; it had left her with a revulsion for any stage-setting.

54

The Batterstone mansion was not lighted with gas. It was lighted in the traditional way: with candles and lanterns, torches and fireplaces. Even the library. And it was in the library that Lord Batterstone had taken refuge after dinner this evening, assuming that he was most likely to be left undisturbed in this room of shelves and books. But he was not left alone for long. The young Reginald B. Sangrail – of all people – came sidling in and almost bumped into the armchair in which Lord Batterstone was incumbent. Having refitted his pince-nez and discovered his reclusive host, Mr Sangrail overcame his initial surprise and seated himself in an adjoining chair, attempting to converse.

The host was just as surprised: Mr Reginald B. Sangrail, whose conversation seldom galloped without horses, foxes and hounds to inspire it, was the last person he had expected to encounter in his library. In any library. Had he been more perceptive, he would have read from the blush on Mr Sangrail's handsome features that he had arranged to encounter someone else – of another age and gender altogether. But not bothering with faces, expert as he was of skulls, the lord asked Mr Sangrail if he, too, was interested in phrenology.

'Yes, sir, what logic?' yipped Mr Sangrail, still recovering from his surprise.

'Phrenology,' repeated Lord Batterstone. He indicated the book he had been looking at, and the shelves in that part of the room – all of them stocked with books on phrenology and related matters.

'Oh, of course, sir,' replied Mr Sangrail, following his general policy of agreeing with people as much as possible, 'I am a great admirer of phrenology. It is an intricate science, sir. Just the other day, I was reading that fellow Coombe…'

It was one of Mr Sangrail's many talents that he picked up references and names in light conversation and quoted them, with much astuteness and deadly effect among females of a certain kind, on singularly appropriate occasions.

'Combe, sir? Now which book was it, and what did you think of the author?'

Mr Sangrail was going to blurt out an inane eulogy, but he looked at his host's expression and, being a careful reader of faces, modulated his reply significantly.

'I cannot claim, sir, that I entirely agreed with the author.'

Lord Batterstone sat up abruptly. For the first time in days, the light of interest flickered in his chimerical yellow-blue-green eyes.

'You were right not to, sir. The man hardly knows what he is talking about, at least not when it comes to the core issues…'

'Exactly my feeling, Lord Batterstone, though of course I lack your knowledge of the matter.'

'So does the world, sir, so does the world,' said Lord Batterstone, feeling a sudden desire to unburden himself to this sympathetic and knowledgeable listener.

Mr Sangrail made soft, obliging noises. Another of his talents was to produce noises so finely modulated that they could be made to carry the burden of any – or no – meaning.

Lord Batterstone grew more expansive. He poured himself and the fine young man some excellent claret.

'It has been one of my endeavours, sir, to prove that man wrong. And I believe it will not be long – perhaps no longer than two or three years – before I crush his supporters under the weight of evidence, of solid proof, sir.'

Mr Sangrail raised himself to the occasion. 'I am sure, Lord Batterstone, that your book will be a major contribution to science and society,' he offered encouragingly.

'Book, sir? I shall not indulge in the vulgar conceit of writing a book. I am compiling something far more extensive and scientific. Haven't you heard of my Theatre of Phrenological Specimen, sir?'

Mr Sangrail, who had not even dreamt of any such thing, hastened to assure the lord that word of this great monument had been circulating, admiring mouth to awestruck mouth, in the upper-most and most intelligent echelons of society, state and civilization.

'You see, sir, my European collection is almost complete, and it proves me right and the Combians wrong. But next summer, perhaps even earlier, I am embarking on a voyage up the Congo which will enable me to expand the collection decisively.'

'I am sure, sir, a voyage to India will be beneficent…'

'India? India, sir? I am talking of the Congo in darkest Africa.

It is there I hope to be around this time of the year, not here, surrounded by…'

Lord Batterstone waved his hands in a gesture of contempt and dismissal, which Mr Sangrail interpreted as aimed at the books in the room. As he harboured a similar contempt for books and never imagined that anyone could evince contempt for people like him, Mr Sangrail hummed and hawed in sympathy, drained his claret as fast as etiquette permitted, and sauntered off to his next rendezvous.

55

Major Grayper rolled the newspaper into a tube, folded it in half and threw it into the wastebasket. The cheek of the man! And to think that he knew him, knew Meadows, knew half the people in their circle… But then, what else could one expect from a pen-pusher, from a grubby little hack!

Mrs Grayper looked up from her breakfast at this act of unusual violence by her spouse. She glanced at the paper lying in the basket. She looked back at the Major.

'You shouldn't let them bother you. They have to write something to sell their rags…'

'It is not that,' said the Major, 'it is the tone… the sower sows the word. It is the tone, and the man.'

'The man?'

'That Daniel Oates.'

'Mr Oates! But he knows you. He knows us.'

'Yes, my dear,' said the Major bitterly, 'yes.'

Mrs Grayper retrieved the newspaper from the wastebasket and after locating the article and smoothening out the sheets with some effort, read it carefully while the Major bit into his bread and ham furiously.

'The cheek of the man,' she exclaimed, neatly echoing the Major's thoughts. 'He implies that you are dragging your feet because the suspect is in the employment of a good friend. He as much as names poor Captain Meadows.'

'Everything but the name, my dear.'

'And it is not even true that the suspect stays with the Captain. Oates knows that Mr Ali moved out weeks, months ago.'

'That is not the issue, missus. The implication is that I am not doing my job.'

'How dare he!'

'Well, my dear, he has, and now I will have to do something about it.'

'You won't do anything rash, will you, dear?' interrupted his good wife. 'I hope you don't intend to challenge him to a duel, do you?'

She asked the question with a brittle laugh and a glitter in her eyes, gasping slightly, for a moment undecided between the rashness of the possibility and its romance.

The Major laughed. 'Those days are over, missus. And in any case, rodents like him cannot be confronted: they crawl away into holes and hide. I will have to do something else.'

'Something else?'

'I shall arrest that man, that thug.'

'Arrest him? But do you believe he is the murderer, the beheader!'

'It hardly matters. He is the only suspect we have, and after this article, it might be safer to put him behind bars than to let him roam free on the streets. That is, if he is still in London.'

'You mean, the murders will stop if you arrest him.'

'Perhaps, my dear, or perhaps not. But I know he will get murdered by some drunken mob if I do not arrest him. This Oates has an eye for detail; his description hardly leaves anything out.'

'The cheek of the man,' Mrs Grayper burst out again, returning to her original sentiment, 'and to think we once invited him to dinner in this very house.'

But by then, the Major, having resolved the matter in his head, was concentrating whole-heartedly on his breakfast. Mary, who always got up a little late, joined them at this moment, and the conversation assumed a merrier tone.

56

Jaanam,

In all stories of great passion – Laila-Majnun, Shirin-Farhad – suffering and loss walk shoulder to shoulder with love. Perhaps that is why I feel a certain dread at times. Having come so long a way, heading into nothing, running away from everything, I had only hoped to survive, not to flourish. For what is the gift of love if not a flourishing? In this bleak climate, under these grey skies, a great blossoming, the rising of a greenness far more luxuriant than anything even the monsoon could bring to my village.

And with it comes a dread of loss and decay.

As when you are late in keeping an appointment.

As when you wake up suddenly at night, reliving that moment of discovery, of your aunt lying dead and beheaded.

As when you sometimes fear that there is someone stalking you.

As when I want to hold you and know that I cannot, that it would be dangerous to do so in the eyes of the world. As when you look at me with the sun of love clouded by doubt, unable to decide between the stories I have told you about myself, and those everyone knows I have been telling Captain Meadows and his friends.

As when the evening deepens into oppressive night, burdened with darkness and fumes, and I try to sleep, not to think of where you might be, in whose home, in what alley, doing God knows what to earn a livelihood.

As when I wake up some morning, terrified not to find you by my side, forgetting that you had not come to me that night.

As when I think of the past and its inevitability, and the future and its fickleness. Or is it the other way round, jaanam, is it the other way round?

As when someone knocks on the door, unexpectedly...

57

Shields, John May observes bitterly to himself, has been given the wrong skull by providence. It ought to be bumpy and dented, with the knobs, or whatever they are, for superstition and credulity exaggerated and the thingummy for logic and rationality absent. Instead, it is smooth and regular, lush with hair, almost noble in its dimensions, if only because the short stature of the man imparts to his head a leonine expanse.

There he sits, twittering about ghosts and spirits, now that he is half drunk. May curses under his breath and plies Shields with another drink. The only way to get him out of this superstitious mood is to get him properly sozzled, for only then will he switch to his other role of excessive bravado. If only Jack would arrive soon: John May needs that drily garrulous man's aura of unflappability. After all, they have a job to do tonight.

Perhaps he is pressing Shields too much, two jobs within the week, but why not; why not strike while the iron is hot? And who knows how long M'lord will continue to pay for the skulls? He has already started showing less and less interest, and once even told John May that he might soon be going away on a scientific expedition to the 'empire'. John May resents this vague empire which, he suspects, serves no other purpose than to drain London of its best minds, noblest names and heaviest purses. He is determined to share a bit more of M'lord's bounty before it is wasted on savages. Already, John May has made more from this enterprise than from all his stratagems and tinkering in the past.

58

Jaanam,

My legs still ache from the blows. There are marks all over my body. Not bleeding cuts, they were far too careful and experienced for that, but bruises and blue marks.

I am to blame, partly. If you are not in your element,

you have to be more careful than usual. The swimmer in the water has to be more wary of drowning than the runner on the ground is of falling. An old lesson, which I thought I had learned years ago. And yet, when I heard the knock last evening, I hastened to open the door without peering through the chinks. I thought it was you, or Gunga and the boys, who had gone for a 'walkabout', which is their word for any activity that involves scavenging, hustling, begging on the streets.

I opened the door, still thinking of you, still holding the feather with which I had been writing in my notebook, and I was faced with three hefty men. At first, I did not notice the colour of their frockcoats. They did not waste words or time. One of them asked me, Are you Aye-mir Al-I? I was too confused to do anything but nod. At that, two of them made to grab me; I resisted, for I still had not realized who they were, and they showered me with blows and curses. It was only after I had been battered into the gutter that one of them said I was being arrested. And it was then I noticed the blue frockcoats, the rabbit-skin high top hats and naval cutlasses of two of the men.

They were Peelers, sent by one Major Grayper to apprehend me, the 'prime suspect' in the beheading cases, as he told the pen-pushers who were already lounging around his superintendent's desk when I was brought there. I think the Major was a little taken aback by the condition in which I was dragged into custody. In any case, he instructed the policemen to treat me properly, reminding them that I was not guilty until proved to be so, and he even asked me if I desired something. This enabled me to ask for some basic things – the prayer beads that Mustapha Chacha had given me, my ink pot, quills and notebook, all of which were delivered to me only this afternoon *by Gunga and Qui Hy's Irish husband. I learnt that Gunga had been denied access to me earlier in the day and had to return reinforced by the presence of Qui Hy's husband. The two of them assured me that they would do all they could to get me out, and that there was no evidence against me, that on most of the nights of the murders I had been with one of them. Not that I think their evidence will hold much water. What witnesses! A beanpole of a lascar; an emaciated Irish soldier obviously given to the habit and known to dance to tunes in his head. I cannot imagine Major Grayper or any respectable jury taking them seriously.*

Of course, Major Grayper, though proper, was not inexperienced in the art of interrogation. He woke me up well after midnight for my first interrogation – after a bucket of cold water had been splashed on me because, it was said, I had not responded to the prodding earlier on. He interrogated me until it was almost dawn, and then had me carted off to another prison. This place: a place that is more frightening to me, for I do not know what it is, or where. What the Major was interested in was the night, just five days ago, when the so-called 'head cannibal' killed his latest victim. It was that night I had to explain away. Where was I that night?

How could I reply to that, jaanam? For you and I know where I was – I was lying with my head in your lap, shaded by the cascade of your brown hair which smelled of vinegar and the husky odour of your body. How could I tell him that? And so, in my silence – my 'sullen silence', as he called it – I have condemned myself in Major Grayper's eyes.

Now I wait in this cold, damp cell for time to decide my fate. The prison they have remanded me to is not very far from Superintendent Grayper's police station. I sensed that much. I was brought to this place hooded and blindfolded: perhaps this was done for my own safety, for everyone assumes that the Rookery Beheader is confined at Superintendent Grayper's station; or perhaps it was done to intimidate me. This place is more like a dungeon than a police station. It is possibly less than fifteen minutes by horse and carriage from the Superintendent's station. This, I fear, is not for my convenience but to enable the Major's men to fetch me easily and at short notice for interrogations, but there is a sense of security in not being interred far away, forgotten and overlooked by the authorities. I have also not been put in with anyone else, though there is a person who often swears at me from one of the other cells, a faceless voice that threatens to break the bars of his cell and devour the cannibal that I am supposed to be. Cannibal, he shouts, beware, for thy doom approacheth; nigger, prepare thyself, for mine is the vengeance. He thinks he is quoting from the Bible. I think he is drunk. If so, this is not a prison but another police station.

What I have confessed in this notebook is something I will never tell anyone else: I will not have them laughing at you, pointing a finger of reproach at you. If I cannot be cleared silently, I will accept my verdict in silence. My only fear is that the verdict will snatch me away, for ever, from you – condemned as I would be to death, or to transportation for life after weeks in those brooding hulks on the river.

59

It is a myth of the lazy storyteller that ghosts primarily inhabit desolate houses and crumbling castles.

No ghost ever walks down the stairs and corridors of my grandfather's house when I visit it now, once every year; no spectre looks in from the other side of the window. The library is empty. My grandmother's keys have been buried with her, as she had stipulated in her will. The house is simply empty, curtains pulled down, windows boarded up. Its emptiness has no voice. But when I return to the bigger cities I now inhabit, I encounter my ghosts: the lilt of a voice from the past, the glimpse of a familiar expression on a stranger's face, the return of a cornice, a windowpane, a gesture, a book. It is in the strangeness of their fleeting presence that I feel haunted; it is in the familiarity of their absence.

No, it is in the big cities that we live with beings that are always there and not there. They live around us, yet we know nothing of them. But they know a little (or is it everything?) of us. Because they are always there, walking past us, living their own lives, watching, shouting, whispering; we live with the knowledge of their presence. These ghosts who fill the streets, who lurk behind shuttered windows.

London is full of ghosts. It is a place of hauntings, of betrayals, hangings, beheadings. And above all, it is a place of dreams and hopes. Ghosts are born of failure, perhaps, but failure itself hatches from hope. If death spawns ghosts then, surely, before death there must be birth, or at least gestation. The ripening of dreams. The swollen belly of hope. And then, well, then comes the knife and the scream, then comes the blood.

Blood has been pouring into the dreams of Shields. He wakes up in terror, choking on the blood of his imagination. He cannot see a knife without starting. He needs half a day to drink himself out of terror so he can accomplish at night, if necessary, if prodded by Jack, tempted by John May, the deed that will soak his nights in blood again. Day after day, night after night.

From a squat little man with few thoughts, Shields has become a thin nervous wreck, haunted by ghosts, trying not to think of damnation. For, unlike John May, he believes in the Devil. He saw the Devil in his dreams one night. The Devil was every inch a gentleman; his face was a mask, but he wore a big, filthy patch over one eye.

60

Nelly Clennam had done her duty. She had reported to Captain Meadows: that girl Jenny, you know, the girl who sometimes gives us a hand downstairs in the kitchen – not that we would ask her often if you had not given instructions about it – that Jenny is asking to see you, sir. To which the good Captain, God bless his soul, had replied, as was to be expected, given her years of dedicated service: 'But Mrs Clennam, surely you can take care of the matter, whatever it might be.'

'So I said to the girl, sir,' Nelly had sniffed, 'but she insists on seeing you, personally. Says it is a private matter.'

The Captain had looked surprised. His broad brow – it ran to his father's side, a receding hairline – had furrowed. 'Private matter? With me, Mrs Clennam?' he had inquired dubiously.

'Yes, sir,' Nelly had replied, her thin lips pressed together to illustrate her disapproval. Come to think of it, she had never really liked Jenny, with her free ways and her precious hair kept cleaner than the starched cap that Nelly insisted the maids wore in the house, and she was sure there had been some hanky-panky between the girl – she had bold eyes and walked and laughed like a man – and that heathen thug who, everyone was saying, had finally been arrested, thank God.

'Well, show her in then, Mrs Clennam,' the Captain had replied.

'Here, sir? In the library?'

'Where else,' said the Captain, putting down the thick book he had been reading a moment earlier.

And now the girl had been in the room for close to half an hour and Mrs Clennam, who never eavesdropped, no, not her, happened to pass the thick door a few times, once detecting a sob, once overhearing the name Aymir, uttered by the hussy; yes, she thought it had something to do with that smooth cannibal. She hoped the Captain would send her off with a good dressing down, the cheap...

But Nelly's hopes were scuttled when the door of the library was flung open and Jenny appeared, drying her eyes, followed by the Captain, who marched out in a hurry, calling for the coach and his hat. Oh well, oh well, one never knew these days, the times being what they were...

61

There are walls. There are voices. The voices come through the walls.

Amir has been given a cell to himself. He is uncertain whether this has been done to torment him or to protect him from his fellow prisoners, for word has gone out that the terrible Indian cannibal who had been feeding off the brains and eyes of the English poor has finally been apprehended.

At first it was just the one man, probably drunk: Prepare thyself, cannibal, for mine is the vengeance. Then other voices joined in. And now there is a storm of voices raging around him. It is quelled for a few moments when one of the warders comes down and strikes the bars or threatens them. But then it starts again.

Not all the voices are hostile. Some are bored. Some are joking. One is, Amir is convinced, merely curious: 'What did it taste like,' this one asks in the quieter intervals, which always sets the louder voices off again. But no matter what their tenor, they are voices, and they penetrate Amir Ali's cell of isolation, making him feel vulnerable and threatened.

It is dark down here, and Amir has been confined for so long that he is no longer sure if it is day or night. His cell has no window, not even a slit. The only light he gets is from the lamp in the corridor outside. He has prepared himself for a long stay. Here, time is a currency he can neither spend nor hoard. He has written off time.

He is surprised when footsteps reverberate up to his cell. This time it is not just a warder or a Peeler. It is Major Grayper himself, flanked by two men. Amir is surprised that he has come to the prison in person. Grayper gestures to the men to release Amir, and Amir follows him dumbly up the stairs. He does not notice one of the men wrapping up his meagre belongings: the notebook, the quill pen, the bottle of ink and his blanket. Upstairs, Amir can sense that it is day outside. He stands there, confused.

'You are free to go,' says Major Grayper.

Amir does not react.

'Go, nigger, go,' says one of the Peelers, thrusting Amir's wrapped-up belongings at him and shoving him towards the door. Amir walks as if in a trance. It is surprisingly sunny outside. For a second, his mind is tricked into believing that he has stepped into India. Then he blinks at the light. His eyes hurt. He does not recognize the street.

62

During his short imprisonment, Amir envisioned various fates for himself: trial, exoneration, imprisonment, deportation, hanging. It was his way of preparing himself for any eventuality, and Amir believes in being prepared. The only eventuality he did not envision was this sudden and unexpected release. He does not know what to do.

The street is not crowded at this time of afternoon, yet Amir knows he has to disappear soon. It will not take long for some passer-by to connect Amir's face with the news of the arrest of the 'head cannibal' and soon he will have a mob baying for his blood. Even as this thought crosses Amir's mind, a carriage rattles to a stop right in front of him. Its door opens and a hand pulls him in. Perhaps Amir would have resisted, were he not so bemused by what had happened to him, this sudden freedom and surprising daylight. He lets himself be pulled in and the carriage sets off immediately, at a brisk pace.

63

Jenny walked the streets alone, as she always had. But she felt lonelier than ever before. Lonelier than she had felt when the shock of her aunt's grisly murder had finally sunk in. How could the disappearance of a man she had known for just a few months, a man from another land, a man who spoke her language with a strange accent and whose language – languages, he would have corrected – she had no inkling of, how could the disappearance of such a person from her life make her feel so lonely? She, who had grown up being alone on the streets and in her head? She, who had learned, since the age of four or five, not to place her trust in anyone – no, not even Amir, for if one's mother could disappear into the vast spaces of life, what was there to keep one's love within reach for ever? And if the man she loved could lie so fluently to Captain Meadows and his much-travelled friends, what was there to prevent him from lying to an illiterate, stuck-in-the-mud girl like herself?

And yet, ever since she had been told that Amir had been arrested on suspicion of murder, she had felt as if the distance between her and other people had increased; as if she was at the bottom of a well, hearing the rest of the world only as an echo. At first, she had reasoned that Amir would be released: after all, she knew, as did Qui Hy and his other friends, where Amir had been on almost all the nights on which the beheadings had taken place.

But the more she thought about it, she realized that Qui Hy and the others would not count as witnesses.

Would her evidence suffice? Perhaps, but only as long as her relationship with Amir was not made public. Once it became public, her credibility would vanish. And how could she vouch for Amir, how could she tell them he had been with her in the middle of the night, without the truth of their relationship being bared? Ridicule she would have put up with, if it gained Amir his freedom, but she was not certain it would. She did not know enough about the world of law and order. It was a world whose steps she had wiped, whose floors she had swept, whose kitchens she had kneeled in, but it was not a world whose language she understood.

Her only hope had been Captain Meadows, and she had gone to him with her story. Captain Meadows who, she knew, had trusted Amir; Captain Meadows, who was one of the very few truly respectable men she had met. Now even that hope was gone, for Captain Meadows had left her in such a rush, as if repelled by what she had – at immense cost to herself – been forced to reveal to him. He had rushed out as if she were a foul smell.

Jenny trudged to her next chore, careless of bumping into other pedestrians or their swearing when she did, not even heeding the tumult in one corner where some street musicians had got a crowd dancing: men and women holding hands and swirling around before the scandalized eyes of gentlemen and ladies stuck in a lock of horses, carts and carriages. It was all so far from her now; so far away that they appeared to be on another continent altogether, a different breed and race of people. She plodded on, forgetful even of that persistent feeling of being trailed or watched occasionally that had sometimes come to her in recent weeks. Solitary, she walked in her mind.

64

As Amir's eyes get used to the gloom of the carriage – all the curtains are drawn – he realizes that the man who pulled him in is Captain Meadows.

Meadows is looking steadily at him, as if trying to see him more clearly. Or, as if seeing him for the first time.

Amir tries to speak but what comes out is an incoherent mumble.

'I thought it would be best to remove you from these parts and take you to some neighbourhood of London where you might not be noticed much,' says Captain Meadows.

The carriage rattles over cobbled stones.

'But...' Amir lets the sentence hang in the air, incomplete. He does not have to frame the questions that rush to his lips. They are, he knows, fully audible to the Captain. After months of answering questions and telling stories, all of them embroidered lies, after months of deceiving the other in ways that are welcome to each, after nights of not quite asking and not quite answering, suddenly, by a process that is impossible to understand, the two men have reached a stage where they can ask and respond almost without the use of language.

'I must be the last person you expected to see, Mr Ali,' says the Captain with a faint smile.

Amir nods.

'I was never convinced of your guilt. No, Mr Ali, let me rephrase that: I was as convinced of your innocence as a person could be under the circumstances. And then Jenny came to me.'

When Amir does not say anything in reply, the Captain continues, 'She told me where you were that night.'

Amir looks alarmed.

'No, Mr Ali, I didn't tell the Major what Jenny told me,' says the Captain gently. 'I gave him an assurance that you were innocent and that, unless proved guilty, you could be released on my word as a gentleman. I think he had no choice but to accept my assurance. There isn't much evidence against you, Mr Ali, nothing but hearsay.'

The carriage jolts at that moment and both men steady themselves.

Amir tries to speak.

'There is nothing to say, Mr Ali. I did what I would have done for any Englishman, had I come to know him as well as I came to know you, had I formed as strong an opinion of him as I had formed of you. It was not what you said, but how you said it; your demeanour, your careful tending of me when I fell ill on the voyage back, your politeness in the face of Mrs Clennam's prejudices, little things like that. I just regret that I needed the evidence of Jenny to make me act on my own convictions. That will remain a matter of shame for me, for I know that I would have acted sooner had you been an Englishman.'

Amir is still struggling for words. His English is suddenly not sufficient. He feels ashamed to look at the Captain.

'Sir,' he says, 'I have to confess, I am not, I have never been...'

Meadows holds up his hand.

'Mr Ali,' he says, 'sometimes I feel that what we are, what we appear to be, what we pretend to be and what we are said to be are four very different things. Such is the nature of life, one of its many imperfections, you might say. But just as one cannot condemn a man, or so I believe, because of a bump or two on his head, surely we cannot write off life because of its imperfections.

I have thought much about these matters in recent months, while preparing my book for the press. But let us not talk about all that. We have driven long enough. If you would now inform the coachman of the address you wish to be taken to, I am sure he will have no objection to driving you there.'

65

There is something deceptive about cities. Qui Hy knew that. And London, this city of cities, how could it be trusted? It hid so many stories and layers, its paths above the ground were devious and twisted, its tunnels and sewers and dungeons numberless and unmapped. Even the one central fact about it – River Thames, Father Thames – was deceptive, for London was not a city of one river. No, it was a city of many rivers, some lost, some lurking. Not just the Thames but also the Wandle and Falcon, the Tyburn and Effra, Neckinger and the Fleet, Stamford Brook and the Ravensbourne.

Qui Hy did not trust cities. She had memories of her own childhood in a village of the Punjab. It was a long time ago. At the age of eleven or twelve – her age was mostly her parents' guess – her mother sent her to work in the kitchen of a rich Sikh family in Amritsar. They moved to Lucknow after a few years, where she was loaned to an English officer's family. The wife had been in childbirth then. After that, Qui Hy passed through three different European families in quick succession, mostly working as a nanny: she was popular with Europeans because of her knack for picking up their languages and her inexplicable skill with children. She had lived in cities since she started working for the family in Amritsar. But she never lost her distrust of cities, or of people who grew up in them.

She tried to say as much to Amir Ali. If a city person, even a gentleman like Captain Meadows, helps someone, there is always an ulterior motive, Amir. People in cities do not help each other unless they stand to gain by it. The ones who do, she said, stitching her pockets by the low fire, without looking up at Amir, the ones who do have come from villages, from small towns.

But Amir was too overwhelmed by the goodness of Captain Meadows to hear her.

Gunga was there too. He sat still, a tall man with a forked beard, thin as a wire, noncommittal. But Qui Hy knew he was worried. She had sensed the bond that existed between this semi-literate, uncouth lascar and the youth, Amir Ali, not a rich man but nevertheless a man of education and culture. Perhaps it was more on Gunga's side, the love of an older man for the son he would like to have had, or perhaps the son he had lost or left behind. Or was she transferring to Gunga her own feelings for Amir? And Amir? Amir, though not inconsiderate, was too wrapped up in the haze of his love for Jenny and now the storm of the fate that was creeping up on him. Qui Hy knew that it was this looming storm that creased Gunga's leathery face with worry and made him pull at his beard in thought.

Like Qui Hy, Gunga knew that the mysterious murderer, the man who was beheading his victims, had to be identified soon. Otherwise, even Captain Meadows' word would not save Amir Ali. His past as a thug would catch up with him. Either Major Grayper or one of the other superintendents would choose to sacrifice Amir to satiate the vengeance of law, or the London mob. Something had to be done. And Qui Hy knew that she was the only one who could do it.

66

Karim flung open the door, entering the room with a gust of wind and noise from the street. Despite his illness, he still opened doors with abandon, as if springing the pleasure of his presence on those in the room. He banged it shut behind him and rushed up to embrace Amir. 'Just heard, just heard,' he gasped, breathless with excitement and exertion, just heard that you have been released. Did they catch the murderer?'

When the matter was explained to him, he grew thoughtful.

'You know what this means, Gunga Bhai,' he said. When no one spoke, he answered his own question: 'It means that Amir Bhai has to get himself a haircut.'

'Haircut?' Amir was surprised.

'Haircut, moustache cut, whatever. New papers, if you can. New identity. You cannot go out into the streets as you are. You never know who you might run into. There are people who might have read descriptions of you. And you will be stopped by every Peeler on his round, every night-watchman with nothing better to do.'

'That is true,' said Qui Hy, intercepting Amir's resistance to the suggestion. 'But we have to do something more. We have to try and find out more about the murders.'

'But how can we? And why us?'

Gunga replied for Qui Hy. 'It has to be us, because the others might just find the most convenient culprit again. And we have a witness.'

'A witness?'

'Jenny. Have you forgotten? She saw the men who were leaving her aunt's house that night. She remembers what they looked like. She has already described them to us so many times…'

'How can we find them if the police cannot?'

'We can find them, Karim,' said Qui Hy, '*because* the police cannot. Why, the Peelers did not even record Jenny's evidence, I am told! Three men, at least one of them from the better classes, walking down a street together, could not possibly be reason for suspicion. What they wanted was a criminal character they could recognize. But these three men will be visible to us, to people like us. They have been taking the precaution of hiding themselves from the police and respectable eyes, but would they even notice the beggar on the street, the lascar in the corner? What we need to do is ask around.'

'But I do not want Jenny involved in this,' Amir interposed.

'She won't be involved. She will only have to identify them when we find them.'

'If we find them.'

'No, Amir, not if. When.'

'And what then?'

'We will see. Let us find them first. There are ways to make them visible to people like Major Grayper.'

Amir shook his head. 'No,' he said, 'no. I do not want this. It will blow away. Let us not do anything. Let Major Grayper find them. I do not want Jenny to be troubled or involved.'

'All right, Amir,' Qui Hy gave in, 'but at least do what Karim has said: change your appearance and name, buy yourself some false papers, references.'

'It is not necessary.'

'Listen to me, Amir beta. Listen to me. I know what is necessary. And it won't cost much: you have more than enough money, but only one life.'

'It is not the expense that I object to…'

'Then just do as I say…'

'You are right, Mai,' said Gunga. He always addressed Qui Hy as 'Mai', though she was not much older than him and could certainly not have been his mother. 'Amir needs another name, another identity. He has to shave off his moustache, clip his hair short, get a tattoo or two on his face and arms, and new papers, papers from old employers, ships, if possible, so that he can pretend to be one of my boys… And you know there is only one person who can do all that.'

'Ustad.'

'Yes, Ustad. But he won't do it, he has disappeared, he has gone crazy.'

'He was always crazy. Fetcher. Fetcher is the only one of us who can get him to listen now… I think he knows where Ustad is, though he won't tell.'

'Perhaps he will take Amir to Ustad.'

'Perhaps…'

67

Daniel Oates opens the one tiny window that allows some light into the garret that he uses as his study. It is surprisingly empty of books. There are reams of newspapers and magazines lying scattered around, and various pamphlets, but not more than three or four books. He returns to his table, dips his pen in ink and begins to scribble:

It has been announced by Superintendent Major Grayper that his decision, reported earlier, to release the Oriental man who was arrested on suspicion of being the 'head cannibal', as the mysterious murderer and beheader who has been stalking fair London is referred to by the public, was based not only on the personal assurances of a respectable gentleman but also on a hitherto undisclosed event. The night after the arrest of the Oriental suspect, a woman, a lady of the streets, was attacked and beheaded by a mysterious assailant in East London. This murder, the superintendent explained, indicated the innocence of the arrested man, which was also vouched for by the aforementioned gentleman.

Various other suspects have been aired by commentators in the period since this revelation by Superintendent Grayper. The mysterious murderer has been identified as a Russian immigrant with a religious mania, which takes the form of murdering Magdalens in order that their souls may perhaps go to heaven. There has also been an attempt to prove that he is a butcher whose mind is affected by the changes of the moon, and who has been much impressed by reading the Book of Ezekiel, c. xxiii, v.25, 26, 33, 34, 46, 47 and 48. The chapter refers to the vicious lives of the sisters Aholah and Aholibah, and verse 25 is the key to the situation: 'And I will set my jealousy against thee, and they shall deal furiously with thee: they shall take away thy nose and thine ears; and thy remnant shall fall by the sword.'

These are, however, nothing but loose conjectures, which do

not take into account such facts as these: that not only Magdalens but also heathens have been killed, and that all the victims have been ceremonially beheaded. Any serious consideration returns us to the original Oriental cannibal theory, first propounded in the pages of this paper by your correspondent.

The Oriental theory of the atrocities is worth thinking out. The Orientals are a sensitive and excitable race, and mental exaltation is not only very common, it usually borders on insanity. We all know how political fanaticism will drive a Nihilist to the commission of murder, but it is not so generally known that religious fervour drives some sects to the most terrible acts of self-mutilation in Asia and Africa. The Orientals are very apt to rush into extremes, and they seem to have an idea that social and eternal salvation can only be obtained by means most repugnant to civilized and well-balanced minds. Orientals, however, unlike Negroes, who are also capable of such acts, are particularly devious, a characteristic evidenced by the Rookery Beheader. All rational consideration and logical thinking points a finger of accusation at an Oriental man, whether or not it is this man, now released, acting singly or in tandem with a larger cult of heathens. It seems hasty to have released the man as early as he has been released.

Daniel Oates dusts the sheets with sand from a wooden box and holds them up, one by one, admiring the words marching along them, his handy, hardy soldiers setting out to conquer the world in print tomorrow. The world of Captain Meadows and Major Grayper and other such born gentlemen. The world that has allowed him entry, though only through a side-gate. But he is a defender of that world; he defends it with the fanaticism of the new convert. For Daniel Oates, there is only this world –

evidence of anything else, whether it is the world of Jenny or of Qui Hy, is a monstrosity or an aberration to be effaced in space and time as firmly as the world, whatever it was, garret or hut, he himself has left behind.

68

In later years, when I started going to university in Patna, my trips to my grandfather's library in that whitewashed house in Phansa grew rather infrequent, confined largely to the summer or winter vacations. And it was only once or twice during the vacation that I would visit that cobwebbed, dusty, gecko-infested room, or read on its veranda. By then, all the interesting books had already been borrowed by my cousins and me; the library only housed unwanted books (in English), such as Mayhew's accounts of London, and of course, many volumes in Urdu, Persian and Arabic. The few Hindi volumes and the easier ones in Urdu had been given away to the children of old family servants, whose gains in literacy were usually marked by fewer visits to my grandmother's house.

But there was one winter – I must have been about nineteen or twenty then – when I spent almost every day of the vacation month in the veranda off that room, studiously retrieving the books that – or so I pretended even to myself— needed to be saved. Mayhew's was one of them.

The reason I was there was not really the books. It was a 'part-timer', an incredibly healthy-looking woman in her early twenties with lush black hair, who had been recently employed in the house. She would arrive around ten in the morning from some remote slum, and so would I from my parents' neighbouring house. She would leave around four in the evening, and so would I. It was my first real love – not an adolescent crush, of which I had experienced a few, but something close to an adult passion. If I had had the knowledge or the courage, I would have invited her into the shady corners of that library room.

She was not unaware of my interest. She took to sitting in the veranda, sunning herself during the afternoon hours when she had no work, and bringing her chores, such as winnowing grain, to the veranda. She sometimes offered to fetch me a glass of water. I was not unaware of her interest either. But there was such a gap between us – of class, clothing, family, education, literacy, even language (for the Urdu spoken in my family was very different from the rough dialect she uttered) – that I could not act on my passion (a passion that often threatened to gag my voice, bedazzle my sight) without the knowledge of betrayal. I would have liked to hold her, kiss her, make love to her; I felt – I knew from the unabashed way she walked and sometimes joked with other (male) servants – that she would know what to do if I so much as reached out and touched her, and that I would not be averse to her display of a knowledge still forbidden to me. But I did not touch her. And once when, by chance, we fell in together on the way back from the market – or, rather, she walked out of a crowd, said 'salaam' and walked back to the house with me – I burned with desire for her, but confined myself to the politest of formal talk. It was not just my ignorance that prevented me; it was also my knowledge – and here I give myself some credit – that our relationship was (in the terminology of the ism that interested me in those years) so 'over-determined' that it could only end in exploitation and betrayal.

That is how, sometimes, I see Jenny and Amir walking; passion holding them apart in the politer parks and avenues of London. And sometimes I see them walking alone, but still full of thoughts of each other; buoyed, disturbed, confused. That is when I stop myself: there is a danger in such retrospective crystal-gazing. I have seen signs of it in the well-meaning talk of Captain Meadows and his closest, kindest friends. Once, during one of those dinners in early Victorian London that I glimpsed from my grandfather's library in Phansa more than a century later, I heard Captain Meadows defend some reviled Asian or African custom by waving his hands, taking in all of the great metropolis that stretched around him with that gesture, and saying, 'This too has been one of the dark places of the earth.'

I had read enough by then, and not just in my grandfather's library, to know what he meant. He meant well. He meant that perhaps a few centuries from now, India or Nigeria would mature into the civilization – the best of it, of course – that had evolved in England since the dark pre-Roman days. Some of my crystal-gazing might depend on this expansive, well-meaning and not entirely blind gesture of his. But unlike Meadows and his friends, I am aware of the dangers, the limitations of all such gestures. I see myself, at the age of, say, forty, looking at a nineteen- or twenty-year-old boy, seeing in his confused maturity a bit of myself, and a bit of Amir Ali. I see a family resemblance, a kinship in the confidence and confusion of early youth. But I hesitate to suggest that the resemblance points to me. For I know that when that nineteen- or twenty-year-old boy grows to be forty, he will not be me. Never. To comprehend his similarity, I have to prepare myself for this ultimate difference. No matter how much like me he seems from my retrospective point of perception, he will never be me; I have to narrate his story not only through claims of knowledge and visibility, which are inevitably based on my knowledge of myself, but also through conjecture, silence, darkness. It is these that make him other than me. It is these that make Amir Ali who he is, and make Jenny, Jenny.

That is how I see Jenny for almost the last time.

She is walking back from work, late again. Tonight she will not go to Amir's house. I can sense that much. It is a chilly night and she does not want to send Gunga and the boys into the streets two nights in a row. She also needs to be alone. Or so I conjecture. She needs to settle the problem that her heart has become. She knows she is in love with Amir, she even shares her bed with him; she wants to marry him. But he refuses to convert to Christianity. And how else can they be married?

Her desire to escape the streets entails that she can marry him only in the correct manner, in the eyes of God and mankind. Perhaps there is suspicion too. How can love across a precipice not contain the fear of a fall? Perhaps her doubts about the stories of Amir Ali make her clutch at conversion, however superficial, as proof of his reality as the man in her life.

She has to think about all this, and it is better to think alone. With Amir, she cannot think of anything; with him, she feels too alive to bother about such matters.

69

Shields is haunted by the business. But he is also addicted to it; the excitement as well as the money it brings. Now, when they walk into a pub, they can buy and eat and drink what they want. It is a new experience for Shields. John May knows this, and he counts on it to keep Shields from getting frightened out of his senses, to keep him from seeing the ghosts that he hears all the time, that make him jump and fret and complain about being trailed.

Jack, on the other hand, shows no trace of their activities. Blood is just so much water off his back. John May wonders if the tall, gaunt man even thinks of their nocturnal stalking and killing. In his own case, it is with an effort of the will and exercise of reason that the ghosts are kept at bay. But Jack, one-eyed Jack, seems to lack that very appendage, whatever M'lord would have called it, which troubles Shields so much and which would afflict John May too, if he were a man with lesser strength of character. He is aware of this difference between his two accomplices. As they leave the table, he watches them from a corner of his eye. They have just gorged themselves on a meal of fried fish and bread, washed down with mugs of ale. With a head to it, Shields had instructed foolishly every time they ordered a round. Shields is drunk, but not drunk enough to stop jumping at sudden noises. Jack is unperturbed, ambling along in his loose-jointed manner.

They step out of the pub in such different ways: Shields looks around surreptitiously, turns up his collar and snuggles his head into his coat; Jack steps onto the pavement briskly, stopping just short of a cab that jolts its way past. The driver curses; Jack curses back. The horse neighs and the carriage disappears into the night.

The street is dimly lit and deserted. As they proceed, saying very little to one another, Shields suddenly clutches John May's arm. May shakes himself loose. Shields grabs his arm again and drags them into a dark alley. 'Hush,' he says, 'hush. They are following us.'

He has done this before. He often suspects others – Peelers, bobbies, vindictive beggars, ghosts – of trailing the trio, seeking vengeance or justice. John May is about to shake him off and step back into the street again, when he spots a woman walking out of the shadows. She does not seem to be trailing anyone, but she does pause, either in thought or to investigate.

Shields gasps as she passes them. 'I told you. I told you they are looking for us.'

John May knows the reason for Shields' conviction. It is a woman they have seen before; at the opium den, where they killed their first victim. It is a woman who would recognize them. John May does not believe she has been trailing them. But he knows that Shields will be even more jittery now.

Shields is tugging at his sleeve again. 'See, see, what did I say...?' John May looks at Jack. Jack is following the full walk of the woman, her sturdy, shapely back, her rounded hips as they recede into the shadows. He is whistling softly.

70

The great stench from the Thames forces Amir Ali to wrap his shawl around his face, muffling his nose and mouth as he used to in India when he went out on summer afternoons. Only, this time, the air is not hot and dusty; it is cold and it smells of putrefaction, caulking tar and fish. There are smoking houses in the distance. And the sun, which was only slightly stronger all day than a full moon in India, has long set.

Fetcher, noticing Amir's gesture, laughs and says, 'Eau de

Thames, guv'nor, Eau de Thames. Bin known to get 'em lords in tha' Parli'ment up there to leave t'umping the'r tables and dis'pear fasta 'n wizard-man headin' for a bafu. But tell-ya-wha', guv'nor, there's money in the Thames and the cesspits, and je'll'ry too. Ask 'em Toshers. Real guld in this spicy sancocho. If ya've the nose for't, *guv*'.

And pointing to his own broken, smudged nose, he lets out a whooping laugh that echoes past the dilapidated buildings, past the steps leading down to the waterside, and slithers like some sea-monster over the slimy surface of the Thames before disappearing into the night. 'Watch't, guv', says Fetcher. 'Good thing the fog's aint stronga tonight. T'way.'

There is an old cesspit, one of the two million that serve the inhabitants of this bloated city, and next to it, a sewer opening. Fetcher looks around, steadies the bag slung over his shoulder, and suddenly ducks into the sewer. As Amir hesitates, he hears a muffled whisper from inside: 'C'mere, tis shorta and no bobby on t'way. Bin clogged for cent'ries, guv'nor.'

The sewer doesn't smell much worse than the Thames. Fetcher brings out and lights a Davy lamp. Its yellow light is just sufficient to show them the way. They wade through a couple of inches of filth; the sides of the sewer are dripping. Fetcher hoots on seeing Amir's revulsion: the laugh goes echoing into the tunnel and splinters into many eerie sounds. 'Thought ya Indoo-laska's were used to ev'rythin' 'n all,' Fetcher sniggers. 'Good I talked ya into making 'em leggin'-csizma, no, guv'? Chapplis won't do 'ere.'

Fetcher is as restless and talkative underground as he is above it. Along with instructions and warnings – watch yer 'ead, guv'nor – he comments on everything, including the large rats that stand on their hind legs, watching the two men pass. Some are as big as cats, and Amir has no trouble believing the stories Fetcher tells of hordes of rats attacking and devouring injured or sick men in the sewers and tunnels.

'Let the beasties smell blood, and yer a goner, guv'nor. Lor', look at that 'un. Wish I had a trap; win me a dozen fights, that monsta there. Worth five d au moins. Look at 'im; look't 'is whiskas. That one's chapard beseff, guv'nor.'

But rats, Fetcher adds, are not the only animals in the tunnels and caverns of London. There are entire herds of pigs, run wild; there are big cats; there are fugitives and criminals; and there are – here Fetcher's voice drops to a whisper – 'them.' They are human, Fetcher avers, but no, they are not from above, not beggars, escaped prisoners or homeless Londoners. They never even go above. They were born and reared in the tunnels under London. Not ghosts, not ghouls; they are human, or half-human. Of that, Fetcher – like others who repeat similar tales – is almost certain. These people can see in the semi-darkness, they know the underground like the back of their hand. They could be next to you anywhere in the tunnels and you wouldn't know, unless they want you to discover them. Small secretive people, albinos. Like a gusano blanco, some say. Who knows? They never go outside; light blinds them. The lost tribe of London, Fetcher whispers. Mole People.

71

John May is against it. He is whispering, since the pub they walked into is still full of workers who were paid their wages in the pub and, except for two who were dragged away by their prescient wives, are spending a substantial part of their salaries there.

'It was a coincidence,' he says.

Shields shakes his head.

John May looks at Jack. The tall man is smiling. 'A comely wench, she was,' he says in reply. And then he adds, licking his lips, 'She can rec'nize us, squire. Shields 'ere is right 'bout that.'

'She won't come across us again. It was a coincidence,' John May hisses back.

'They are tracking us, I tell you, John May. I have sensed it in the small of my back for weeks now, the small of my back. They are watching us...'

John May is going to ask in exasperation, and for the hundredth time, who 'they' might possibly be, but One-eyed Jack interrupts him. 'You don't have to come with us, squire,' he says. Then he adds, and for the first time John May detects the steel of a threat in his tone: 'It is a free country, after all, ain't it, squire?'

72

They have been walking for at least fifteen minutes now, squeezing through openings that are just large enough for one man, hunching through arches of brick, once cutting across a catacomb with lead coffins warped and twisted like paper with time, darkness, humidity, some of them leaking viscous pools of ichor. Some tunnels are dry and some wet, in some there is a draught that makes Amir shiver under his coat and shawl, but all seem to lead away from the Thames.

A couple of times, the darting, rambling Fetcher has come to a sudden halt and hissed Amir into immobility too. They stand still for a minute, Fetcher dimming his lamp until the tunnel is dark and eerily silent. Had it been daytime, Amir is sure he would have heard the bustle of the city above, the clatter of wheels, the hooves of horses. But even such sounds of familiarity are absent at night.

When this happens for the second time, and they start scuttling through the tunnel again after their minute of stillness and silence, Amir asks Fetcher the reason for it. Fetcher lowers his voice. '*Them*,' he whispers, 'they've got their checkpoints. Ojo, ojo ev'rywhere. No one comes 'ere without the permission of the'r king...'

'You are joking,' Amir replies.

'Oh no, guv'nor, cross my heart. I seen 'un sometime back.' Fetcher is adamant, though his voice is still a whisper.

'Yes? What did he look like?'

'Naked as Adam; stark nu. 'N schwartz, blacker 'n me – except that it was earth, filth, kul dust. God knows what was unnerneath. 'Is 'air was mostly reddish, I think, 'n his eyes, guv', lor' his eyes...'

It is difficult for Amir Ali to follow Fetcher's conversation, not just because of the way he speaks but also because of the sediment of other languages – all that have ever been deposited in the nooks and crannies of London – swirling around in the muddy torrent of his English. Amir has never been able to figure out how many of these are languages Fetcher understands, at least in bits and pieces, and how many are just sounds, embedded like gold nuggets in the stream of his conversation.

'Like a hvid sheet. Pale, guv'nor, pale. Y'see, *them* people can't take much light. They aint have t'eyes for't. Not outside, that is, guv'nor. But 'ere: they know what's goin' on. Ev'rythin', guv'nor, they 'ear ev'ry footstep. 'Tis the'r kingdom, this 'ere. Who do ya think has connected all the sewers 'n tunnels we bin walkin' thru'? The'r kin'dom, guv'. And ya gotta show 'em some izzat.'

Amir recalls a conversation on this same subject during one of the rare gatherings at Captain Meadows' house: a lady had said they were a prehistoric people, and an officer laughed at that and said that they were just idle beggars with nowhere else to go. Amir is more inclined to agree with Captain Meadows, who considers the Mole People to be a tall story concocted by those who live mostly on the surface of cities.

At that moment, the tunnel they are walking through comes to an end. It is blocked by rubble. But Fetcher is not put out; he starts scrambling up the rubble heap. Right at the top, he gropes around and opens what Amir later realizes is a trapdoor. Then he pulls himself up through the door and stretches out a hand for Amir.

Amir finds himself in a dry room, paved with stones and bricks, with low brick arches. There is a candle burning in it and a slight draught that indicates some sort of connection to the world outside. The candlelight is enough to reveal the extent of the room, but not enough to dispel the shadows lurking all around, the darkness obscuring the roof.

'It's Fetcher, Ustad, it's Fetcher that's fetched ya 'nother hazraan cust'mer.'

'Out, out, you spawn of Satan,' comes a rasping voice from the shadows in a corner of the room. 'How did you get in here, you incubus of Iblis? Out. I told you, I do not want anyone to know where I live.'

Aw, Ustad, it's me, Fetcher, yer fav'rit, an I got a cust'mer fra yer own land, yer watan. He aint know where you live; we come longlongway, unnerground…'

A string of curses in Urdu and Farsi follows.

'An what's endnu mere, ustad, he is nob'lity fra yer watan.'

There is a silence; suddenly, an old man, almost spectral, darts out of the shadows from where the curses ensued. For a moment, perhaps because of a similarity in age, voice and posture, Amir thinks it is Mustapha Chacha, risen from the dead in the bowels of this foreign city. But this is another man, a man whose resemblance to Amir's murdered uncle has long been twisted into something else, something bitter and underground. The man, Ustad, is dressed in a long flowing robe, once white. He is completely hairless, bald and without whiskers. His face and body are tiny, as though shrunk, and there is a mad glitter in his eye. For a moment, it occurs to Amir that Fetcher's image of the Mole People is based on this pale old man.

The man thrusts his face close to Amir's, and Amir has to make an effort not to turn away from the sweet stench. Then Ustad spits into a corner and murmurs: 'Jis sar ko gharur aaj hai yaan taajwari ka…'

Amir cannot help completing the sher for him: 'Kal us pe yehin shor hai phir noha gari ka.'

'Ah,' says the old man, grimacing, 'no nawabzada I am sure, what would a nawabzada do here, but educated, cultured. Even that is rare in these godforsaken parts.'

Then, turning to Fetcher, Ustad curses him again: 'Shaitaan ki aulad! Spawn of Satan, son of a dozen fathers, I will do it just once. I will make the papers for your man – but it will be expensive.'

'He can afford it, Ustad; he is amir, that's 'is name, guv'nor: rich.'

Ustad laughs. 'Cultured and rich? Now that is even rarer. What is the world coming to!'

He moves away to turn up two lamps and Amir sees that he is in a bare room, with cold, stone walls, bleak and austere. But the walls are covered with the most intricate calligraphy, lines from the Quran and verses from Persian and Urdu poets mixed together, couplets and stanzas and entire poems flapping around and around the walls, dipping like birds, blossoming like flowers, ebbing like the sea.

The mad old man's eyes gleam with an unearthly light as he observes Amir Ali. 'They cannot stop me,' he says, lighting a third lamp. 'They have tried. They have done everything they could to stop me. But I have cheated them. Here, I still do what I was born to do, what I am capable of. They would have me do this and that. They would stop me. They would have me do other things, the servants of Shaitaan who infest these lands and are always taking over the world. And when that doesn't work, they tempt me with money. They send to me people like you, to distract me from my work. But I cheat them. Always I cheat them. I take their money when I need to, and I cheat them. Always I go back to my real work. Look around you, you pimps and devils, look around and despair of victory. Even here I am what I was: the greatest calligrapher east of Samarkand. Behold, devious stranger, behold my master work and despair!'

He holds the lamp closer to the walls and roof, and Amir is startled to see that even the ceiling is covered with reams and reams from the Quran and from the work of poets such as Mir Taqi Mir and Wali Mohammed Wali: the beautiful cursive script in silver and white and gold, spreading its wings on the stone and plaster, fluttering like a bird caught in a net, filling the room with silent noise. Elaborate fragments from lost cultures that have coalesced to create this aviary of shrieking, silent alphabets, shored against the ruin of a mind, and somehow still preventing Ustad's glittering eyes and bony hands from being exposed in full madness on the streets above, mouthing obscenities, casting stones.

73

Jaanam,

Sometimes you ask about my night in prison. Perhaps it reminds you of the fate of your mother, the mother you do not recollect but who you know was imprisoned and deported. And I hesitate to tell you the story. You assume that it is because I do not want to recall an unpleasant experience.

But that is not really true. There is another reason I do not wish to talk of those hours.

Let me tell you. I can explain this better in my language than in yours. Perhaps one day you will read these pages – and why not, for you grasp things very quickly when you apply yourself to the task – and you will have the real answer.

You see, jaanam, in those hours of imprisonment, a frightening thought crossed my mind. I felt that I had become my own story; my life had turned into the lie I had narrated to Captain Meadows. Suddenly, I was the thug I had claimed to be.

It felt strange to become something else. Is that all it requires? A few words, a few stories? Is our hold on reality so weak, so insecure? Can stories – told by yourself, told by others – turn us into something else? Why is it that, no matter how we grasp reality, no matter what reality we grasp, we need to don the glove of stories? Is that all we are: stories, words, breath?

Perhaps it was the suddenness of the events, the circumstances I found myself in, the taunting voices from the other cells, but thoughts crossed my mind like the delirious images one sees when tossing in a high fever. I almost came to believe that by deceiving Captain Meadows and his circle, I had become the master of deceit that he wished me to be; a thug. It frightened me: I feared that by hatching a thug in words, I had brought to life a real thug, one who was now stalking London and beheading victims. For a moment, I was no longer sure if the story I had told the Captain was not, after all, the true one, and the stories I told you and myself, simply lies.

Now that I have been released, and especially when I can hold you and feel the evidence of your reality as something not defined solely by words, I find my fears diminishing. But when I look back on my hours in prison, I find myself staring into a mirror, and from the mirror stares back someone who is me and not me. I find myself unable to say who I really am, if I am not also the thug brought into being by stories of my own making.

Are we then nothing but the playthings of language? When do we tell stories, and when do stories tell us?

Oh, my love, I wish you were back now, so I could touch you and dispense with words.

74

Lord Batterstone finished labelling the latest skull that John May had procured for him. He placed it gently back in its place on the shelf. The room was full now. He had all the varieties he could have hoped to find on this fair isle, almost all. His theatre was complete.

Or was it? Why then this sense of disappointment, of dissatisfaction? Why the feeling that there was something lacking?

Would the voyage to Africa that he had started to envision fill this lack? Would it make him feel that his theatre was finally ready to be revealed to the public?

There was only one way to find out.

He had often thought of it, but now he would have to do more than think about it. He would have to start organizing the expedition. Yes, that was what he had to do. That, he was convinced, was his mission in life: a glorious voyage of discovery into one of the few remaining blank spaces on the map.

75

Qui Hy had wanted Amir to be nearby, within easy walking distance of her dhaba, but she had also wanted him to change his place of residence. She did not trust Major Grayper or Captain Meadows.

The basement she found for him was in a building that had been abandoned and was now used by beggars and other homeless people who paid, in kind, cash or service, a 'rent' to Bubba Bookman. A large man, dressed in a bowler hat and an eclectic assortment of loose clothes and robes that somehow gave him a regal bearing, Bubba Bookman claimed to be the direct descendant of a witchdoctor called Bookman who had led the great slave revolution in Haiti half a century ago. He also claimed, with greater evidence to back it, to be the Badshah of Beggars in Central and East London, a self-assumed title he had once defended with blows against two contenders simultaneously, who had since quit his kingdom for other parts of London. After that, potential usurpers left Bookman alone, and his reputation as an ex-prizefighter in his youth remained untarnished despite his greying hair and increasing girth.

Bookman had made out a full royal description for himself. All those who swore allegiance to him (which they had to do in order to 'rent' a place in any of the dozen or so abandoned buildings in the Mint and London rookeries that he owned) had to address him, on their first meeting, with the full title: Badshah of Beggars, Tiger of Tinkers, King of the Cursed, Helper of the Homeless, Rajah of the Rejected, Duke of the Damned, Pope of Paupers, His Royal Highness, Lord Bubba Bookman the Brave.

That was how Amir addressed him now, in the company of Qui Hy. Amir had been allowed basement space in the building because of Qui Hy, to whom Bookman (like so many other people) owed a favour or two from the mysterious past, but he still had to present himself at the court of the Badshah of Beggars. Bookman sat regally on a broken wall outside the building, his many-coloured robes and dresses billowing in the gust. He had hung an umbrella from a section of the broken wall and spread a large neat handkerchief on the broken masonry and now he sat delicately on the handkerchief.

Bookman held tightly, like a missionary might hold the Bible, a thick bound book which, Amir had already been told, was a collection of plays by Shakespeare. Bookman, though barely literate (unlike his namesake, the revolutionary ancestor who, Bookman insisted, was a learned man), had a way with words and a love for Shakespeare. He either remembered entire pages from Shakespeare or was lucky in his flipping of pages, for he was reputed to find the exact page he wanted every time he opened the tome. And he opened the tome regularly, either to prove a point or to consult it for auguries. He often recited the lines by heart, always at the right page; and sometimes he got others to read them out for him.

Bookman listened to Amir's story without batting an eyelid: he was reputed to have a disconcerting ability to stand or sit unmoving, looking at you without giving any evidence of hearing you out. Amir had been encouraged by Qui Hy to tell Bookman of his troubles, explain why the police had been after him, and protest his innocence. If Bookman believed him, he would stand by him, and Bookman had more places in which to hide people than the Metropolitan police had men to look for them.

After Amir had recounted his story, though only from the point when he arrived in England (for Bookman was not interested in anyone's story from before their arrival in London), he made the usual, formal appeal for Bookman's patronage.

'For a lascar, you speak English well, young man,' said Bookman in a booming voice.

'He can even read English, Bookman,' Qui Hy quipped.

'Read! A lascar who can read English! This I must see for myself, sister.'

Bookman opened his tome randomly, and thrust it at Amir, pointing to a section with a thick finger. 'Read, my man, read what it says here on this page. Let Shakespeare decide your fate, East Indian.'

Amir read, with some difficulty:

'O, reason not the need: our basest beggars
Are in the poorest thing superfluous:
Allow not nature more than nature needs,
Man's life is cheap as beast's...'

Bookman held up a regal hand. 'You read well, East Indian,' he said. 'And the bard is pleased. The bard has spoken. All glory to the bard. Welcome to my kingdom, son. But remember, you yourself are the surety for your rent, for this is also what the bard wrote:

A pound of man's flesh, taken from a man,
Is not so estimable, profitable neither,
As flesh of muttons, beefs, or goats.'

With this softly sinister threat, Bookman jumped off the pile of broken masonry, surprisingly light on his feet, and neatly folded and pocketed the handkerchief on which he had been sitting. He walked away, jauntily swinging his umbrella, whistling a tune from the dancehalls. Two men who had been lurking nearby fell in with him as he walked into the street. The Badshah of Beggars had his courtiers.

76

John May is scolding his wife. The leg of mutton is slightly burnt. Waste of good money, he grumbles. You do not seem to care, woman, for the fact that I slog day and night, earning money for the victuals that you so casually burn.

His wife apologizes, blaming it on the butcher and the girl they have recently hired, and scuttles away to bring in the pudding. Their dinners have improved in quantity and quality over the past few months. The pudding, she hopes, will distract John May from her previous culinary failure, for it has turned out perfect and golden.

From experience, she knows that her dishes, well-cooked or not, are not the reason for her husband's irritation. It is something else, something at work – whatever that might be. She never dares to ask John May about the nature of his work. He is not given to sharing matters with her, and lately he has fallen into even greater, and sullen, secrecy. He has put a padlock on the door of what he calls his 'study': that foul-smelling room in which he shuts himself for hours at a stretch on some days.

She does not really care. He is bringing in so much money that for the first time she feels they have money to see them through old age. That is her only concern: old age. She does not want to end up in a poorhouse and a pauper's grave like both her parents had. If that means living with someone who comes home and slaps her because something has gone wrong at work, well, she has taken slaps from people who had harder palms and gave her much less in return.

When she walks in with the pudding, John May is lost in

his thoughts and muttering to himself. She thinks he is saying something to their children or to her. But he is talking to himself, as he sometimes does, without even being aware of it. Damn Shields, he is saying, damn Shields. I just hope the fools do not make a mess of it.

77

None of the houses Jenny worked in was as impressive as Captain Meadows' house. They were usually two- or three-room places, and never had more than one full-time maid. They had rooms full of old and broken furniture, which tended to disappear for periods, and sometimes for ever, when they were pawned for the purchase of more urgently required commodities. They contained children who were undernourished and either too mature or too childish for their age. Jenny did not like working in such households, though she did not have the education or the contacts to be hired as a maid in households like that of Captain Meadows. But even these dirty houses, where a knock on the door sometimes sent the husband and father scuttling into a cupboard to avoid the bailiff even such houses were politer places to work in than the marketplace.

Or so Jenny felt.

The place where she is employed today – it is her last chore of the evening – is no different. There is an ailing wife who seldom leaves her couch, except to scold one of the children or Jenny, and there is a husband, a much older man not averse to touching parts of Jenny's body whenever he can. Jenny hurries through her chores; she had hoped to go to Amir's place in the evening, but it is already too late. It is dark, and her room is closer to this neighbourhood.

She wishes Amir could come to meet her at the end of her chores. But, of course, that is out of the question. Servants are commanded not to encourage 'followers', let alone a follower from another land.

Jenny bends down and... I cannot see what she does. From my grandfather's library in Phansa, in the ghostly white pages of the books here and elsewhere, there is much that I can see and much that I cannot. Yet, I know she must be doing something similar to what I have seen the servants do in my grandfather's house. Working. Bending. Cleaning. Sweating. And at the same time thinking about something else, someone else, somewhere else.

I know she is thinking of Amir. She is thinking of what he is: the reformed thug he is said to be, or the lover she knows him to be. Could the two be the same? Are they mutually exclusive? And how many names does he actually have? I see her bent figure, musing, while outside the shadows of the night gather, the noise of the street peters out, lamps flicker in the rising wind and one or two go out, doors begin to close, shutters are pulled down.

78

The evening has loosened the shadows from where they lay, pinned down by the buildings and posts, bridges and walls. Now they spread like ink: darkness oozes from under the ground and crawls up the houses and chimneys, the bridges and towers until it finally creeps into the sky, where the last flicker of the sun goes out like a candle starved of wax.

The houses here are grimy with soot: some still have clothes strung out of garret windows, drying in the air, now that the sunlight has vanished. These are houses struggling to survive, each containing more families than they would have in a better neighbourhood, each containing more hopes and aspirations than will be met by fate.

In this scene of shadows, stand Shields and One-eyed Jack. They make an odd couple. In size and deportment, they differ to a degree that would have made them noticeable anywhere. Perhaps that is why they are keeping to a dark corner of the emptying street. Or perhaps it is for some other purpose.

'She works here. She will be out any moment. I know it: I have watched her for many evenings now,' Shields whispers to One-eyed Jack.

'Just give me ten minutes with er, Shields. You stay back. I'll do it fer yer.'

'But no hanky-panky, Jack. I will not have her molested. Your word on it, man. Swear to it. Swear.'

Jack swears, laughing inwardly at the strange morality of this nervous man.

79

Jaanam,

It is late. I am alone now, in this basement, on my cot. There is no Gunga, none of his boys, in this place. I seldom go out during the day. Qui Hy is afraid I will be arrested or attacked, though I do not look as I used to. I remember how you laughed when you first saw me like this. I even feel different.

With the papers that I have, the short hair, the clean-shaven face, will even Kaptaan Meadows recognize me again? Will the stories about the past that I told him still return to haunt my present, fashion my future?

I had hoped you would come tonight, and I could lose myself in the cascade of your hair. But I know that there are evenings when you cannot get away early enough to come to me. Each such night is a dark emptiness to me, and I cross that emptiness only in the hope that there will be other nights...

This is where the Farsi notebook that I found in my grandfather's library peters out and my narrative is plunged into darkness. It is a darkness as sudden as the black of the powercuts which, with the years, have become epidemic in Phansa. Houses would be humming with activity – children playing, students reading, women cooking, men talking or working – when suddenly the lights would go off, the fans would clatter to a stop. Load shedding, someone would announce unnecessarily. The many threads of our activities would unspool and fall inert on the floor. The stories we were living out would be dunked in darkness. But, of course, the stories never stopped. There were sounds and smells and movement; sight is not all. And then someone would light a candle, or the moon would show from behind the clouds, sending a sliver of silvery light through the curtains. The darkness was never absolute.

No, the darkness is never absolute.

Time Future: Conjecture

80

Paddyji this, Paddyji that, oh, she can go on for ever, worse than the most anti-Papist Englishman, ignoring my real name – not that it is my original name – and pestering me with the nickname I used to hate before she turned it into something else. Not Paddy, but Paddyji. All right, I said to Qui Hy, all right, all right, all right, you Punjabi gorgon. There was no point in pretending to be asleep. Qui Hy was too perturbed to make me my pipe, and even I was disturbed despite my grumbling. I remember that much.

It must have been a little later when we woke up Amir Ali with the news. I went along, because Qui Hy insisted on it. Her knees were acting up again and she could not walk the distance. So, for some Oriental reason beyond my comprehension, I had to go in her place.

When Amir was shaken awake in the dark basement of the house in the Mint where Qui Hy had tucked him away, he knew something was very wrong. Because I had come to wake him up. He rubbed his bleary eyes and looked at my face; a handsome face once, I must say, but now scarred with age. Beside me stood Gunga and Karim.

At that moment, he looked vulnerable and wary, in a way that only the very young, who are still tentative about life, can look. Surprisingly, his face also displayed the weariness of the aged, of people to whom bad news has come more than once.

'Have they arrested her instead?' Amir asked me. The boy never calls me Paddyji; strangely, none of them do, despite hearing Qui Hy address me as Paddyji. None of them calls me by any name. I know that, among themselves, they refer to me as Qui Hy's husband. Or, if inclined towards greater precision, Qui Hy's Irish husband.

I shook my head in response to Amir's query. 'Come with me, son,' I said 'Come to the dhaba. Qui Hy will tell you.'

The streets were deserted. It was still half dark. The clouds piled up in the sky, like bales of hay dumped into a grey sea. We walked quickly from corner to corner until we reached the narrow house they all call Qui Hy's dhaba, though it belongs to me. Not that I mind: let it be known by Qui Hy's name, which is as much her real name as Paddyji is mine. Names are like clothes: you wear them only as long as they are not too tight or threadbare.

A parsimonious fire had been lit in our small stone fireplace. Tea – boiled with milk, spices and sugar, the Indian way – was bubbling over it, stirred absent-mindedly by Qui Hy.

81

When Amir Ali is given the news of what happened to Jenny, he feels as if he has been through it all before: the voices of concern, the faces that reflected some, if only a fraction, of the pain, anger and frustration that he feels. He recalls the morning in his village when Haldi Ram and his people intercepted him and told him of the fate of Mustapha Chacha and his family. Once again, he is surrounded by people who barely know him, and with whom he can claim no kinship. Their unmerited concern for him, the crudeness of their decency, is visible in their faces. Their past is as murky, if not more; they must have known hatred and anger and jealousy; they must have manipulated, betrayed, perhaps murdered. But at this moment, by a strange twist of circumstances, they stand with him in the essence of their crude humanity.

Amir has imagined many possibilities. Getting married to Jenny, not marrying her, leaving her behind in London while he makes a fortune elsewhere, taking her with him, perhaps even to India, staying on in London and seeing her occasionally, as he already does, as he moves from job to job. He has imagined almost every possibility. All except this. Even death would have been imaginable, but not in this shape, not a death like this.

He feels bewildered; if the news had come to him from other people, he would not have believed it. This is the capital of the power that is seeking to bring law and order to the world. This is the city of light. How can such things happen here?

For a moment, such is his bewilderment that he almost comes to see himself again through Major Grayper's and Nelly's eyes: he fears he has brought and unleashed the ghosts of his narrated homeland in this place of reason and science. As if the spectres with which he paid for his passage to England, the soucouyants with which he revenged his uncle and family, all those bloodthirsty ghosts of his narrative have come alive in this city. He has brought them here. And now they have chosen their victim, for what they want is not just blood but suffering.

82

I was surprised at how calm he was. It is strange, isn't it? One does not expect an Oriental to be calm. There is something about how they talk perhaps, their hands like birds, their faces like waterfalls. Perhaps that is how the English see us Irish too. And how differently people react under pressure: Irish or Oriental, they always escape your idea of them at the crucial moment. As did Amir. He remained frighteningly calm.

'Her head?' he asked Qui Hy.

It was Gunga who understood first. 'No, no, Amir. She was clubbed and perhaps garrotted. It was someone else. Her body was found intact...'

'Thank God,' he muttered. Then he burst out, in the first and only sign of anger: 'I will kill the person who did it. I swear I will kill him, if that is the last thing I do.'

'But carefully, son,' I said, stirring the chai, 'this is not India.'

83

This ain't inja, said Qui Hy's Irish husband.

Amir looks up at him, startled, as if seeing him for the first time. He feels like shouting, yes, it is, this is the India that Captain Meadows wants from me. This is India as you people imagine it. You have made it come alive here in the streets of London.

But even as the thought forms in his mind, he feels a sense of shame. He thinks of Captain Meadows in his carriage, and hears Qui Hy speak, slowly, softly like she always does, stitching together her words in English with the slow care with which she stitches pockets, her voice sometimes revealing a slight Irish brogue just as her husband's voice sometime betrays a North Indian lilt. Qui Hy, always cautious, is urging them not to be hasty.

84

We all understand revenge. Even I, an opium-befuddled white man though I might seem to them, a half-crazy Irish man with tunes running in his head, an ex-soldier with tall tales of colonial campaigns who never leaves his house except to get drunk in the pubs. We understand revenge because we do not fully trust law and justice. From where we stand, I and they, justice is the revenge of the rich and the powerful. And, by inverse logic, it makes revenge our only justice.

Not that any of them saw this: they came to revenge as their last recourse, a violent urge. But then, they had not lived with a woman like Qui Hy and learned to turn thoughts over, examine the nature of each necessity, the artificiality of every urge.

85

Amir hears himself demand vengeance. It is like hearing a ghost. The jaws of the past have gaped wide again. The words are similar to those he uttered in the presence of Haldi Ram and the other villagers so long ago. He can see their faces react in sympathy and understanding, even Qui Hy's addict of a husband. But Amir feels a hollowness in his words. His loss and anger are as great as the last time, when his uncle and aunt were murdered. Still, there is a hollow ring to his cry for vengeance.

86

Qui Hy calmed them down, as much by her words as by returning to her fireplace seat and to her meticulous stitching of pockets. But over the next few days, she also tried to find an eyewitness to Jenny's murder. She was convinced someone would have seen it. When you have lived with the woman as long as I have, you come to mirror her convictions without noticing it. She is opinionated at times, no doubt about that. But she is also almost always right.

In this case, she was convinced, with her Indian peasant logic, that someone must have seen the murder. It was just that no one had come up and told the police. The sort of people who were out in those parts at that time of night were unlikely to go to the police, she reasoned. I felt that in this she was more Indian than she realized, her mind still terrorized by memories and tales of Oriental despots. But perhaps she was right. Perhaps we are all more Indian than we realize.

No, she proclaimed, such witnesses would not go to the Peelers.

Instead, they might come to her. So, once again, she summoned her ragtag army of ayahs, lascars, whores, opium addicts, gypsies and servants of the lowest order. Such an invisible lot they were; before I fell in with her, even I had looked through them on the streets of London. Even I, an opium-addled ex-soldier, not a gentleman by any means, had failed to see them. But they were there; I knew this as surely as Fetcher claimed to know that the Mole People lived in the tunnels, ruins and caverns of the city. And so the word went out: Qui Hy wants information. And I, her lawful husband for years, know exactly how far into the many realms of invisibility Qui Hy's word can reach.

It didn't take long. On the fourth night, a woman walked in. Qui Hy was reclining in her rocking chair, as she always did in the late evening, stitching pockets for those new contractors who had started distributing work: a pocket stitched here, a seam there, the buttons put on somewhere else, and hey presto, a dress was ready to be sold to the affluent classes, a dress brought into existence by the magic of a dozen invisible hands all over London. Qui Hy, with her mysterious connections and her Indian love for silver, had caught on early and was now meticulously stitching pockets for three different contractors in her spare moments. My pocket money, she would call it, shaking silently with laughter. I never understood how that woman could laugh so heartily without emitting a single sound.

So, as I said, on the fourth night, a woman, an English woman, walked in. I watched her; I always watch them from the cot in my room, smoking my sweet pipe. She wasn't Cockney; she spoke with a genteel accent, mostly. It was either an accent she had meticulously tried to learn without entirely succeeding, or it was an accent she had picked up as a child, but whose sheen had been dimmed by years of disuse.

Gunga and Amir, who usually joined us late at night, were the only other people there when the woman entered. She was around fifty, garishly painted and dressed in the faded style of an older generation, in a worn silk paletot. It was obvious that she was a streetwalker, and Qui Hy, who did not like her place being frequented by whores she did not know, made a gesture of repugnance. Place closed, luv, she said to the woman.

'I am looking for Qui Hy,' the woman replied in a slurred voice. She was more than a little drunk.

'You have found her,' Qui Hy said, putting aside her thread and needle.

'Qui Hy, the Chinaman?'

'There is only one Qui Hy, luv, and that's me.'

'You are the one who wants to know what happened in, you know, the alley.'

'Yes, luv. But you didn't see anything, did you?'

'Maybe I did. Maybe.'

'Or maybe you imagined it because you want a drink?'

The woman looked at Qui Hy for a moment, then burst out laughing. She had a deep, frank laugh, an infectious one, and Qui Hy's broad face relaxed into a smile.

'A drink will make me remember better, missus,' the woman said with a wink.

At this, Qui Hy laughed in turn and indicated to Gunga to get the bottle of gin that she kept for her own use in a cupboard.

Cups and glasses were filled all around, the gin diluted with water. The woman gulped her drink down in one go, gave a satisfied gasp, and extended the glass again. Qui Hy filled it and said, 'The story now, Miss...'

'Miss No One, ma'am,' said the woman. 'Miss No One. You get my story but you do not get my name.'

'Fair enough.'

'And I want to see that shilling you promised. I want to see it exists.'

Qui Hy took a gleaming coin out of the many folds of her dress and tossed it once. It glinted in the firelight and disappeared into Qui Hy's fleshy fist again.

'There, Miss No One. It exists. But you get to feel its weight only if we believe you. Now, your story if you please.'

87

'I don't usually work late, ma'am,' said the woman. 'There was a time when I used to go to the Alhambra and the Argyle, and would be escorted back in a coach. But it is hard now. I usually work in the Haymarket area and have to walk all the way back home. The times change and we change with the times.'

She squared her shoulders and gestured with her hands, as if to suggest stoic acceptance of the great wrongs inflicted by time.

'That night I had stayed a bit longer at a pub and, after a long day's work, you can imagine, ma'am, I was very tired when the pub closed. I decided to take a shortcut, but halfway into the... alley, my feet could no longer support me. I had worked long and hard all day, ma'am, and I decided to take a short rest in a dark corner, you know how it is, ma'am.'

Qui Hy nodded impassively, but I noticed that Gunga had to tug at his forked beard to prevent himself from smiling.

The woman continued, but only after some hesitation, as if she were no longer certain that she wanted to confess to this gathering.

'So, you see, ma'am, I was very tired and half-asleep when I saw what I am going to tell you. I remember it only hazy-like...'

Qui Hy nodded, impassive and understanding, and absent-mindedly brought out the shilling again, twirling it between her thumb and fingers as if about to perform a magic trick.

The woman looked at the shilling and gave a short laugh. She squared her shoulders again.

'But, of course, I remember enough, ma'am: one gas lamp was working further down the alley and it was not a dark night; there was a moon behind the drifting clouds. There were sounds of footsteps, and a pretty young filly came running. She was looking over her shoulder, and to be honest, ma'am, it did sound like there was someone running after her. But just before the turning up front, where that red-tiled house with dragon-shaped water pipes juts into the lane, a man jumped out in front of her and tried to grasp her just as she turned to look back. He was a short man, broadly built. The girl was taken by surprise, but she was a quick one, slippery and strong. She twisted in the man's grip, half bending over and lifting him off his feet. She threw him over her hips, but he grasped her ankle and pulled her down too. They grappled in the mud, but she managed to thrust him down, and grabbing a brick or a stone, hit him on the head. At this the man let go of her, cursing, and she sprang up, ready to run away. It was then that another man, a tall one, stepped out of the shadows with a bludgeon and hit the girl a nasty blow on the head. I think she died right then, though of course, they did things to her that I will not narrate in the presence of men...'

Qui Hy was not convinced. She quizzed the woman closely about the girl and the men. Amir could not bear it and twice walked to the door, only to come back again. But as the woman answered, it became clear that she had certainly seen Jenny that night. Her description of the girl was accurate. Her description of the men who had assaulted and murdered Jenny was less precise until she said, with a start, 'Oh yes, ma'am, I forgot to say this, but the man who hit her, the tall man with the bludgeon, he had a patch over one eye.'

At that, Qui Hy tossed the shilling to the woman. The woman grabbed it and disappeared with a hurried curtsy: she could sense the tense atmosphere in the room.

'You were right, Amir beta,' said Qui Hy quietly. 'It was not just any crime.'

The description offered by the woman had tallied too closely with the description of two of the three men Jenny had encountered in her aunt's den: she had often described the men to Qui Hy and Amir.

Amir was sitting with his face in his hands. Qui Hy went up to him and put her hands on his shoulders. The young man – not much more than a boy, I thought – was sobbing. Then Qui Hy looked in my direction. She knew I had been watching, and I knew that later in the night, when they had all left, she would ask me to repeat what I had observed, matching it against her own observations. She is a meticulous woman in her own way, a deep one.

88

It was a strange gathering. Take my word for it. See, I have nothing against niggers, lascars, head-hunters and the like. Dammit, I live with one of them, don't I? You won't catch me wrinkling my nose at attar or burnt incense or fried curry smells. But Qui Hy's gatherings still take some getting used to. They always have some religious excuse: a kirtan or a millaad, she is not exclusive in her choice of deities to flatter. But when a gathering is called, say once a year, everyone knows that there is something in the air, something more solid than religion.

And the crowd that turns up: you cannot imagine a more villainous-looking and motley band of savages. You should hear the din they raise, in a dozen different languages. Had our house been in any other neighbourhood, the neighbours would have gone to the Peelers or the priest with nervous reports of the Devil's Sabbath!

This was one of those occasions. Qui Hy's place was packed with lascars, ayahs, beggars, some impossible-to-place oddities like Fetcher, and riff-raff, mostly but not entirely from the lands of Hindoostan. Many of them had come on short notice, informed by word of mouth or fetched by Fetcher. One ayah even had a pram with a white baby in it: she was supposed to be taking the frilly baby out for a walk in some nearby park. It was obviously an occasion, you could tell even if you were new to the gathering. Qui Hy had put away her baskets of pockets and threads for the day; I was up too, hunched in a corner of the room. Only Amir Ali was missing and I knew that Qui Hy had arranged for him to be absent.

After the chanting from the Ramayana or the Koran or some other heathen Bible was finally over and sticky sweets had been distributed and consumed with relish (by everyone except me – I survive such occasions of infernal music by puffing on my pipe more strongly than usual), it was time for the real business. Qui Hy cleared her throat and leaned forward in her chair. The conversations in the room – in different languages, various pidgins of English and, I suspect, sheer gibberish for the bloody heck of it – subsided into an expectant hush. Qui Hy did not beat about the bush; she never does on such occasions. She got to the point directly.

'We have to find them,' she told the gathering, and not just because it is the only way to clear Amir of the charges that might be laid on him every time those murderers collect a head for whatever devilish purpose they need such things.

'No,' added Qui Hy, 'now we have to find them not only to clear Amir Ali's name, but also to prevent the boy from murdering someone or getting killed in the attempt.'

Gunga cracked his knuckles. 'Why prevent him,' he said. 'Why not help him?'

'And be strung up like chickens?'

I knew that Qui Hy was law-abiding to a fault: the fault being that she was willing to break almost any law but only if she could be certain of getting away with it. Paddyji, she told me on one occasion when I was contemplating a harsh action on some English provocation that I no longer recall, Paddyji, the law requires names, and neither I nor you want our real names to be discovered, do we?

Now she continued, softly, in the tone of someone discussing a recipe, 'Look, I like Amir: he is a nice boy. But do not think I am doing this just for his sake. I am doing this because we have to. If the beheadings go on and, God forbid, if Amir does something rash, he will invite attention to all of us. From one thug to a gang of thugs – look, look at yourself, you, me, we are a band of thugs. Every man-woman of us has thug branded on his face! Every sooty inch of us is terrifyingly thug-like! But even without that, do we want their attention, Gunga? I have this small place here, with my husband. It took me years to set it up: I do not want soldiers and policemen nosing around. You must have your own nest egg, Gunga; Zaibun Ayah there has her little business that is not entirely legal, so do you, Thapa Bhai, and you, and you. Look around you: this place you call Qui Hy's dhaba, is it only a place we meet for a cup of chai, or will it seem far more sinister a place in the eyes of the Peelers? What is there to prevent them from seeing thuggery in this place, or devilry, or conspiracy? So, when I say we have to help Amir, I mean that we have to help ourselves. Not land ourselves in deeper trouble. No. That is not what I want to ask of you, and of those you know who are not here. I know that each one of you has his or her own circle of confidantes. Go to them and ask about these men: the man called John May, whose name we know because he bribed a lascar in the opium den, a lascar who overheard the three men talking but unfortunately came to us only now.'

'Who was it?' asked a tiny, sharp-featured, white-haired ayah, famous in the crowd for her malicious gossip and her trips as an escort between India and England: on eleven different voyages she had nursed the children of various British families being sent 'home' for schooling.

'That is my concern,' said Qui Hy, just a little sharply. 'When you came to me with your, ah, little problem after your fourth voyage, did I ask you for names? Have I ever asked any of you for names? Let me keep the names this time. Trust me. Instead, ask around for John May and his two accomplices, the short, squat man and the tall, one-eyed one, who sometimes carries a stick or a cudgel. Looks like the Devil, they say, so it should be easy for us, devils that we are, to recognize him.' She broke off to chuckle silently.

Then she continued. 'We have an idea where they meet, the pubs and beer-rooms. But we need to know where they go afterwards. Mark my word, they are doing this for someone else. It does not make any sense otherwise. There is something or someone bigger behind them. And those of you who work with English families, try and find out why the English might want to collect heads. Is it some secret rite, like what the Tantrics do back where I and some of you come from? Is it some rare custom that we do not know about? Let me know what you hear, but remember – say nothing. You are my eyes and ears, but we do not have a mouth. A mouth is something we cannot afford in this place...'

89

Sometimes I am surprised by my wife of so many years; I am surprised by Qui Hy. The English collecting heads? Tantric rites in Stonehenge? Voodoo in Westminster? I had to stop myself from laughing.

How much of it was just talk, I wondered, and how much of it was exactly what she meant?

For Qui Hy knows this city intimately, and yet can evince swathes of ignorance, as if her elaborate map of the place contains unexpected blank spaces. On occasion, I know she is only pretending, but sometimes she is in dead earnest. Things that an English woman, even a tune-crazed Irish ex-soldier like me, would take for granted, small mundane things, suddenly they loom in front of Qui Hy, totally illegible, or she reads them in a way that I could never imagine, a way far from the truth as I see it. Tantric rites! Skulls placed at the altar of an idol wearing a demon's face?

Overhearing and watching them, as the others now joined in with a cacophony on inexplicable England, I had to stifle a laugh more than once.

But I agreed with Qui Hy's plan. We have always agreed on the important matters of life. For different reasons, we do not want the bobbies here. It is not just what we may have to hide. It is best not to be forced into a defence of your habit, an accountancy of your hours – which is what the law will demand. Once you have to explain, defend, justify yourself, it hardly matters whether you lie or speak the gospel truth – every word rips a bit of you out of yourself and strews it where anyone can trample on it.

90

Daniel Oates, intrepid journalist, had just returned after witnessing the latest crime. Not just any crime: a new horror by the Rookery Beheader. For about eighteen months now, London's reading public had thirsted after news of the Beheader and his crimes with such avidity that Oates, who had set himself up as the authority on this particular criminal, had become a household name. News of other events paled in comparison; it needed something like the People's Charter or the Myall Creek Massacre in Australia or Grace Darling's heroism in rescuing survivors from SS *Forfarshire* for public attention to be momentarily diverted. Otherwise, the London Beheader – with his fourteen recorded victims till date (though there was some chance that one of them had been killed in a common drunken brawl over a dog fight and then beheaded to mislead the police) – was what everyone wanted to read about.

Oates almost looked forward to the Beheader's crimes. In the weeks when nothing happened, he felt disappointed, as if the criminal had let him down personally. Nothing had filled Oates' life, and furthered his career, as much as the mysterious beheadings. They had even given him the idea of going to the colonies to write about the murderous cults of superstition and irrationality. He was negotiating with another paper for a series of articles titled 'Crimes from the Colonies'. He would like to start with places in Africa, then move to India and finally, perhaps, go to Canada and the Caribbean.

And wouldn't it be excellent if the London Beheader turned out, as Oates had depicted him, to be a Hindoo thug or a cannibal from Africa? Oates wished Major Grayper would pay more attention to his theories.

91

I read out from the ripped sheet to her. She was perched at the foot of my bed, still stitching a pocket. She asked me to read it out again.

'It is not by that Danny Oates, is it, Paddyji?' she observed at the end of my second reading.

'No,' I confirmed, 'he writes for a rag; this is a poster put out by the police.'

'Read it out once again, will you,' she said.

'It is not a bloody Hindoo mantra, woman,' I growled, but I looked at her and was shaken by the sadness in her eyes. Qui Hy is not a woman given to melancholy. What was it in this poster that had moved her: the memory of a woman she had known, or the glimpse of a fate that might have befallen her too had we not met by accident so many years ago? Whatever it was, I looked away and did as she had requested. I read it out again.

GHASTLY MURDER

IN THE EAST-END

DREADFUL MUTILATION OF A WOMAN

CAPTURE: ROOKERY BEHEADER

Another murder of a character as diabolical as that perpetrated in Back's Row on Friday week was discovered in the same neighbourhood on Saturday morning. At about six o'clock a woman was found lying in a backyard at the foot of a passage leading to a lodging house in Old Brown's lane, Spitalfields. The house is occupied by a Mrs Richardson, who lets it out to lodgers, and the door which admits to this passage, at the foot of which lies the yard where the body was found, is always open for the convenience of the lodgers. A lodger named Davis was going down to work at the time mentioned and found the woman lying on her back close to the flight of steps leading into the yard. Her body appeared broken, as if smashed on the ground or hit with terrible force a number of times, and not only was her throat cut but her head was also missing. An excited crowd gathered in front of Mrs Richardson's house and also in the mortuary on Old Montague Street, where the body was quickly conveyed. As the headless body lies in the rough coffin in which it has been placed in the mortuary, it presents a fearful sight. The body is that of a Creole or Gypsy woman at least forty years of age. The height is estimated at five feet. The complexion is sooty but not negro black and there is a foreign-looking tattoo on the left arm.

92

Major Grayper was not fooled by the occasional lull in the murders. By now a pattern had emerged: there would be no murder for weeks, a month or two at times, and then suddenly there would be two gruesome beheadings in the same week. The Major felt that the lack of a proper and independent all-metropolis detective service was the main obstacle in clearing this mystery, for even with his special mandate it was not easy for him to obtain full cooperation from the other superintendents.

He was convinced that Amir Ali had nothing to do with the murders, though he still had his men looking for the absconding thug, if only to keep them busy and create the impression, so necessary for the preservation of public order, that he knew more than he did. The Major also did not like the idea of the former suspect disappearing into thin air: it made him feel that his grip on London was not secure enough.

He had evidence that at least one of the murders had taken place when the thug was in custody and he had the word of his future son-in-law, Captain Meadows, for the innocence of Amir Ali on the night of yet another murder. He also knew that on at least some of the other occasions, Amir had been seen in a very different part of the city than the one in which a beheading had taken place. It was difficult to imagine a recently arrived East Indian knowing the city so well as to strike in different parts of it, at random and always without witness. Still, he wished he knew where the man had disappeared to. Of course, he could have shipped out, or gone into the provinces, but the Major doubted that.

On his table, Major Grayper had spread out a detailed map of London. Painstakingly, he marked the site of each murder with a red spot. Then he marked the sites of other unsolved murders of a similar character – involving the slicing of a limb or an appendage – with blue spots. The blue spots, he noted, were spread much more widely than the red spots. He was convinced that the blue spots had nothing to do with the red spots. The red spots clustered around central London, seldom, if ever, moving farther out, while the blue spots appeared more randomly. This confirmed the Major's suspicion that the beheading murders were a special case, perhaps the work of some religious cult after all, or at least some fanatic or lunatic, as that man Oates kept suggesting in his articles.

The main problem in understanding the murderer was the eclectic character of his victims. If they had all been women of the street, Major Grayper would have been able to imagine and perhaps trace a certain kind of man. If they had all been foreigners, he would have had another sort of clue. But the victims of this murderer were so mixed: an old woman who ran an opium den, a lascar, a nigger beggar, a gypsy or whoever it was, and so on. There did not seem to be any connection between them.

Major Grayper paused in his thinking. Of course, there was a connection. It was surprising he had not seen it before. All the victims were the very dregs of society. Was their murder then the work of some vigilante, someone who wanted to cleanse London of its sores and pus? The Major had come across such thinking aired over too many drinks in polite circles: the poor should be removed, sent to the colonies, etc. He himself believed that some drastic action was long overdue. London was swarming with the poor and the useless, not just indigenous folk but from all over the empire. Just last week at the club, one of his friends was complaining of the burden of empire, as he put it: we ship them civilization, he had said, and they ship us problems. Perhaps some other citizen, some vigilante, had felt more strongly on the subject.

But Major Grayper was also a pillar of society. He might sympathize with the feelings of this vigilante, but he would uphold law and order. What was wrong with people who wanted drastic solutions was exactly this, he thought: they did not realize that their solutions would unravel the intricate network of law and justice. It would be like opening Pandora's box.

Major Grayper lit another cigar. This would be a difficult matter. It might even involve someone from the better circles of London, perhaps a medical man or a tradesman. But he would find the culprit. That was his job. Search, and you will find. Though it would have been easier if the poor of London had not been so suspicious of authority, so unlikely to give full answers to the superior classes – for surely someone or the other must have witnessed the gory murders.

93

The Head Cannibal Strikes Again

Sketch by Daniel Oates

There are officers to inspect and certify the goods that are downloaded at West India and East India docks at the Isle of Dogs and the London Dock Company's docks at Wapping. But only if the goods are dead and inanimate. Every day hundreds of living goods are downloaded at those very docks, and they slip into the great city of London with hardly any inspection. There is no one to test if these living goods are of sufficiently high quality or not, to certify that they are undamaged and not rotted.

In the old Royal Exchange, there were separate walks even for merchants in the American, Italian, Norwegian, Irish and other trades, but the living goods shipped into London jostle with the rest of us on the same streets and alleys. Every day we meet these goods on the streets of fair London: men and women from every corner of the Empire who are now in our midst and can be often found associating with the worst of our own native crop of scoundrels. From the far points of the globe they come, from places with wondrous riches and sights but also, as our missionaries and colonists remind us, with strange rites and heathen customs, with extreme political views like anarchism, with devilish practices like cannibalism and suttee and thugee. Why then do we throw up our hands in horror and surprise when another person – this time a beggar from the West Indies – is found murdered and decapitated in our streets?

This morning your correspondent was called to witness, in an indescribable corner of Bethnal Green that reeked of misery and manure, the latest handiwork of the Rookery Beheader. During the night, this monster had fallen upon, battered to death and decapitated an old beggar from the West Indies who was often seen in the streets of London, dressed in a tall hat with green tissues shaped to resemble palm fronds and singing a jolly tune in a kind of English.

Once again, there are no witnesses to the crime. But it has been whispered in the streets that the murderer is some heathen, recently imported into our parts, who either practices a devilish and esoteric rite or consumes human flesh. The practice of some island tribes that shrink the skulls of their enemies has also been raised as a clue to the identity of the monster who is often called the 'head cannibal', for his victims have all been found without that vital appendage.

Whatever may be his identity, perhaps it is time to think about the nature and significance of all the goods that are brought into the docks of England by its mighty fleet of globe-spanning ships.

94

I enjoyed observing how Qui Hy went about her investigations, for – need it be said – this was not the first time I had seen her embroiled in solving someone else's problems. She always had a rational argument for it. No, it was never due to the goodness of her heart, the devils of Hindoostan forbid! She always had a reason. Whatever it was, for me her cases were an education every time. But this time the matter was much more in the public eye than any of her earlier cases.

Of course, Qui Hy never left the house; she seldom does, now that she suffers from gout and swollen knees, but even when she was younger she would wait for people to come to her. She would sit there, her eyes hooded and appearing only vaguely interested, patiently stitching her pockets, and they would sit with her, sipping tea or munching the paan she prepared. If you did not know, if the surroundings were not so different, and especially if her guests were ayahs or women, you would think it was a scene in India. She would ask them about their health or about news from 'home' or of 'family', if they had family. They would ask after her health. She would complain about her knees: that took at least ten minutes. And so the conversation would continue. Somewhere in the middle of this flaccid banter would be inserted a kernel of information. After the guest or guests had left, she would come into my room and make me a new pipe or fetch me something I needed. Then she would say, write this down, Paddyji, will you. Out would come the name of a place or a pub, some detail to add to what she knew already, nothing more than a word or two usually, and I would add it under the appropriate heading in the notebook that she had bought and now kept, with a stub of pencil, on the floor under my bed.

She is illiterate. Lick lora, per patter, she says, confessing her absolute illiteracy and laughing silently when one of her people asks her to help them read out or write a letter. She speaks five or six languages, most of them Indian dialects, as also passable French along with English, both of which she picked up while working as an ayah for various families. She cannot read or write a word in any language, though. 'Likh lorha, parh patthar,' she corrects me.

Once a week, she would ask me to read out all that I had written, heading and all, from the first page to the last. I would do so. She would sit there and sometimes she would nod or shake her head. I would ask her if the reading had helped. She would smile slightly and say, 'It helps, don't worry, everything helps, Paddyji.'

I would not press her for more. I knew she would tell me first when she felt she had the answer. I know she will have the answer. She always gets what she wants. I have been with her for two decades now: I know that. She is a deep one, this woman, my Indian wife.

95

It is a strange time for Amir Ali. After his initial angry outburst, he has started to feel a kind of lethargy, as if the idea of vengeance, perhaps even the notion of justice, is tiring. He misses Jenny more than he ever missed Mustapha Chacha and his family, but he feels a reluctance to do anything about it. It is only in the evenings sometimes, when he sleeps in the basement and is entirely alone with his thoughts, that he jolts up, sleepless, filled with anger at the senselessness of it all. He is happiest when, using the forged papers he received from Ustad, he accompanies Gunga to the docks, looking for work on one of the ships, any kind of ship plying the seas or the river, even the new steamships that none of them has any experience of. Gunga wants him to join his gang of lascars. Sometimes Amir feels tempted, but he knows he cannot leave London without finding out what happened to Jenny and why. Qui Hy has told him a little more every week, but he suspects she has told him less than she knows. When he accuses her of keeping back some information, she says, 'But Amir beta, do you think I am God?'

'Not God, Qui Hy,' he retorts, 'but surely someone from His inner circles!'

At that she shakes with soundless laughter and talks of something else.

96

Look at the man. Look at the blasted man, thinks John May. He turns to Shields and says it aloud. 'Look at yourself, man. When did you last shave? When did you last change your shirt? You are more jumpy than a bloody bean. Even your hands are shaking...'

Shields mumbles something.

'Speak up, man,' John May barks at him. 'Speak up. There's no one else here.'

One-eyed Jack sniggers.

'They are here, John May,' Shields replies, looking around furtively. 'They are always around.'

'Who?' John May shouts at the shorter man. 'Who, you goddamn peasant? Who have you seen now? Another trailing maidservant?'

Jack laughs aloud this time.

'It's not right, John May,' Shields mumbles back.

'What, man? Speak up. Speak up, damn you.'

'What we are doing. It's not right.'

Jack laughs again. But for a moment John is silent: he has qualms of conscience too, at times. Despite himself. Despite his iron will. But it is a matter of a few weeks now: M'lord is barely interested any more. John May has to make elaborate promises – strange skulls, stranger skulls – in order to keep him interested. It is only a matter of weeks before M'lord stops paying, stops appearing at the pub. John May senses this. M'lord is paying less and less; he acts distracted, like he has other matters on his mind. Very soon, he will vanish as suddenly as he appeared, mask and all. Why not make as much as one could until then? A beggar here, a lascar there, who would miss them?

97

The night Bubba Bookman burst into Qui Hy's parlour was different. He did not come with information. And he did not enter gently. He threw the door open violently, and entered with two of his men. I was so startled that I reached for the dagger I keep under my pillow, an old army habit. I cannot fall asleep unless I feel the sheathed dagger under my head.

'Who are they?' he shouted at Qui Hy.

Bookman has a booming voice, a sound that reverberates from the deep well of his being. Shouting comes naturally to him and it is not pleasant to have a man of Bookman's size shouting at you.

But Qui Hy remained in her rocking chair, stitching as usual. She did not even look up.

Bookman said again, 'By God, Qui Hy, you tell me who those men are. I know you know of them. You give me the names and I will kill them with my bare hands (He made as if he was twisting off heads). No one murders the poor buggers who pay me for safety, and that too, behead them in my own territory. They have gone too far. One I could have ignored. But two. Two! They killed poor old Crazy Abraham last night...'

Qui Hy looked up then. 'I know,' she said.

'You tell me, now, now,' Bookman thundered. 'Names, names, names...'

It was seldom that Bookman lost his sense of being on a complex stage and slipped into a singular emotion like anger. The beheadings had shaken him. Qui Hy set aside her basket.

'I always speak to people I know and trust, Bookman,' she said calmly, looking him squarely in the eye.

'Then tell me, Qui Hy, tell me.'

'I know you, Bookman. But do I know the men with you?'

'They are my men.'

'Do I know them, Bookman?'

Bookman made a gesture of exasperation. Then he grunted and spoke to the men in the reversed English that they used among themselves: Veal im own. Yrruh. Yrruh.

He looked back at Qui Hy, his eyes flinty, amused. 'You are a hard woman, Qui Hy,' he said in a voice that had recovered some of its sly humour.

Qui Hy waited until the door had closed behind the men. It was only then that she started speaking. Though I had been keeping her notes for her, I had not been able to put together the entire picture as well as she had. Even I was surprised by what she claimed to know.

Over the next thirty minutes, interrupted only once or twice by Bookman, who remained standing, massive and immobile as an oak, she told him what she had found out. She had all the names, all except that of the tall, one-eyed man. She had all the descriptions. She had the address of John May. She knew the pubs where they met. Somehow, by piecing together the evidence and getting people to overhear the conversations of John May and his companions, a modus operandi that appeared confused and disorganized to me but evidently contained its own method, she had figured out that the men were collecting deformed skulls for a masked gentleman. She told Bookman about the masked man, known in the Prize of War as M'lord, who met John May at irregular intervals.

At the end of it, Bookman sat down in a chair. He finally took off his trademark bowler hat. He whistled a pensive tune for at least half a minute.

'What are we waiting for?' he asked Qui Hy finally.

'The masked man,' she replied. 'We do not know who he is. We do not know where he goes.'

'What does it matter, Qui Hy?' Bookman retorted. 'That masked man is not the murderer. He might be buying skulls, but he has not killed my people. We should just get this John May of yours.'

'No, Bookman,' she warned. 'We have to find out about the masked man: never unravel a knot unless you know where the loose ends go. I need to know more. And you, brother, will stay out of it.'

'Why?'

'I am taking care of it.'

'How?'

'That, brother, is my concern. But I will tell you. I have procured letter paper through one of the ayahs – she has stolen it from her mistress – and I am getting Mrs Duccarol to write anonymous letters about the men to Major Grayper.'

'Mrs Duccarol? Captain Duccarol's widow? Why should she write your letters?'

'She is from my parts, Bookman.'

'Mrs Duccarol is Indian? She is fair, woman; she has blue eyes; she dresses and speaks English like some Duchess. You are pulling my leg.'

'She is Indian, Bookman. She was a very young Brahmin widow. Captain Duccarol saved her from a life of widowhood on the ghats; she repaid him by converting and becoming more English than the English.'

'Damn, this beats anything I have ever heard! You bloody women never cease to surprise me… But what if these letters fail?'

'Give me time, Bookman.'

'One month.'

'Four months.'

'Two months. That's it, Qui Hy. Two months, and that's stretching it.'

'Three months, Bookman.'

I stared at them in amazement: there they went, haggling, haggling, haggling over time, as if they were selling or buying a fowl or a bloody vegetable! What is it about niggers, whether from the East or the West, good or bad, man or woman, what is it that makes them love haggling so much?

'Two-three months, it is. Two-three months. But after that, I settle it my way. My way, Qui Hy, my way, the Bard willing.'

With that, Bookman put on his bowler hat and went out in a flurry of colours. Qui Hy looked at me and grimaced. 'You men, Paddyji,' she said with a sigh. 'Always impatient, always in a rush.'

'Not me, Qui Hy,' I replied from my bed. 'Not me. You know me. I even wait for you to fetch me my pipe…'

98

Shields sometimes sees ghosts in his dreams. But, in real life, even Shields sees only what is visible to him: he sees white men and women. Other kinds of people he often sees through.

That evening, he sets out to meet the other two. Had he looked around the corner into the next street, he would have noticed the one-legged beggar he passed run suddenly, on two legs, scampering across the streets until he meets a gypsy who takes his message and runs to a blackamoor, who runs with it all the way to a large man in a bowler hat and flowing clothes of many colours and cuts.

99

Major Grayper handed the latest letter to Constable Watson, who had been entrusted with the task of maintaining the records of the murders that the press were attributing to the 'head cannibal'. Gutter press was bad enough, thought Grayper; these letters were worse. There was a letter almost every day: letters giving advice, suggesting suspects, ranting about the Beast, talking about mysterious African or Maori rites. The Major had to go through all of them, using his famous detective skills to decide which ones, if any, were useful or legitimate.

'Take for instance this letter, Watson,' said the Major, gesturing at the letter he had just handed the constable. Watson paused in the process of filing it away.

'Do you know this is the third such letter by the same correspondent?'

Watson did what he was expected to do. He had been selected for this role because of his ability to follow cues. He shook his head.

'Read it, read it out.'

Watson took the letter, held it at arm's length, for he was longsighted, and read it with some effort.

Dear Sir,

The correspondent begs to bring to your notice that in all the places in which the so-called 'head cannibal' has consumed his victims, you may, if you enquire of those who, unfortunately, often have no other roof over their heads but the blue vault of the sky, you may, sir, come across the description of three men who have been seen with the victim or in the vicinity in the days before each murder. These three men are all, contrary to popular supposition, English: one of them fairly well-dressed to be considered a gentleman or an affluent tradesman, and the other two probably belonging to the working classes. One of the men is short and broad, and the other is tall but lacks an eye: he wears a patch and has on some occasions been seen carrying a cudgel. I am sure if your men ask around, they will be able to determine the identity of these three men. These three men are not mad, nor are they part of a mysterious cult. Their purpose is simple and can be ascertained by seeking information – the streets will supply you with much information in the shape of gossip – about the nature of the skulls that were severed and are yet to be recovered. The actions of these three men, your humble correspondent makes brave to suggest, might even be performed at the behest of someone else, a hidden hand too powerful to be easily seen. It is to be feared that these are the men behind the murders and decapitation that have lately tarnished the fair image of Great London.

Yours sincerely,

Truth

Watson looked up, eyes watery with the effort of reading.

'What do you notice about this letter, Watson?' asked Major Grayper.

'It is admirably well-written, sir.'

'That is good, Watson. Yes, it is fairly well-written; it is obviously the work of an educated person, and certainly not a foreigner. Not a Chancery hand though, or a Text hand. What else do you notice?'

Watson looked suitably blank.

'Smell it, Watson, smell it.'

Watson smelled it.

'Well, Watson, what do you think?'

'It smells nice, sir.'

'Perfume, Watson. It is perfume. Not a cheap one, either: it is lavender. And what does that tell you, Watson?'

'Tell me, sir?'

'Yes, Watson.'

'That the writer of the letter dropped perfume on it. Perhaps he works in a perfume shop, sir.'

'Why not in a fish market, Watson?'

'Sir?'

'Your logic could work that way too: a person in a fish market might need perfume at home to overcome the smell of his labour!

No, Watson. The answer is obvious. It tells us that the writer of this letter is a respectable and rich woman.'

'Yes, sir.'

'And what else does it tell us, Watson?'

'What else, sir?'

'What else does it tell us about the authenticity of the letter, Watson, the facts narrated in it?'

'Sir?'

'I will tell you, Watson. It tells us that this letter, like the other two, which were worded exactly alike and smelled of the same perfume, is inauthentic.'

'It does, sir?'

'Yes, Watson. You see, the letter has been written by an affluent English lady. How would she know about things that even you and I, having walked the streets of this city, have never heard of?'

'Perhaps her servants, sir...'

'And how would the servants of a lady know? No, Watson, this is another one of those letters written by a bored young lady for her own entertainment. File it away. There is nothing to it, but file it anyway. One has to be scientific and methodical. Always. That is the first rule of modern investigation.'

Watson filed it away.

100

One evening, with Gunga and Amir there, Qui Hy disclosed the identity of the masked man who had been buying the skulls.

I was surprised. 'How did you find out?'

The coach, she said, and his coachman. Once we had him trailed to the coach, it did not take very long to find out who owned such a coach and with such a coachman.

'So what do we do now?' I asked.

'Nothing,' she replied. 'We wait for the letters to have an effect on Grayper. It will all come out once those men are arrested. The short one, especially, he will blurt out everything.'

'Those three do not know M'lord's identity. That is what you said. And the Peelers would not arrest M'lord in any case. Dammit, woman, we are talking of Lord Batterstone; he is not just anyone!' I expostulated. 'And, in any case, he has not committed any murder.'

'That hardly matters,' said Qui Hy. 'M'lord is not our concern. He is not a loose end any more, Paddyji. Now that we know who he is, we can ignore him; he will pose no danger to us. Once the three are arrested, the murders will stop and we can get back to normal activities without fear of anyone backing the three or seeking revenge for the arrests.'

But Amir differed here. He argued that the three were not important, that they were hardly even guilty of the murders they had committed; it was M'lord who was the culprit.

'I know such people,' he said, suddenly very angry. For a young man, I had always considered him surprisingly even-tempered, some might even call him sly – I wouldn't, for I saw the suffering in his eyes in the days after Jenny's murder. Though, he remained remarkably calm even then, apart from that first evening. Then suddenly, on a matter of almost no importance, he got all upset. 'I know such people,' he shouted at us, 'they always act through their henchmen.'

Qui Hy and Gunga had trouble calming him down. But

after this, Amir started keeping away from us, disappearing for long periods without telling us where he was going. Qui Hy sometimes worried about him getting arrested, though by now it was obvious that his disguise and the papers forged by Ustad were not easy to see through. Unless one of us blabbed to the authorities, he was unlikely to be identified as Amir Ali.

101

Head Cannibal Finds a Stranger Victim

Sketch by Daniel Oates

The Head Cannibal, who started his bloody career in the Rookery by murdering and beheading an old woman, has struck again. And this time his victim is almost as strange as the murderer must himself be. This time the unknown beheading monster appears to have murdered a freak.

The body was found on the banks of the Thames in Deptford, by the mouth of a sewage opening. Enmeshed in green dank deposit and rotten wood and next to a dust heap abandoned by tosh-hunters and rag-pickers, it was, to put it with a modicum of decency, in an extreme degree of undress. In fact, like the head, which was missing, the dress, if there had been one, was also gone. Modesty forbids a full description.

The victim is yet to be identified. It is a male of indeterminate age and a very pale texture, so translucent a skin that, experts say, it indicates a life led solely in places not much exposed to the sun. Local people claimed that the victim was one of the Mole People, the lost tribe that is reputed to infest the underground caverns, tunnels and pathways of London.

This, of course, is a tall tale, and was dismissed by Major Grayper, who has assured your correspondent that the murderer will soon be apprehended.

We know more about the identity of the murderer than we can reveal to the public at this juncture of our investigations, the Major told your correspondent. He added that the murderer will be identified very soon and trapped in the net that the Metropolitan force has been weaving for him. The Major declined to comment on a recent letter published in this newspaper by an anonymous correspondent who claimed that the murderer is a cannibal from one of the tribes that shrink heads in the South Pacific, originally for ritual purposes and now for sale to those in our beloved islands who suffer from the inexplicable and unchristian fad of collecting heathenish curios.

102

Amir looks at the house. He has to be careful on these streets: there are more gaslights here than in other parts of London. It is a fashionable quarter; people like him are unusual here. An ayah or a black footman, yes, but not a lascar hanging around, doing nothing.

He knows that the house he is watching is far more impressive than the one Captain Meadows lives in. He saw M'lord drive up once; his coachman, a giant of a man, jumped down and opened the door for him. Standing across the road, Amir watched the man he considered responsible for the death of Jenny. The others can go looking for the henchmen, but Amir believes that he can spot a Mirza Habibullah even in this land of different faces. And if Amir has scores to settle, he surely has scores to settle with the Mirzas and M'lords.

Amir does not know how to avenge the death of Jenny. He does not even know if he wants to seek revenge once again: revenge, he feels, always changes you into something else, something much worse than what you might otherwise be. But he cannot tear himself away from the house. Evening after evening, he comes back and watches it. He does not know why.

103

Qui Hy shook me awake. 'Too early,' I muttered and tried to turn around, though I knew it was afternoon. She would not let me go back to sleep. 'Paddyji, wake up,' she said, 'wake up. I need to discuss something with you.' I murmured in irritation and ignored her. She went off and returned with a wet cloth which she threw on my face. 'Get up, Paddyji, you hooligan,' she said. She knows I hate being called a hooligan. I gave up. I sat up reluctantly and rubbed my eyes.

'What is it, you Punjabi gorgon,' I asked her.

'I want your advice.'

'Yes,' I said, 'I gathered as much. Why else would you wake me at this unearthly hour?'

'It is well after midday,' she replied.

I shook my head.

She continued. 'I want to ask you. Why isn't Major Grayper reacting to the letters?'

'How would I know,' I retorted.

'He is one of your people, Paddyji,' she said.

'He is not one of my people, Qui Hy.' I was offended. 'He is bloody English.'

'You know what I mean.'

'You want me to tell you why I think Major Grayper is not acting on the letters you have had Mrs Duccarol send him?'

'Yes, yes, yes.'

'How would I know? These are strange people. They do not think like you and me.'

'You worked for them, Paddyji, you fought under them,' she retorted. 'You used to be a soldier; he used to be an army officer.'

'I never understood my officers.'

Qui Hy paused for a moment. 'I think I will have to try something else,' she said.

'Why,' I asked her.

'Why?'

'Yes, why?'

'Because otherwise they will kill more people.'

'Oh, come off it, Qui Hy. Don't tell me you have a bleeding heart. I have known you too bloody long to believe that.'

'Maybe it bleeds more than you know.'

'And maybe the Queen is Irish.'

'It's Bookman,' she said then. 'I am worried about what he might do, or what Amir might do.'

'That is their headache,' I retorted. I quite like that boy, Amir, but I did not see why we should be so upset over his travails.

'No,' she replied, after a pause. 'It is our headache too. If they get arrested in the process, we will all be involved. Maybe that Oates whose articles you read out to me will make us out to be a heathen cult of cannibals. Whatever happens, we will have our places, names and lives poked into. And you do not want that, do you, Paddyji?'

I shook my head. We had had this discussion before. We always have this discussion when she gets embroiled in one of her cases. No, I do not want that. All of us have a past and all of us have reasons – small but inevitable reasons – not to want it back.

104

Gunga, Karim and Tuanku lit up the chillum that they had between them: Gunga had managed to obtain some tobacco and opium. They passed it around carefully. It was ages since they had been able to afford a smoke.

There were several bundles scattered in the dark room which they shared with five other lascars. Eleven marooned men slept every night in that foul, dank room, streaked with coal dust: the room had been used to store coal in the past. It was bare of furniture but littered with bundles of rags, newspapers and blankets. Some of these bundles belonged to another gang of abandoned lascars, who were now out on the docks or scavenging in the streets. Both the gangs had come together, the flotsam and jetsam of gangs that had been abandoned, and Gunga was once again hopeful of finding work on a ship. At least he had enough men to offer, though he knew that most of the ships leaving London already had their required quota of sailors. It was ships sailing back from Asia and Africa – decimated by illness or by the better job prospects offered by local princes to European sailors who knew, or pretended to know, new technology and army drills

– that took on lascars more readily. Still, Gunga kept looking. He was not a man who gave up easily.

'Two winters. Two winters in this city. I tell you, by God, two winters are two too many. I would like to feel real sunlight on my back just once more,' said Karim, coughing, not this moonlight that passes for the sun. Who would even believe that winter is over?'

He pointed to the narrow, barred window.

'A drunken pig at the docks told me that the English have won in Afghanistan,' Tuanku replied.

Gunga was going to say something, when he stopped himself. Why had they started speaking like this, no one really talking to anyone else, each conversation a boat set adrift in the sea? Was this what happened when jahaajbhais started dissolving the sacred links that bound them each to each, before they started moving apart?

105

Just when you think that you have got used to people, that they cannot possibly do anything to rattle you any more, they go and spring on you a horrific surprise. I had been out drinking with the blokes and came in, not drunk, you understand, not drunk but happy. I opened the door – have I mentioned that my house used to be a shop, and hence the door opens directly into what they (and at times even I) call Qui Hy's dhaba? – so, yes, I opened the door at midnight, expecting the place to be empty, unless Qui Hy was still stitching away a fortune in pockets by the fireplace and, Lord help me, what did I find? Not only were there three or four people in the room, Gunga and that boy, Fetcher, and one or two others, there was an Indian I had never seen before. Seen him? No, let me be honest. I had never seen anything like him before.

I had seen ugly people, deformed people. Believe me, I had lepers dangling their faces before me for baksheesh in India, their skin dripping like sweat; I had seen soldiers with noses or ears cut off and faces sliced into ribbons. But never had I seen a face so naturally ugly. A great brute lump of a skull on a lascar with lips and eyes that had been slapped on in a God-almighty hurry. I shuddered. I might even have screamed.

'You have had a drop too much, Paddyji,' Qui Hy whispered, coming up to me and guiding me firmly to my room.

I knew what she meant; she did not want me around. There was some heathenish devilry going on. I let her guide me to my room and light my pipe for me. I knew she would come to me with news of her devilry when the time was ripe. She always does.

106

Amir has a strange feeling the entire time he is out on the streets near Lord Batterstone's mansion: not so much during the evenings or the nights, when the neighbourhood is hooded in darkness and mystery, but during the mornings and afternoons. At first, he thinks it is merely his fear of being accosted or identified. But then he realizes that it is something else.

Night fits in with his expectations of the mansion, so glorious on the outside and so hideous inside. Day does not.

In the daytime, the neighbourhood fills with tokens of

normality – carriages, men on horses, babies being taken out to the park, children, ladies going for a stroll, porters, servants, dogs, birds, vendors, tradesmen. Amir has lived in London long enough to identify such things with the quotidian. And it is this that imposes on him a sense of unreality. For in such a setting, Lord Batterstone's imposing, impressive mansion is a monster.

In it, or so Amir imagines, are hidden piles of skulls, bone gleaming white like ivory, while from the outside the mansion appears the very epitome of all that is honourable, cultured and beautiful, and from it emerges, on occasion, Lord Batterstone, a man honoured and rich, but in Amir's eyes, a thing monstrous and free. There is something disturbing about the mansion, its elegance and freedom, the fact that its monstrosity is not revealed or shackled. There is something monstrous about the very normality that envelops it.

So Amir Ali prefers the night, for it restores a semblance of balance. It claims neither more nor less than what is: it obscures both monstrosity and normality from sight, momentarily erasing distinctions.

107

There were days when I thought Qui Hy had forgotten all about her investigations, about the beheadings, so tranquil was she as she sat by the fireside, stitching pockets.

Then one day Qui Hy turned to me and said, 'We will do it tonight.'

'Do what?' I said.

'Get the three.'

'Kill them?'

'Don't be a fool, man. Don't talk like one of those damnfool lascar boys.'

'What then?'

'We will get them arrested. Just don't smoke yourself asleep this evening…'

'I am not needed, I am sure,' I said.

'Oh yes, you are. And you have to bring along two or three of your boys.'

'What boys?'

'Those Irish pals of yours, the no-good ones you go out to drink with every Friday.'

'Why them?'

'I will tell you,' she said. 'I will tell you later today. Just bring your boys along to the pub at the corner, you know the one under the sign of that goat man…'

'Pan,' I said.

'Pan or pot,' she replied, 'who cares? Just be there with as many of your drinking chums as possible, and don't tell them anything now or later.'

108

Captain Meadows watched Nelly fuss over the flower arrangements. Now that he was formally engaged, Nelly made every visit by Mary into something of a dress rehearsal for their forthcoming wedding. He smiled.

The Captain was in a joyous mood. He had just finished revising his book. He had settled on a title for it: *Notes on a Thug*. Maybe he ought to add a subtitle too: *Character and Circumstances*. He would ask Mary about it. He trusted her judgement even when he differed from her, as he did on the issue of Dumas' French romances, which she had started devouring ever since the Papal ban against them had been announced. But though their reading differed – the book he was currently perusing was titled *A Summary View on the Principle of Population* – Mary was receptive to his commentaries and not at all a bad advisor, when it came to that.

If only the matter of these beheadings could be cleared up. He could not possibly publish a book based on interviews with someone who had been, and was still popularly suspected of being the Rookery Beheader. Especially someone who had disappeared, skipped port, as they say. This did not surprise the Captain. He had always known that Mr Ali intended to return to his homeland.

But it would not be out of order to wait for a few more months before sending the book to the printers. It was a precaution worth taking: the Captain did not want to start his married life embroiled in controversy. Yes, he would wait until the murders were cleared up. His prospective father-in-law, Major Grayper, never ceased to say that it was only a matter of time before the culprit was caught. He would not say more than that. He was incredibly tight-lipped over the details these days. When pressed, he would only stare levelly at you and say, the trap will spring shut, the trap will spring shut any day now. Then he would tap the ash off his cigar with immense authority.

109

The normality of Lord Batterstone's excellent neighbourhood has not shattered, but Amir can sense ripples under its surface. He knows something is happening, or about to happen. Twice he sees boxes being brought into M'Lord's house. Once, he sees boxes being carted away by hired men. He follows them to a ship at dock.

The ship is called *Good Hope*. It stands tall and stark against the cloudy water, the brooding sky. It is being loaded.

110

I have to hand it to that woman. You cannot beat her at planning and intrigue. If she had been a man, she would have made a famous general.

I heard her lay out the plan. She had long given up hope of getting Major Grayper to respond. Instead, she decided to stage the arrest of the three. It was a simple plan. She knew that they went for destitute people with strange or damaged skulls. So she had found a lascar with a strange skull and thrown him into their path so often that they were now trailing him.

'That devil you had tucked away in here that night, the night I almost screamed?' I asked, and she nodded absent-mindedly.

'Thank God,' I said, with some bitterness. 'For a moment I thought you had finally gone and sold your soul to Ol' Nick, woman.'

'No firangi Nick can afford my soul, Paddyji,' she retorted. 'But listen to me now.'

Qui Hy continued her tale. She had arranged for the lascar to sleep regularly in an abandoned house on Draper's Alley, a dark street on the other side of the Mint: it was full of abandoned buildings and cheap lodging houses. Somehow, through her eavesdropping spies, or a sixth sense, or some witch's brew she had cooked in an off-hour, who knows, she was convinced that the three would strike tonight. And she wanted us to be stationed nearby, so that we could come running when the lascar raised an alarm.

'Why us?' I asked. 'Why not you?'

'We will be there. Gunga and his men will be there. That boy Fetcher will be there too: he or one of the lascars will give you the signal. But they will only detain the three until you all get there. We cannot get Peelers to arrest white men. You know that. You have to hand them over.'

'But what if the three simply deny what they were up to?'

'They won't,' she said.

'Why?'

'You will see. I know them now. I have had them trailed and watched for weeks. At least one of them will fall to pieces, and he will pull the others down. They are men, Paddyji, just men. We know how you men are. You just have to shout loud enough that they are the beheaders, get an angry mob going and, for all our sakes, bloody well keep them alive until the bobbies get there. At least one of them will confess. And then they will have to look into their backgrounds and living quarters: they will find enough there. You just get your boys there on the quick when you hear the signal.'

She was referring to the boys – most of them ex-soldiers like me – with whom I occasionally go for a drink in the pubs. She seldom lets them come to this place because, she says, they get drunk and start fighting the battles of India and Africa all over again in front of her guests. (To be honest, most of them do not feel comfortable drinking in the company of niggers.) But now, quite unabashedly, she was requisitioning them.

Then she added, 'Do not say anything to Amir. I do not want him to know before all this is over. He should not even be in the vicinity.'

111

John May walks past St Paul's on his way to Draper's Street. He had agreed to meet Jack and Shields at the corner. He walks slowly. There is no rush; it is not even dark yet. He looks up at the impressive dome of the cathedral. He had climbed its iron stairway once. The view from the top had been strange: the fog was like a brown sea. It covered the houses, so that only the chimneys, spires and towers jutted out of the brownness, making London resemble a vast graveyard of ships, ships sunk in the water with just their masts and top sails and steam funnels jutting out of the waves.

This evening, John May knows, will be their last evening of profit. Unlike Shields, he has few qualms about it. The lascar they have been trailing literally fell into their clutches. He crossed their path at least twice, with his large globe of a head, with knobs and depressions that John May knows will thrill M'lord.

But, of course, it was difficult the last time even to get M'lord to meet him at the Prize of War. Their usual method of leaving a message with the one-armed publican, which would be collected by a large, gypsy-looking man, has entailed greater and greater delays in eliciting responses from M'lord, and John May, despite being tempted, has avoided trailing his mysterious customer. He is too much in awe of the aristocratic masked man and his class to take such a risk.

John May knows that M'lord will not buy any more skulls: this is the last one, and were it not such a strange sample – John May waxed poetic in his message – it is certain that M'lord would not have agreed to a meeting five evenings from now. John May is not entirely disappointed. He has accumulated a small fortune from his dealings with the masked aristocrat, and though he is not averse to earning more, one part of him is relieved to have the temptation removed from him. He is not euphoric about this loss of enterprise, unlike Shields, who burst into rapturous prayers of deliverance on being informed that M'lord had stipulated that no further contact could be made between them after this transaction. But he is not morose about it, either, unlike Jack, who suggested that perhaps they should look for another customer.

But what kind of customer? Shields, because he is too obtuse, and Jack because he wants to, still believe that the skulls are sold to some school of surgery or club of medical students; they see it as a strange version of the older profession of selling 'Things' to surgeons and students, a profession that has almost disappeared in recent years. But John May, who knows that the skulls have to be prepared before being handed to M'lord, understands that this is a different sort of collection, a unique one. They will find no other customer.

A street Arab runs towards him, attempting to hustle last week's, or perhaps even an older newspaper, in the bad light of the dusk. The headline is something about the death of the Ottoman emperor. John May shoos the urchin away.

Tomorrow, John May knows, the paper will carry news about a beheaded lascar. London will be abuzz again. The Rookery Beheader strikes again! The Head Cannibal consumes another victim! John May will go about with the knowledge of being better than his betters, of knowing more than them, of tricking them with his strength of will and intelligence, his cautious enterprise. He will miss that feeling in the future, but still…

112

The things that woman has made me do in the past. You wouldn't believe it.

Here I was, at the Head of Pan, not my favourite place I must say, regaling my chums with lies about the small inheritance that I had just come into. I had to invent that inheritance. They would have been suspicious of my standing them free rounds otherwise, and I would not have been certain of getting more than a couple of them to join me without the carrot of free drinks. As it was, there were seven of us in the pub now, and I was the only one not really drinking.

I had to remain alert, ears tuned for the signal that would be shouted from the streets – or perhaps by one of Gunga's men running into the pub screaming, murder, murder. I could not afford to miss the signal. So, not only was I paying for the bloody drinks, I was not drinking half as much as my chums were. That woman and her scheming!

113

Night descends on London once again. Descends? No. It rises slowly, in the overlooked nooks and crannies of this teeming metropolis. First, it crawls like a spider between the cobblestones. Then it spills like ink on the ground, between the buildings, from the walls, under the bridges. It grows out of the corners. It builds a net of shadow in the parks and between the lamp posts. It turns the water of the Thames blacker. It darkens the facades of the houses, mean or majestic. It is only when the land has been conquered that night rises up into the sky, the cloudy, smoky London sky, and snuffles out the last traces of day.

The city is at home in this night. It knows the night as one of its own. Night makes the city more of a city, stretches its expanse, deepens its anonymity. At night, the city dons a mask and steps out in another character, whether it is in a room full of skulls and candles, the room of a thousand and one flames in Lord Batterstone's mansion, or in the feeble light of a fireplace in Qui Hy's dhaba, where Qui Hy sits alone tonight and stitches, stitches, stitches, or in the fumes of the gas-lit pub under the sign of Pan, where Paddyji regales his old and withering friends, or in the shadows of the streets outside, where steps approach, eyes watch: if night is not sheer blankness, surely it is a place for masquerade.

114

Mary was already at breakfast with her mother when the Major returned. He had been away from around midnight when the news had been brought to him. He had been woken up in bed by Watson, as he had instructed: anything to do with the Rookery Beheader had to be reported to him immediately, no matter where he was.

'Oh, poor Pa,' said Mary, jumping up and embracing him as he entered the room.

'You must be tired,' added Mrs Grayper, putting down the knife she was using to butter her slice of thick bread. 'Would you like to eat something, or should I have your bed made ready again?'

The Major shook his head and sat down at the table. He knew what the two women really wanted to ask him as they watched his grim, tired face.

His face broke into a broad grin.

'What?' said Mrs Grayper. 'Is it true? Have they been arrested?'

The Major nodded. 'All except one,' he replied. 'One of them escaped.'

'Are they the culprits, the beheaders?'

'It looks like it,' said the Major, helping himself to the bacon. He had his doubts, but he was not going to express them if the beheadings ceased.

115

Gunga was worried. He had not seen Amir for two or three days. Amir had not participated in the farce organized by Qui Hy and Fetcher last night: despite his disguise and false papers, Amir's presence would have been too risky. The farce, Mai be blessed, had gone well; Gunga was sure that Amir would feel justice had been done. In any case, Qui Hy was relieved that it was all over, the suspicion, the danger. She believed in a quiet life, a quiet life of steady profit. Gunga was relieved too. But where on earth was that boy Amir?

He should have been back by now. It was evening again. Gunga also had news for Amir. Not just the news of the arrest of the beheaders – he was sure the boy must have heard of that by now, London was talking of little else – but other news. He had done as Amir had asked him to do when they last spoke together: he had gone to the docks and enquired about the ship, *Good Hope*. He had found out that it was bound for Africa.

It had been a lucky break, actually. His enquiry had led to something Gunga had almost given up hoping for. It appeared that for some reason or the other, the skipper was determined to sail the following morning instead of the following week, as scheduled. He was so desperate that he was hiring any dog of a sailor to fill in for those who could not report on time. Gunga and his boys had been hired immediately. Gunga was ecstatic. He was tired of England. He was sick of land. Even Karim, who had been lying in bed, coughing blood for weeks now, had roused himself. They were hoping to take Amir along too. Why leave him here? What did he have left to do here?

But where was the damn boy?

In any case, Gunga had to take his gang of lascars aboard *Good Hope* now. The ship had just been loaded and moved to another dock for some mysterious reason. All of them had to be aboard by dawn. The skipper was determined to sail at first light.

116

I have seldom seen Qui Hy show such visible signs of happiness. She has an Indian peasant's suspicion of providence. Providence, she thinks, is a bully always on the lookout for smiling people, so that it can bash them in the face.

But when I read out Daniel Oates' account of the events last night, her broad face creased into a smile. 'Finally,' she said, 'finally, the son of a pig is writing something vaguely close to reality.' And then she shook with silent laughter.

This is what the report by Daniel Oates said:

Gracious Reader, this morning your correspondent brings to you news that will set you dancing in the streets. The Rookery Beheader has been apprehended. It had been suggested in this paper that the beheadings which have plagued our fair city could be attributed either to the old and deplorable profession of Resurrectionists or to some Oriental cult. We are glad to report that our first conjecture has been proved entirely correct.

Last night, when the respectable citizen had retired from the dark and the unusually thick fog, three desperate men walked with murder in their minds to an abandoned building in the Mint. There they attacked a beggar from the East – how correct was your humble correspondent in predicting the Eastern connection! – with the intention of murdering him and selling his head (and perhaps other bodily parts) to students and doctors of surgery. The beggar would surely have forfeited his life had he not woken up in time. He raised an alarm in his own tongue, for he is not acquainted with the English language. Fortunately for the man, the abandoned building contained other illicit sleepers who came to his aid. The alarm carried to a neighbourhood public house, where a group of brave Englishmen, some of them retired soldiers, were having an honest drink. Acting quickly, these heroes repaired to the spot and nabbed two of the attackers, who have since confessed to their crimes. However, one attacker, a man identified as John May, managed to escape the custody of our brave ex-soldiers before policemen arrived on the spot.

It is reported that some men ran after Mr May. He was pursued through a number of dark alleys, until he was finally lost in the fog. Some of the men, however, claimed that he was not lost in the fog, but grabbed by strange figures and dragged into a tunnel or a doorway. They heard him shriek and then all traces of him were lost. Need we state that wild speculation is a trait of the mob; such credulity is fortunately not shared by your correspondent.

The police, who arrived on the spot with admirable efficiency, gave assurances that the escaped man would be captured soon. Major Grayper, who came personally at that unearthly hour of the night, took over the final investigations, which we believe cannot rest in more capable hands.

Thus, honoured Reader, ends the mystery of the infamous Rookery Beheader: the seventeen or eighteen murders committed were all the work of this gang of Resurrectionists, a profession that, it was hoped, had been eradicated after the public outcry over the case of the Italian boy. However, once again, the honest citizens of our magnificent metropolis can walk its streets without the angel of terror hovering over them.

I read it aloud to her. Then I put aside the paper.

'Strange figures,' I observed, raising an eyebrow. 'Bookman's people?'

'So I think,' she replied. 'But Fetcher swears it was the Mole People. That damnfool boy sees Mole People everywhere! And Gunga, who is old enough to be the boy's grandfather, also hums and haws. The fog, he told me, was like a cloud fallen on the street. I saw him run into it, Mai, Fetcher and me had just turned the corner; then something happened, Mai, the fog grew darker, denser, as if there were things in it, it filled with movement, and I heard him scream, Mai, such a terrible scream. In all my years I have not heard the like, Mai, so, by all the gods, I do not know, I do not know, perhaps there are Mole People living under these streets, Mai, who knows?'

She looked at me, undecided and scoffing. 'Have you ever heard the like, Paddyji? You who have lived here half your life? Mole People!'

I did not care. A tune was already playing in my head. It grew louder. I could recognize it now. I did a light jig. Then I danced to where Qui Hy was sitting, in her usual chair. I curtseyed to her, elaborately. I offered her my hand, inviting her to dance. She would usually turn down such invitations with a grimace. No tomfoolery for me, she would say, slapping away my hand; she was no dancer. But today she grasped my hand and pulled herself up.

Qui Hy is heavier on her feet than I am. Younger but heavier, with bad knees. I led her. The tune flowed out of my head and flooded the room. And we danced together, holding each other, King and Queen in our impregnable castle.

117

Amir has stood watching the house all night. He has stayed in the neighbourhood for two nights now; his coat and shawl affording him enough protection from the balmy, foggy May nights. He knows he should get back to Qui Hy. But he also knows that something is afoot in M'lord's mansion. The house has been bursting with activity all day. He has seen the butler, whom he now recognizes by face, and the coachman, bustling about, supervising this, having that carted out, covering the furniture inside, closing windows. Then suddenly, late in the afternoon, M'lord came out and, after shaking hands all around (which was unusual), drove away in his fly.

The butler and the servants went inside after that, and quiet descended on the house. Now, with darkness falling, the imposing house looks asleep. It is less brightly lit than usual. Has Lord Batterstone gone away somewhere, out of the city? The thought has crossed Amir's mind before: he knows someone is about to leave, what with the boxes being carted in and out, but he expects the departure to be formal and more elaborate. Great men do not sneak away in a fly; they are seen off by friends and family; there are dinners and farewells. This, Amir believes, is as true of London as of India. Why should a nobleman like M'lord leave all of a sudden, without any dinners, speeches, announcements in the newspapers?

It begins to drizzle, and Amir seeks shelter under a ledge. The fly passes him on its way back to the house. There is only the coachman; no M'lord descends from it.

Amir walks up to the coachman, who is leading the horses to

the mews. 'I need to see His Lordship,' he says boldly to the giant. The coachman is surprised. He laughs. 'Come back in a year or two,' he replies.

'A year or two?'

'A year or two, lascar; his Lordship is on his way to the dark continent…'

Amir starts running towards the docks even before the coachman has completed his reply. The slight drizzle cuts into his face. The emptying streets of London seem to fill with his footsteps, as if he were a monster chasing himself. He brushes past the few pedestrians; he runs into the wet darkness.

118

Gunga and his men were given the usual quarters: the worst in the ship, well below the deck. Gunga did not mind. He was used to it all. Even this ship, with its drunken skipper, its motley crew, not one of whom Gunga would show his back to if he could help it, its mysterious owner, some rich lord who had filled the hold with crates full of equipment for some 'scientific expedition' in Africa.

Good Hope, the ship was called. Good hope for whom, Gunga wondered; perhaps for the Lord-owner and perhaps for Gunga and his men, who could finally start the long journey home, for he doubted the crates contained hope for wherever they were headed. He had sailed the seas long enough to know that hope does not ship well; it is usually spoiled across long distances.

But that was not what worried Gunga. He was worried

about Karim: he did not know if Karim would last to the Congo, though perhaps warmer climes would revive him. And he hoped that he would be able to go out just once at dawn and look for Amir. He had told Qui Hy and Fetcher to send the boy to these docks.

119

Amir wakes with a start, and that is when he realizes he must have fallen asleep. The wood is cool and hard against his body, the sound of the waves soothing despite the stench. All is still and clear. By the stillness he knows it to be late in the night, perhaps just a few minutes before the first light of morning. For the docks – with their pubs and taverns, biscuit bakers and block makers, pawnbrokers and rope spinners, knocking shops and grog shops – are never quiet until long after midnight, and they come alive again with the faintest light.

He is not surprised that he fell asleep. His last memory is of the men in the tavern. He had run without stopping when he left Lord Batterstone's mansion. The drizzle had stopped by the time he reached the tavern, leaving his clothes moist rather than wet. He rushed up to the sailors and dock hands in the drinking den, jostling the crowd so that one of them spilled his ale. Luckily there was a man, a recently arrived Burmese lascar, who knew him from Qui Hy's place; knew him not as Amir Ali, but by his new Ustad-given identity. It was this man who answered Amir's desperate, madly repeated question.

'No,' the lascar replied in the jargon that Amir can just about comprehend. '*Good Hope* sailed hours ago. It is not docked here any more, bhai.'

Amir cannot believe it. He scrambles to the piers – to be met by an empty, dirty stretch of water where he saw *Good Hope* anchored a few days earlier. He rushes around, peering at the names of the ships still anchored here, hoping against hope to find on one of them the cursive letters of *Good Hope*. There are so many ships, but not one of them is *Good Hope*. It is then that fatigue falls on him like a cloak, and he sinks onto the wooden planks of a pier, resting his tired body on a pile of ropes, his fists clenched, his mind undecided between frustration and relief. He has failed Jenny. It is too late now. And yet, a burden has been lifted from his soul. It is then that he falls asleep without even realizing it.

Loneliness wraps the dock, its closed stalls and shacks like sightless eyes. With dawn now limning the horizon, the dark masts of ships seem to stand solitary and mute, aspiring to heaven but failing to reach it; the riggings are spread like empty nets. Water laps against the ships, dirty, but mysteriously insistent, as if it is telling the caulked planks stories that are beyond human hearing.

Slowly an eyelid lifts in the sky. The sun is rising in the east. Waves of light spread behind the clouds, pulsing like a mighty heart.

Then Amir hears Gunga shouting for him. He knows in that instant that *Good Hope* has not sailed. Perhaps it was moored somewhere else; perhaps the lascar was misinformed. Gunga is shouting for him, asking him to hurry up, they are going to lift anchor soon, they have to go aboard now, he cannot wait any longer, all the other boys are already there, where are you, jahaajbhai? Oh, where are you, nawabzada?

He half turns towards the voice and hesitates. He hesitates, and half turns towards the voice.

Nawabzada, jahaajbhai, where are you?

At that instant, the morning or the wind passes a thin blade across the belly of the clouds to the east and sunlight spills out like blood.

120

The sudden stab of light after a powercut was always greeted with shouts and comments. Allah be praised, my grandmother would mutter, not without irony. The bulbs and mercury tubes would burst into light, blinding us for an instant. Darkness would be defeated, but sight would still take a few seconds to be restored. No, let's put this differently: eyes that had gotten used to seeing in the darkness would be blinded by light. Who says only darkness is blinding?

As the dawn bursts over Amir Ali in London, I am blinded by it. I see him hesitate and turn towards Gunga's voice; I see him turn and hesitate. The sunlight falls on him. He stands drenched in sunlight.

Amir Ali knows he can duck into one of the corners and the ship will sail without him. Or he can respond to Gunga and sail with the ship. But whatever he does, he has already embarked on a new story – the Hindustani from Patna, the thug of Captain Meadows' science, suspected murderer in the streets of London, a lascar in Gunga's gang, the instrument of love's revenge... There are so many possibilities, some already visible, some still lurking under the surface of reality; some half-visible in darkness; some half-hidden by brightness.

Not one of the possibilities is Amir Ali, and yet he is in all of them. No choice can ever be embraced whole-heartedly, no story will ever tell all of what he was, but one or more of the stories would have to be chosen, uttered, lived out. Any choice would leave him with the option of spinning another set of stories, stories that would sweep him on to other voyages, other destinies. But he knows now that all stories are not equivalent, no, not at all; each story relates to his illegible reality in a different way, each also relates to different realities. Perhaps he turns towards the voice. My sight fails me; the library in Phansa fails me; all libraries fail us at this instant of decision.

Forgiveness and vengeance are easy only in thought, when language pretends to tell us all about life.

But face to face, say, aboard a ship off the coasts of Africa, still some moments away from sighting land, a ship smelling of a long voyage, a stale, rotting, confined smell that even the brine of the sea breeze cannot blow away, on a ship like that, when one of the lascars turns and stares at the nobleman who has financed the voyage, what is it that appears in his eyes: vengeance or forgiveness? Does Lord Batterstone read the face on that skull, the new face of Amir Ali the Lascar? A squall has blown up. The sailors are running about on deck, pulling down sails, scampering up and down riggings. What happens when Amir Ali faces Lord Batterstone? Can my language dare to choose between the options? Can my language claim to tell all of Amir Ali? Or should I let the squall blow in the blind whiteness of a sea fog behind which I can hide my choice of words, the fact that what I have chosen, what I can choose is never enough, never complete?

I see Amir Ali look at Lord Batterstone, seasick and soul-weary. The sea is choppy; the wind is howling; the heavens press down on the earth, heavy with clouds. Lord Batterstone steadies himself against a sudden lurch and looks back at Amir Ali. He sees a lascar. He sees no story worth reading.